SURVIVE

THE

DOME

Also by Kosoko Jackson

Yesterday Is History

SURVIVE
THE
DOME

KOSOKO JACKSON

Published by Sourcebooks Fire, an imprint of Sourcebooks
P.O. Box 4410, Naperville, Illinois 60567-4410
(630) 961-3900
sourcebooks.com

Library of Congress Cataloging-in-Publication Data

Names: Jackson, Kosoko, author.
Title: Survive the Dome / Kosoko Jackson.
Description: Naperville, Illinois : Sourcebooks Fire, [2022] | Audience:
    Ages 14. | Audience: Grades 10-12. | Summary: "A high school junior
    teams up with a hacker during a police brutality protest to shut down a
    device that creates an impenetrable dome around Baltimore that is
    keeping the residents in and information from going out"-- Provided by
    publisher.
Identifiers: LCCN 2021042559 (print) | LCCN 2021042560 (ebook)
Subjects: CYAC: Race relations--Fiction. | Protest movements--Fiction. |
    Hacking--Fiction. | Police--Fiction. | African Americans--Fiction. |
    Hispanic Americans--Fiction. | Gays--Fiction. | Baltimore
    (Md.)--Fiction. | Science fiction. | LCGFT: Novels. | Science fiction.
Classification: LCC PZ7.1.J285 Su 2022 (print) | LCC PZ7.1.J285 (ebook) |
    DDC [Fic]--dc23
LC record available at https://lccn.loc.gov/2021042559
LC ebook record available at https://lccn.loc.gov/2021042560

Printed and bound in the United States of America.
LSC 10 9 8 7 6 5 4 3 2 1

2021

Daunte Wright, 2001–April 21, 2021

Marvin David Scott III, 1995–March 14, 2021

Vincent "Vinny" M. Belmonte, September 14, 2001–January 5, 2021

Patrick Lynn Warren Sr., October 7, 1968–January 10, 2021

2020

David McAtee, August 3, 1966–June 1, 2020

Daniel T. Prude, 1979–March 30, 2020

George Perry Floyd Jr., October 14, 1973–May 25, 2020

Dreasjon "Sean" Reed, 1999–May 6, 2020

Michael Brent Charles Ramos, January 1, 1978–April 24, 2020

Breonna Taylor, June 5, 1993–March 13, 2020

Manuel "Mannie" Elijah Ellis, August 28, 1986–March 3, 2020

Rayshard Brooks, January 31, 1993–June 12, 2020

Carlos Carson, May 16, 1984–June 6, 2020

Tony McDade, 1982–May 27, 2020

2019

Atatiana Koquice Jefferson, November 28, 1990–October 12, 2019

John Elliott Neville, 1962–December 4, 2019

Elijah McClain, 1996–August 30, 2019

Sterling Lapree Higgins, 1982–March 25, 2019

Javier Ambler, October 7, 1978–March 28, 2019

2018

Emantic "EJ" Fitzgerald Bradford Jr., June 18, 1997–November 22, 2018

Charles "Chop" Roundtree Jr., September 5, 2000–October 17, 2018

Chinedu Okobi, February 13, 1982–October 3, 2018

Botham Shem Jean, September 29, 1991–September 6, 2018

Antwon Rose Jr., July 12, 2000–June 19, 2018

Saheed Vassell, December 22, 1983–April 4, 2018

Stephon Alonzo Clark, August 10, 1995–March 18, 2018

2017

Aaron Bailey, 1972–June 29, 2017

Charleena Chavon Lyles, April 24, 1987–June 18, 2017

Fetus of Charleena Chavon Lyles (14–15 weeks), June 18, 2017

Jordan Edwards, October 25, 2001–April 29, 2017

Chad Robertson, 1992–February 15, 2017

2016

Deborah Danner, September 25, 1950–October 18, 2016

Alfred Olango, July 29, 1978–September 27, 2016

Terence Crutcher, August 16, 1976–September 16, 2016

Terrence LeDell Sterling, July 31, 1985–September 11, 2016

Korryn Gaines, August 24, 1993–August 1, 2016

Joseph Curtis Mann, 1966–July 11, 2016

Philando Castile, July 16, 1983–July 6, 2016

Alton Sterling, June 14, 1979–July 5, 2016

2015

Bettie "Betty Boo" Jones, 1960–December 26, 2015

Quintonio LeGrier, April 29, 1996–December 26, 2015

Corey Lamar Jones, February 3, 1984–October 18, 2015

Jamar O'Neal Clark, May 3, 1991–November 16, 2015

Jeremy "Bam Bam" McDole, 1987–September 23, 2015

India Kager, June 9, 1988–September 5, 2015

Samuel "Sam" Vincent DuBose, March 12, 1972–July 19, 2015

Sandra Bland, February 7, 1987–July 13, 2015

Brendon K. Glenn, 1986–May 5, 2015

Freddie Carlos Gray Jr., August 16, 1989–April 19, 2015

Walter Lamar Scott, February 9, 1965–April 4, 2015

Eric Courtney Harris, October 10, 1971–April 2, 2015

Phillip Gregory White, 1982–March 31, 2015

Mya Shawatza Hall, December 5, 1987–March 30, 2015

Meagan Hockaday, August 27, 1988–March 28, 2015

Tony Terrell Robinson Jr., October 18, 1995–March 6, 2015

Janisha Fonville, March 3, 1994–February 18, 2015

Natasha McKenna, January 9, 1978–February 8, 2015

2014

Jerame C. Reid, June 8, 1978–December 30, 2014

Rumain Brisbon, November 24, 1980–December 2, 2014

Tamir E. Rice, June 15, 2002–November 22, 2014

Akai Kareem Gurley, November 12, 1986–November 20, 2014

Tanisha N. Anderson, January 22, 1977–November 13, 2014

Dante Parker, August 14, 1977–August 12, 2014

Tyree Woodson, 1976–August 2, 2014

Ezell Ford, October 14, 1988–August 11, 2014

Michael Brown Jr., May 20, 1996–August 9, 2014

John Crawford III, July 29, 1992–August 5, 2014

Eric Garner, September 15, 1970–July 17, 2014

Dontre Hamilton, January 20, 1983–April 30, 2014

Victor White III, September 11, 1991–March 3, 2014

Gabriella Monique Nevarez, November 25, 1991–March 2, 2014

Yvette Smith, December 18, 1966–February 16, 2014

McKenzie J. Cochran, August 25, 1988–January 29, 2014

Jordan Baker, 1988–January 16, 2014

2013

Andy Lopez, June 2, 2000–October 22, 2013

Miriam Iris Carey, August 12, 1979–October 3, 2013

Barrington "BJ" Williams, 1988–September 17, 2013

Jonathan Ferrell, October 11, 1989–September 14, 2013

Carlos Alcis, 1970–August 15, 2013

Larry Eugene Jackson Jr., November 29, 1980–July 26, 2013

Kyam Livingston, July 29, 1975–July 21, 2013

Clinton R. Allen, September 26, 1987–March 10, 2013

Kimani "Kiki" Gray, October 19, 1996–March 9, 2013

Kayla Moore, April 17, 1971–February 13, 2013

2012

Jamaal Moore Sr., 1989–December 15, 2012

Shelly Marie Frey, April 21, 1985–December 6, 2012

Darnesha Diana Harris, December 11, 1996–December 2, 2012

Timothy Russell, December 9, 1968–November 29, 2012

Malissa Williams, June 20, 1982–November 29, 2012

Noel Polanco, November 28, 1989–October 4, 2012

Reynaldo Cuevas, January 6, 1992–September 7, 2012

Chavis Carter, 1991–July 28, 2012

Alesia Thomas, June 1, 1977–July 22, 2012

Shantel Davis, May 26, 1989–June 14, 2012

Sharmel T. Edwards, October 10, 1962–April 21, 2012

Tamon Robinson, December 21, 1985–April 18, 2012

Ervin Lee Jefferson III, 1994–March 24, 2012

Kendrec McDade, May 5, 1992–March 24, 2012

Rekia Boyd, November 5, 1989–March 21, 2012

Shereese Francis, 1982–March 15, 2012

Jersey K. Green, June 17, 1974–March 12, 2012

Wendell James Allen, December 19, 1992–March 7, 2012

Nehemiah Lazar Dillard, July 29, 1982–March 5, 2012

Dante' Lamar Price, July 18, 1986–March 1, 2012

Raymond Luther Allen Jr., 1978–February 29, 2012

Johnnie Kamahi Warren, February 26, 1968–February 13, 2012

Manuel Levi Loggins Jr., February 22, 1980–February 7, 2012

Ramarley Graham, April 12, 1993–February 2, 2012

2011

Kenneth Chamberlain Sr., April 12, 1943–November 19, 2011

Alonzo E. Ashley Jr., 1982–July 18, 2011

Kenneth Harding Jr., August 5, 1991–July 16, 2011

Derek Williams, January 23, 1989–July 6, 2011

Raheim Brown Jr., March 4, 1990–January 22, 2011

Reginald Doucet, June 3, 1985–January 14, 2011

2010

Derrick Jones, September 30, 1973–November 8, 2010

Danroy "DJ" Henry Jr., October 29, 1990–October 17, 2010

Aiyana Mo'Nay Stanley-Jones, July 20, 2002–May 16, 2010

Steven Eugene Washington, September 20, 1982–March 20, 2010

Aaron M. Campbell, September 7, 1984–January 29, 2010

2009

Kiwane Carrington, July 14, 1994–October 9, 2009

Victor Steen, November 11, 1991–October 3, 2009

Shem Walker, March 18, 1960–July 11, 2009

Oscar Grant III, February 27, 1986–January 1, 2009

2008

Tarika Wilson, October 30, 1981–January 4, 2008

2007

DeAunta Terrell Farrow, September 7, 1994–June 22, 2007

2006

Sean Bell, May 23, 1983–November 25, 2006

Kathryn Johnston, June 26, 1914–November 21, 2006

2005

Ronald Curtis Madison, March 1, 1965–September 4, 2005

James B. Brissette Jr., November 6, 1987–September 4, 2005

Henry "Ace" Glover, October 2, 1973–September 2, 2005

2004

Timothy Stansbury Jr., November 16, 1984–January 24, 2004

2003

Ousmane Zongo, 1960–May 22, 2003

Alberta Spruill, 1946–May 16, 2003

Kendra Sarie James, December 24, 1981–May 5, 2003

Orlando Barlow, December 29, 1974–February 28, 2003

2001

Nelson Martinez-Mendez, 1977–August 8, 2001

Timothy DeWayne Thomas Jr., July 25, 1981–April 7, 2001

2000

Prince Carmen Jones Jr., March 30, 1975–September 1, 2000
Ronald Beasley, 1964–June 12, 2000
Earl Murray, 1964–June 12, 2000
Patrick Moses Dorismond, February 28, 1974–March 16, 2000
Malcolm Ferguson, October 31, 1976–March 1, 2000

1999

LaTanya Haggerty, 1973–June 4, 1999
Margaret LaVerne Mitchell, 1945–May 21, 1999
Amadou Diallo, September 2, 1975–February 4, 1999

1998

Tyisha Shenee Miller, March 9, 1979–December 28, 1998

1997

Dannette "Strawberry" Daniels, January 25, 1966–June 7, 1997
Frankie Ann Perkins, 1960–March 22, 1997

1994

Nicholas Heyward Jr., August 26, 1981–September 27, 1994

1990

Mary Mitchell, 1950–November 3, 1990

1987

Yvonne Smallwood, July 26, 1959–December 9, 1987

1984

Eleanor Bumpers, August 22, 1918–October 29, 1984

1983

Michael Jerome Stewart, May 9, 1958–September 28, 1983

1979

Eula Mae Love, August 8, 1939–January 3, 1979

1978

Arthur Miller Jr., 1943–June 14, 1978

1976

Randolph Evans, April 5, 1961–November 25, 1976
Barry Gene Evans, August 29, 1958–February 10, 1976

1973

Rita Lloyd, November 2, 1956–January 27, 1973

1968

Henry Dumas, July 20, 1934–May 23, 1968

1950

Eugene Burt (46)
Lorenzo Best (32), June 19, 1950

1948

Theris Rudolph Wood (19)
John Johnson (42)

1946

Harrison Lee (39)

1945

Denice Harris (22), June 6, 1945
Ervin Jones, August 21, 1945
Moses Green, September 9, 1945
Wilbert Cohen (14), November 1, 1945

1943

Knox Fail (40)

Sources

Ater, Renée. "In Memoriam: I Can't Breathe." On Monuments. May 29, 2020.

Chughtai, Alia. "Know Their Names." Al Jazeera. 2020.

Thomsen, Ian. "The Untold Stories of 143 Black People Killed by Officers in One Alabama Town." News@Northeastern. July 30, 2020.

Patterson, William L., et al. "We Charge Genocide." Quoted in Glenn, Susan A. "We Charge Genocide: The 1951 Black Lives Matter Campaign." Mapping American Social Movements Project, University of Washington. Accessed 2021.

CONTENT WARNING

This book contains death, police violence,
and slur words toward Black and brown minorities.

PROLOGUE

Science had never been Governor Ambrose's forte.

She had a passion for it, though. She loved that others found pleasure in understanding the world at large. But there were too many unknowns, and she wanted answers. To her, science was nothing more than an ocean waiting for the bigger, smarter, more well-funded fish to come around.

Sitting in the governor's mansion, with the first pink light of summer washing over the hills and illuminating her study, she sipped her tea. One part milk, four parts water, a splash of sugar. Her laptop was pristine, like everything else in her life. The screen flickered once, as if the reception was poor, and then came into focus: video from one of the testing rooms down in Fort Meade, streaming clearly and directly to her computer. To the untrained eye, there wasn't much to see: simply a thick white ring, roughly twenty feet in diameter, with a bull standing in the center of it.

Outside of the ring, by a panel, stood a man—a scrawny one,

with glasses too big for his face and a face too small for glasses—who gave a thumbs-up to the camera.

Governor Ambrose tapped her nude-colored nails against the hardwood desk.

The screen flickered again. The bull seemed agitated. The man seemed unbothered.

Governor Ambrose smiled. Any moment now.

Finally, something happened. The screen filled with blinding white light, like a hundred bulbs had exploded at once. For a moment, everything was out of focus, just white and static.

Governor Ambrose paused mid-sip. Was this it? Had the billions of dollars she had secretly funneled from the Maryland budget over the past four years with the help of several like-minded individuals, been wasted on this? No. That couldn't be. She had hired the best scientists because she wasn't a scientist. This had to work. She wouldn't—she couldn't—take no for an answer.

What other choice was there for her? She had won the election by the skin of her teeth. She wouldn't win another one. Running on a platform of law and order was tough, especially for a woman. It had been a results-driven campaign that had threaded a careful line between being too tough on crime for the liberals and not tough enough for the conservatives. She needed an ace in the hole. She needed surefire results. She needed to make a name for herself. She needed to make a bang.

And what better way than to create something that would eliminate crime in the third-most-violent major city in America? She could practically taste the air of the White House right now. Maybe even a Nobel Prize.

But the path to the presidency was paved with men who made backroom deals and sacrifices, and most such rooms were closed to people like her. She had to come out with something so brazen, so bold, so useful that no one could ignore her.

That's how the Dome was born. A shield to contain threats within until they could be neutralized and dealt with so their poisonous influence didn't infect everything else.

Putting the half-drunk cup of tea down slowly, she leaned forward. After a few taps on her keyboard, the camera zoomed in. The bull hadn't moved, but at least it seemed fine. That was more than she could say for the first four test subjects.

Without looking, she reached into her black suit jacket and pulled out her phone. *What is going on*, she typed, but she didn't get a chance to send it. The bull twitched, shaking its head violently, and then charged.

Her breath caught in her throat. This could be it. This could be the moment.

Perhaps someone else would have been more concerned with the well-being of the man in the room. Governor Ambrose was not that person.

The video had no sound, but she could practically hear the whining whirl of metal and electricity. She could feel the tension in the room as the muscular bull charged toward the scientist.

This was the moment everything could change.

The distance between the bull and the scientist was less than twenty feet, but it felt like it took hours for the bull to reach him. Well, the bull didn't *actually* reach him. There was a pulse of light that rippled outward from the horns when they made contact with *something*. Again, the bull attacked, shaking its head in frustration. Each time it slammed its horns against the invisible barrier, another pulse of light rippled out, revealing the shape of a fifteen-foot dome for a fraction of a second.

Governor Ambrose was not an expressive person. That was what the polls had said about her. *How can a woman who doesn't show any emotion be trusted?* Then again, other polls had said, *How can a woman who shows too much emotion be trusted?* There was no way to win.

Right now, she wanted to jump up and scream. But instead, she sat quietly, reveling in her joy.

Project ADP was a success.

Her phone vibrated. She looked down, expecting to see a text applauding her victory. But instead, she was met with a simple message from her press secretary.

A trial date has been set.

6
MONTHS
LATER

ONE

Today's the day everything changes.

I go through my bag for the tenth time, making sure everything is neatly packed inside. Water bottle? Check. Candy? Check. Notepad and three pens? Check and check. And most importantly, my camera that uses actual film: check. I reach into the side pouch, feeling around and counting. Two extra batteries, just in case. That should be more than enough for tonight.

Zipping up my backpack, I slip on my most comfortable shoes—a pair of worn checkered slip-ons—and grab a light blue raincoat. Maryland in the summer can be as unpredictable as…well, weather, I guess. It might be seventy degrees now, a nice cool reprieve from the previous two weeks of ninety-plus days, but that doesn't mean a sudden rainstorm isn't coming.

"Better to be hot for a bit than soaked for hours," I mutter. At worst, I'll leave it in the car.

I pat around on the bed, feeling for my phone, and check it for messages: none. Biting my inner cheek in frustration, I pull up my text thread with Damien. No response since this morning.

Dozens of thoughts swirl through my head. Has he decided he doesn't want to talk to me anymore? Has he moved on to...what's his name, Liam? Is he dead in a ditch somewhere?

Instead of getting swallowed by the pit of *does Damien West like me or not*, I pocket the phone and push it down, along with my worries.

He said he would join me. It was his idea to go. He'll come, I tell myself. And that's that.

Besides, I have bigger things to worry about right now.

Maybe I should just sneak out of the house. That might be easier, right? Better than having to deal with Mom right now. Or I could just run out quickly and say, "Heading out! Love you!" and leave before she can ask any questions or make me feel guilty.

I know she doesn't approve of me going. Heading out to a protest is already scary enough. But a protest against police brutality because a cop got off for beating a man to death? In Baltimore? That's a whole different beast. It took me all week to convince her to be even slightly okay with it. This is the final hurdle, the final boss to slay before I can be on my way.

I settle on a middle ground. I won't make it obvious I'm leaving without saying goodbye, I just won't...go out of my way to see her. That's fair. Slowly, I tiptoe down the carpeted stairs, careful to skip the fourth step from the bottom, which is far too noisy for anyone's good. Almost there, and I'll have enough time to stop at Panera before heading into the city. Maybe get an iced—

"Jamal," my mom says like it's just a common noun, no inflection to give away any of her feelings. "Come here."

It isn't a request, but a maternal demand I have no hope of ignoring. Instead of trying to fight it, I take a deep breath, drop my bag, and slink into the living room.

Mom's on the couch knitting, because that's what she does when she's nervous. It's always been that way. Her fingers move like some charm master's hands casting a spell. I can't tell what she's making, but judging by her use of bright pink and green, it's something for our next-door neighbor, Brenda. She loves those noxious colors.

The TV displays clips of riots all across the country. Atlanta. New Orleans. Chicago. Oakland. Tempe. Even Washington, DC, about forty-five minutes south. A map appears, showing another half dozen locations.

"As you can see, Chip," the female reporter with the blond bun says, "all over the country, people are standing up in protest against the acquittal of Baltimore police officer Damon Kyles. His trial, which lasted only two short weeks with less than a day of deliberation, has sparked another ripple of Black Lives Matter protests. And though Damon is the one who shot Jerome Thomas, a thirty-five-year-old single father of two, when a routine traffic stop turned into an altercation, most people blame Police Chief Ian Coles for the no-mercy atmosphere; he's known for demanding an iron fist of justice from his subordinates.

"Chief Coles, a decorated army veteran who served twice in Iraq, has served for more than fifteen years on the police force—"

Mom turns off the TV before the reporter can finish. We all know what happened, especially me—I read every report and article I could get my hands on. Because it happened less than thirty minutes from where I'm standing right now…and because Jerome looked like me. Dark skin, strong features, slightly-above-average height. But most of all, he was Black. And that, in America, seems to be a death sentence sometimes.

"So, you're really doing this," Mom says.

"I'm going to be safe," I promise her. Like I've promised her the past three days. "I'm also not going alone. Damien is going with me."

That seems to help. The tightness in her shoulders relaxes a notch. Damien's white, and life is always easier when you have a white guy by your side.

Maybe that's part of the reason I'm interested in dating him? Damien isn't at all my type, let me be clear. He doesn't care about politics or social justice like I do. He doesn't see beyond what the news—or anyone, for that matter—tells him. He doesn't seek out information so he can make his own decisions. But he's handsome, he's smart, and he's kind.

Plus, as every Black person knows, proximity to whiteness helps us succeed in life, whether we like it or not. At least Damien gives me that.

"And you'll have your phone with you?"

"Yes."

"Charger?"

"Yes, Mom," I lie. It wouldn't fit in my bag. Candy is more important, anyway. Got to keep my energy up.

"Water?"

"Yes."

"Contact list of—"

"You, Grandma, and two friends." Also a pro bono legal group I found online that is giving free legal help to anyone arrested at the protests, but she doesn't need to know that. "I also have my camera. I'll show you the photos when I get back, if you want?"

That's why I'm doing this in the first place. It's not just to protest injustice, though of course that's a big part. But this is also to better myself—to better *us*. If I can get awesome pictures at the protest, it'll bolster my Columbia photojournalism application. My guidance counselor said I'm close to being competitive for a full ride scholarship. I just need a little something extra.

If I can capture these protests, the anger and hurt, the rift between people and the police? That's the kind of *something* she means. I just know it.

"Do you have a mask? I'm sure there's going to be tear gas."

I pause. That's something I don't have—and didn't even think about. Shit.

My mom glances over, my own dark brown eyes looking back at me. "You didn't pack a mask."

Again, not a question—a statement.

"I forgot."

"You forgot," Mom mutters. Her words are soft, but they stick like a thousand knives. Mom is a master at that. You'd think she had a history working for the CIA as an interrogator or something. But no, she's just a Black mother raising a Black son in America.

"You know there are going to be police there, Jamal," she scolds. Slowly, like the weight of the world is pressing down on her shoulders and joints, she stands and frowns at me. "They are going to be look-ing for any excuse to throw things at you. Rocks, tear gas—"

"Rubber bullets," I finish for her.

"Exactly." This isn't the first time we've had this talk, because this isn't the first time I've wanted to go to a protest, because this isn't the first time a cop has overstepped. Just eight months ago, there was another incident in DC. A year and a half ago, there was one in Richmond. This is just the first protest Mom has let me go to.

Let is probably a strong word.

She shuffles over to the cabinet where we keep the good linen and the plates we use for Thanksgiving. She reaches into the third drawer and pulls out a peach-colored cloth.

I know that cloth well. It's a shawl Grandma used to wear all the time. It was only thing Mom wanted when she passed away.

Mom holds the fabric to her nose and takes a deep breath. She sighs and walks past me to the kitchen, then lays the cloth out on the table, grabs the scissors from her knitting kit, and cuts it without hesi-tation. The action is merciless. I don't even have time to tell her to stop.

She hands the smaller section to me. "Betty will keep you safe while you're out there."

It takes me a moment to put two and two together and under-stand what she means. I examine the fabric, then bring it up to my nose, mimicking the inhale Mom did, like there is some sort of hidden power inside of it.

Before I can tuck the fabric into my back pocket, Mom wraps her sinewy arms around me, holding me so tightly I think our flesh might fuse together.

"You be safe, Jamal," she demands. "You come back to me, you hear?"

I should be more afraid. I know I should. There's no difference between me and any of the other men and women who have been on the wrong side of the police, who have been deemed a threat just because their skin is dipped in midnight. What I'm doing for a photo opportunity is dangerous. Stupid, even.

I don't expect Mom to understand. I just expect her to support me. And she does. I know, deep down, that she does. Because even if she wants to chain me to my bed or slap some sense into me, she knows I have to do this. Not only because it'll help me get into a good college and pursue my dream of working in journalism, but because being there, standing up for what's right, letting the police and the state of Maryland know that they can't fail to deliver justice—actual justice—is important to me. It's important to almost every Black and brown teen I know. This can determine the type of future we're going to make. Are we going to be a generation that just lets the status quo continue, or are we going to stand up for our rights no matter what? I know what type of person I want to be. Going to this rally is the step in the right direction.

And Mom isn't going to stop me.

I pull back, smile as bright as I can, and kiss her cheek. "I'll be okay, and I'll come home before it's too late. It's only a forty-five-minute drive. And remember, Damien is coming with me. I have a white boy. They aren't going to hurt me."

That's at least what I'm gambling on.

Damien's house isn't far from mine. Usually, when we're "hanging out," I just walk. It gives me time to decompress, to analyze my thoughts and still my anxiety.

But tonight, my anxiety is at an all-time high.

I park and walk up the steps to his house. I knock on the door. No answer. I raise my hand, about to rap my knuckles against the worn wood again, when the door bursts open.

"Hey," Damien says.

"Hey, yourself."

Unlike me, dressed and ready to take on The Man and record history, Damien is…not. His hair is a curly mess, he's wearing a worn, stained T-shirt—what he wears when he's doing his woodwork—and a pair of gray sweats and slides.

"That's not revolutionary attire," I tease. "Didn't you get the memo?"

He forces a smile that doesn't reach his eyes. "About that."

Uh-oh.

Nothing good ever comes after *about that*. Damien has a special ability to twist my heart when he says it. I know whatever is about to come out of his mouth is going to hurt.

Damien sighs, rubbing the back of his head awkwardly. "I don't think I'm going to be able to make it tonight."

"Oh." The words don't hurt as much as I thought they would. Honestly, I was surprised he wanted to go to begin with.

"Yeah." A beat passes, and the space between us, only a few inches, feels like it's getting wider by the moment. "It's not like I don't want to come."

"Sure. Totally get it."

"It's just…have you looked at the news? The protests are going to be crazy."

"Mm-hmm."

"It's going to get violent."

"Yeah."

"It's probably not a good idea to—"

"—go down, yeah, totally get it. You don't need to say anything else."

Damien's shoulders relax. "Cool, thanks for understanding."

In that moment, I feel my blood boil. It feels like he's happy to get out of it, to not have to stare in the face of what's going on in Baltimore. How nice it must be to just…check out and be happy with ignoring the world. How easy it will be for him to close his door when I leave and go back to whatever he was doing.

"No problem." I step back, needing to put some distance between us. He may be pretty, but the way he disassociates from what's happening? Ugly.

"I'll see you around at school?" he asks. "I wanna see your photos fr—"

"Yeah. See you."

I hurry to my car, turn the keys so hard and fast I'm afraid they'll spin around in the ignition, and drive toward the chaos, cranking up Lauryn Hill to drown out my own thumping heartbeat.

TWO

The ride from Annapolis to Baltimore only takes me thirty-seven minutes, eight minutes less than the expected forty-five. Thank you, speeding. The only downside is the fact that the police keep me from parking inside the city center.

I keep still as I wait my turn in a long line of cars, like an animal caught in the lights. *Five rules, Jamal*, I remind myself.

One: never make any sudden movements.

Two: never talk back.

Three: if you have to speak, keep your sentences short.

Four: never give them a reason to think you're a threat.

Five: remember that you're loved, you're valued, and you're important.

"Please be a Black cop. Please be a Black cop," I chant as the line of cars being checked slowly advances. There are about a half a dozen officers leaning into cars, having brief conversations with drivers trying to enter the city, and then directing them into different lanes. What those divisions mean, I have no idea.

I examine my car quickly. I made sure to clean it before I left, so the interior is devoid of anything personal. Only my book bag, a three-day-old Starbucks cup, and my license and registration remain on the seat next to me. I even used Febreze and put scented air fresheners in the car so it didn't smell like anything they could use as a reason to search me.

My heart skips a beat as a white cop with small facial features approaches my car. I take a quick deep breath. Mint mixed with evergreen. Green. Weed. Jail. Will this cop know that artificial smell isn't some illegal Kush? Am I going to be yanked out of the car and slammed against the ground? *Shit, shit, shit.*

The cop approaches the car, rapping his knuckles on the window. Quickly, but not too quickly, I roll it down.

"Are you going to the protests?" he asks, leaning against the glass, his steel-colored eyes scanning me and then the inside of my car.

My throat turns dry, and the words are like a whisper when they leave my mouth. The cop—Officer Duncan—leans in a bit. "Speak up, son."

Son. A three-letter word that has so much weight to it, especially when spoken by someone who is only a few years older than me. He has the power to control my future or end my life if he chooses. With great power comes great responsibility. I wonder if he treats his life-taking ability as the powerful thing it is.

"Sorry," I say, forcing more bass into my voice, like that'll help him relate to me. "Yeah. For the local high school."

He arches his brow, silently urging me to elaborate. Did he ask anyone else to explain themselves, or just me?

"I go to Hunter."

"That fancy private school?"

I want to correct him, tell him it isn't that fancy, but I feel like that violates rules two, three, and maybe four. Being an "uppity" Black man definitely violates rule four.

"Yeah," I settle on.

"Didn't know they had reporters or anything there."

"I'm part of the journalism club," I say, which isn't a lie.

"Hmm," he curtly replies. He gives the car one more look. "You're not going to make any trouble for us, are you?"

What kind of loaded question is that? I'm a seventeen-year-old kid with a camera, a lanky frame, and an anxiety problem. What problems am I going to cause?

"No," I say.

He arches his brow, another silent request. It doesn't take me long to realize what he's asking for.

"No, sir."

"Good." He nods and steps back. "Go on to that lane." He points to where a few other cars are going. "Have a good day."

"You too."

The words feel hollow. Do I want him to have a good day, or do I want him to rot in hell? I don't stay long enough to think it over before driving as quickly as I can to the right area, gripping the steering wheel tighter than usual since my sweaty palms make it hard for me to gain traction against the leather.

There isn't designated parking for the protests, but there's an area about ten blocks away where most cars are parked.

By the time I make it downtown, the streets are flooded with people. I can't get a good view as I merge into the sea of protesters along with about twelve others who parked around the same time. Signs of all different colors made from all different materials cover the streets. If you looked from the skies, it would be a sea of colored signs. People are chanting like everyone was born knowing the words, as if we're sharing one hive mind:

"Take it to the streets, defund the police! No justice, no peace!"

The words have so much power behind them, the glass buildings around us seem to rumble. Metal warps, and the ground shakes as the protesters and I thump our feet against it.

I push through the crowd and find a lamppost. On the second try, I grab it and pull myself up, and I'm suddenly able to see the hundreds—no, thousands—of protesters all around me.

"It's endless," I mutter in awe.

Fumbling with one hand, I pull my camera out of my bag by the strap and toss it up. I easily catch it, using my other hand to hold on to the pole while I snap some photos. I trust they'll look good. That's what I love about not having a digital camera. It's only you and the subjects of your photos. You can't get distracted with all the fancy buttons. You have to trust yourself.

I wait until the crowd thins just a bit, jump off the lamppost, land in a crouched position, and rejoin the group. The energy is infectious, and within half a block, I'm chanting with everyone else.

The crowd splits off into three different groups when we reach the end of the four-block march. One, according to my limited knowledge of Baltimore, seems to be heading toward the water. One is heading toward one of the parks, and one is heading toward City Hall. The water is where the organizers of the event told people to go if they need food, water, or legal help. The parks are where most of the people who want to cause trouble are probably going. Mom would want me to stay away from there. And City Hall—that's where the action will be. The best shots. The protests. Everything.

That's where I'm going.

Which reminds me, who *did* organize this event? I can't write an article without knowing that.

While walking toward City Hall, I pull out my phone and do a quick search. Every one of these marches has an organizer and money behind it, even if it's just community funds. I need to—

"You're not going to find it through Google," someone says to the right of me.

I jump when I hear the voice. Baritone, confident, and way too close. How did he sneak up on me?

"Always know your surroundings. That's how you keep yourself alive, Jamal," Mom had told me months ago when I first started talking about wanting to go to these protests. I know why she doesn't want me to go—one part parental concern, one part history. Back in the day, on the tail end of the Civil Rights Movement, her older sister was a Black Panther and got herself killed. Mom never recovered.

I quickly pocket my phone and turn to face the man. Not a man—a boy. He's only an inch or so taller than me with wild curls, tan skin, and a mischievous smile. He's wearing a basketball jersey, a pair of tattered jean shorts, and Chucks with specks of paint on them.

"And how do you know that?"

"I just know."

"That's not good enough, and it's a bit creepy."

He shrugs. "Nemesis doesn't put their info online. They say it—"

"Wait," I interrupt. "Go back. Did I hear you right?"

"Hmm?"

"You said *Nemesis*."

"Mm-hmm."

"*The* Nemesis?"

He arches one bushy brow. "Do you know of another one?"

I push my lips into a thin line, wanting to snap back at him. His sarcasm has no place here. But the idea that this march might be funded by Nemesis? That's enough to steer my focus away from any sarcastic jab I could throw at him.

Nemesis, one of the leading activist groups in the country, organized this? How does no one know that? How does *this guy* know it?

That information doesn't come cheap. He has to have some sort of in.

"How do you know?"

"How do I know what?"

"Who organized this march," I clarify, annoyed. "Are you one of them?"

He makes a *psh* sound and puts his hands on his hips. "Do I look like a hacker? Plus, you say that with such disdain, like being a hacker is a bad thing."

Absolutely not, I think, *on both accounts.* But not every hacker wears a shirt that says HELLO, I'M A HACKER! GIVE ME ACCESS TO YOUR COMPUTER.

"I'll take your silence as an answer," he says. "I just know things. Information comes easy to me."

"Sounds like another way to say you're a hacker."

He only smiles and extends his hand to me like a peace offering. "Marco."

"Jamal," I say, shaking it.

Over Marco's shoulder, I see a burly-looking cop with too much muscle for his body pushing through the crowd like an icebreaker ship. While everyone else is moving north, he's coming from the west, disrupting the flow of the protest. And his eyes are locked directly on me.

Instinctively, I take a step back. Marco notices and looks over his shoulder.

"Shit," he whispers. "Act cool."

How am I supposed to act cool when—

"Hey!" the cop yells, loud enough to be heard over the noise around us. He's not alone. Seemingly out of nowhere, six other cops, most of them plainclothes officers, join him in formation. Attack formation. "What is that?"

I know what he's pointing to without having to look down: my camera.

I raise it up, showing him it's no threat, the safest and easiest thing to do. If I show him I don't have a weapon, everything will turn out all right. That's how this works.

If only that were always true.

Marco steps to the side as the cop approaches. He gets close, but not too close, keeping about five feet of distance between us. Marco and I have been standing and talking long enough that most of the procession has already moved downtown, meeting up at City Hall for the rally led by a local civil rights leader.

"I said," the cop growls, "what. Is. That."

"Camera," I croak out. "I'm here taking—"

"Photos aren't allowed during protests. Hand it over."

That's not true at all, I think. But does what's true really matter right now?

I stand there, completely still.

Move, Jamal, my brain urges. *Just give him the camera. It isn't worth it.*

No, the other side of my brain argues. *You haven't done anything wrong. He's just worried your camera has evidence on it of any wrongdoing he's done. A guilty conscious, that's all, Jamal. Play it cool. He won't do anything. Not with so much media attention on the city right now.*

But what if he does? People have been shot for less.

He isn't going to risk that. This is a rally about someone being shot and killed. You think this cop is going to do exactly what we're accusing him of?

Yes. Yes, I fully think that.

The cop growls, puffing out his chest and taking a step forward, wrapping his thick white fingers around his half-holstered taser. "I said, hand over the—"

"Officer, Officer, Officer," Marco interjects. He takes a half a step forward, hands raised, and squints at the man's badge. "Officer Daniels."

Suddenly, the thickness in the air, the coldness and isolation that the black hole of the cop created, just disappears. It's like everything comes rushing back—the sound of those around me, the thumping of my heart, all of it.

And most importantly, my awareness of the crowd growing around me, the cop, and Marco.

Relief washes over me. Nothing will happen now, not with people watching. The cop isn't that stupid. Then again, cops have done worse things and gotten away with them. What makes me, or anyone, think I'll be different than any other Black man who died unnecessarily?

"I'm going to tell you this simple and easy, because none of us have time for this," Marco says slowly. I can't see his face, since his back is facing me, but he sounds…relaxed? At least he's smart enough to keep his hands up, palms facing the cop.

"There are hundreds of people watching you—do you really want to do this?" Hundreds might be a bit of an exaggeration. There's closer to maybe four dozen, but all of those people have phones and social media accounts.

As if on cue, the other stragglers pull out their phones. Some turn on their flashlights, putting a makeshift spotlight on Officer Daniels to reiterate the point.

"Thank you all," Marco practically purrs. He turns back to the officer. "Do you really want to be the cop who assaults a Black teen during a protest about how cops are assaulting Black people? Really? Optics?"

The cop opens his mouth to speak, his face swelling red with anger, but Marco cuts him off.

"Sorry, sorry, not done yet. What I'm trying to say is, there's no way you can win this, and it isn't worth it. What my friend here has is just a camera. People are angry. And angry people not only make mistakes, they come at you with a vengeance. And I promise you, if you do what I think you're about to do, this march won't be about Jerome Thomas, it'll be about Officer Daniels."

The cop's body gets more rigid as he pauses less than five feet away from me. His jaw is tight, his bright blue eyes burning like fire. His right hand, the one closest to his gun, twitches.

I don't really know why, but all I can think of is *Doctor Who*.

I remember watching it with my mom when we were trying to pass the time in a hotel room a few years back. The doctor was talking about fixed points in time, how some things in history can't be changed once they happen. They are defining moments. Am I cocky enough to think this moment, right here and now, is a defining moment? That whatever choice this cop makes will alter history and determine the direction humanity takes?

There's no proof of that. How many times have Black men and trans women been shot with no consequences? Nothing ever changes. I'd be just another statistic. Another hashtag. Another poster. Another talking point. Another—

"Fine," the cop says gruffly, pulling his hand away. "But if I see either of you again…"

"Mm-hmm," Marco says. "Sir, yes, sir."

Before Marco can say something that'll get us in trouble, I yank him along, moving far away from the cop.

"Where are we going?" he asks.

"It doesn't matter."

"Jesus, you're hurting me. Loosen up, will ya?"

"No." We need to put some space between us and that guy before he changes his mind. I don't want to be anywhere near him when or if he does.

My brain is sharp with alertness. Every bit of information is funneled through and sorted into the correct bin. Thousands of pieces of data per second pass through, all rapidly organized. Hyperawareness is a symptom of something; I remember reading about it in AP Psych. But what—

"Hey!" Marco finally says, ripping his arm from my grasp. "We're far enough away. Jeez."

Marco literally just talked down the cops. How did he *do* that? It never happens, as far as I know. I sling my camera over my shoulder and quickly pat myself down.

"What are you doing?" he asks.

"I must have gotten shot," I reason. "I'm dead or something. None of this is real."

I can't find the bullet hole. No sore spots, no wounds, no nothing. Is this what the afterlife feels like? How many times have we seen stories in the news about Black people having run-ins with cops, lesser run-ins than that, and not making it out alive?

So how did I just stand by and watch as Marco berated a cop and not end up dead? It doesn't make sense. It's not logical. It—

"Hey, hey, HEY!" Marco barks. When I snap back to reality, I feel his hands on my shoulders, gripping me firmly but not *too* firmly.

"You're okay," he says. "You're here. You're alive. You're okay. Say it with me."

"I don't need—"

"Humor me?"

I sigh and take a deep breath.

"Good. Hold it for five seconds, and then breathe out."

I follow his directions, breathing out the words, "I'm safe. I'm alive. I'm okay."

I didn't notice how far we'd walked until that moment. We were on Fifth Street before, and now we're on Ninth. Well, not *on* Ninth—in the alley between Ninth and Tenth. How did we get here so quickly?

Marcos looks at his right arm, frowning. He thrusts it in my face. "What do you see?"

"Nothing, because your arm is—"

"Bruises!" he barks. "With a grip like that, you've gotta be into football or something."

"Did you say that because I'm Black?"

He rolls his eyes. "Please don't make this a thing. I asked—"

My phone vibration catches me off guard. "Hold on." I hold up one finger, silencing him, pulling my phone out.

"You did not just—"

Four texts from my mom. Two missed calls. When did these happen? *Probably during the incident*, I think. I must have been distracted.

"I need to take this," I say to Marco. "Then we're going to talk."

"We are? As in, like, a scolding talk, or an I'm-the-star-of-your-film talk?"

"I'm a journalist, not a documentarian. And besides, who says I'd want you on camera?"

"Oh, come on." He flashes a cheeky smile and flexes his sinewy right arm like a bodybuilder. "Who wouldn't?"

"Mm-hmm. Sure. Give me a minute."

I answer the phone, preparing myself for whatever tirade Mom has prepared, but I don't get a chance to speak. Instead, all of her words jumble together.

"Wait, wait, hold on, Mom, slow down. Start from the beginning."

"You need to get out of there," she says, slowing down barely enough for me to understand her. "Now."

Had she seen what had happened between the officer and me somehow? She couldn't have, right? I didn't clock any cameras, and there's no way the news would focus on me, anyway. We're not even in central downtown yet.

"I'm fine. Really. I'm not going to be here much longer." One of those vague answers that'll keep her at bay long enough. At least, that's what I think.

"You're not listening to me," she says, more and more static cutting through her voice. "I...something...news...dome..."

"Mom?" I pull the phone back and look at it. The bars dwindle from five to two to none. And then the call cuts out.

Marco glances back at me. "Everything okay?"

"Probably," I admit, pocketing the phone. "Mom's freaking out."

"Isn't that what parents do? You told them you're coming down here, yeah? Mine would be freaking out too."

"She was just going on and on and said something about a dome. I think she—"

"Wait," Marco interrupts. "What did you just say?"

I want to bark at him for cutting me off, but the seriousness on his face matches the panic I heard in my mom's voice.

"She said something about a dome," I say slowly. "I wasn't able to make out the rest of it."

"Shit, shit, shit." Marco pulls out his own phone. "No reception. *Shit!*"

He kicks the brick wall hard, hard enough that I know it hurts, and that's what scares me. He's more concerned about whatever this dome thing is than his foot.

"You going to tell me what—"

Marco turns to me, wincing as he puts weight on his right foot. "Shut up and listen."

"Okay, you do not—"

"Shut. Up," he says, firmer this time. "You need to get out of here. Right now. Head back to your car."

A high-pitched sound pierces the air. Marco and I both cover our ears, and I can only imagine he's experiencing the same pain I am. Everything turns blurry as the noise, like a knife, rips the lobes of my brain apart.

And then, as quickly as it started, it stops, only its echoes filling the air and bouncing around in my head.

"So this is what a migraine feels like," I mutter. Somehow, I have fallen to my knees and scraped them up so much that they're bleeding. I hiss, watching the skin move over the wounded flesh. Slowly and carefully, I brush it off with my fingers. Mom is going to kill me.

But I don't have time to think about that before Marco grabs my arm again, tugging me like an overeager animal.

"We have to get somewhere safe," he urges.

I want to protest. I want to *demand* that he give me answers—my mom taught me not to trust strangers, and Marco is still very much a stranger. But there are more important things to worry about right now.

Like the booming, crackling voice that seems to come from the skies.

"Citizens of Baltimore," the voice says, rumbling through the streets and making the glass buildings quiver, "this is your chief of police, Ian Coles. With the power granted to me by the governor of Maryland, I am placing this city in isolation. I repeat: Baltimore, Maryland is now in isolation. Report home immediately, or there will be consequences. You have been warned.

"You have ten minutes to disperse. Good luck."

THREE

"What the hell was that?"

I'm not the only one on the street who looks confused.

"*Now* do you believe me?" Marco asks.

"No! I believe you *less*. You think that"—I gesture wildly at the sky—"is going to make someone trust you *more*?"

"Yeah, honestly, I was hoping it would!"

I check my phone again, ready to call my mom, or at least ready to see a dozen texts from her. But I still have no bars.

I turn it off and on again: nothing. It's like I'm in a dead zone. Before I can try something new, like putting it on airplane mode and turning it off, Marco slaps the phone out of my hand.

"*What the*—" I watch as my expensive new iPhone falls to the pavement. The screen cracks, a spiderweb appearing almost instantly. Valid anger boils up from the pit of my stomach and floods my system, but Marco grabs my shoulder, and his words still me.

"We don't have time," he says with venom in his voice. "I'm

begging you, please listen to me. I promise I'll explain everything. I swear it. But right now, you have to trust me."

Marco is asking me to trust him? That's rich. He hasn't given me a single piece of information since we met. And he wants me to just blindly believe him?

I look around quickly, getting a sense of how the other protesters are reacting. No one seems to know what's happening. Murmurs and low rumbles fill the streets, a heavy veil of confusion lingering over everyone.

All right, I think. *Let's work this through logically.* Information is power. If I want to understand anything, I need to know what I'm up against, create some sort of baseline.

Which points back to Marco. Cussing mentally, I lean down, pick up the phone, and pocket it.

"Fine," I say. "But the moment—"

"I'll tell you what you want to know. I keep my promises," he says.

He suddenly seems calm. At least *someone's* calm. But it just confirms that he knows more than he's letting on.

"What time is it?" he mutters. "All right, we've got eight minutes. What street is this?"

"Charleston."

He nods. "Good, good. I know where we can go. It's not far from here. Come on."

Marco's long legs keep him about half a step ahead of me.

"What did they mean?"

"What's going on?"

"Is this some sort of joke?"

"What are they up to?"

"I need to get home."

"I'm scared."

The voices blend together, like how I imagine Hades would sound with its river of souls—each of them distinct, but all of them forming one homogenous sound at the same time. I stay close to Marco, like he's some sort of lightning rod of sanity.

"We're halfway there," he says a few minutes later. Or at least I think it's a few minutes later—I have no concept of time. My phone's screen is so cracked that I can't even make out the numbers on it. But having it feels like a lifeline, and I grip it a bit tighter.

It feels stupid to worry about a piece of technology right now. Mom will be pissed that it's broken, sure, but she'll be even more pissed if…whatever Marco thinks is going to happen happens to me. She'll understand about the phone. Focusing on it is just an excuse my mind is using to ground itself.

"There," Marco says, pointing. "It's another quarter of a mile or so, but we're going someplace where we'll be safe."

"Your home?" Seems like the reasonable answer.

He laughs. "I wish. Come on. We don't have much time."

"How long is *not much time*?"

He doesn't stop walking; in fact, Marco picks up his pace, forcing me to almost jog to keep time with him. "Two minutes."

"Two minutes to go a quarter of a mile?"

He smirks. "You up for a jog?"

"I don't run unless I'm being chased."

"I think that applies now, indirectly."

Without asking permission, Marco takes my hand and tugs me along. His long legs pick up speed, and it feels like I'm flying across the pavement.

We're not the only ones hurrying. It's like all the protesters have a hive mind, knowing our time is almost up.

And right then, I notice something I didn't see before.

I yank my hand out of Marco's and stop in the middle of the street. Marco makes it a few steps ahead of me before realizing our connection is broken and turning to face me.

"Where are all the police officers?"

Why didn't I deduce it earlier? At a time like this, when they are trying to enforce law and order, I would expect to see dozens of them. But I can't see any. It's like they've cleared out, leaving us to fend for ourselves.

He looks around two, three, four times. "They're getting suited up," he whispers. I want to ask what he means, but at the same time, I don't.

All I can think of in that moment are images of protests in the sixties. Cops in uniforms, spraying down Black people in the streets with hoses.

"Shit." Marco checks his watch again before saying those fateful words no one in any situation wants to hear: "We're not going to make it."

"I'm sorry, what?" I hiss back.

Marco looks over his shoulder. He turns back to me, about to say something, but the loud sound in the air, like metal sliding against metal, makes him frown.

"Focus on your breathing," Marco mutters. "We'll get through this, I promise. Then we'll get to the house. We'll be safe there."

I want to push back, to ask what the hell he's talking about. But something deep in the pit of my stomach, that nagging feeling, that voice of logic, tells me I should listen. And this time I do.

A harsh boom fills the air. It's so loud it makes my bones ache. I can feel it deep in my inner ears, threatening my gag reflex and making me want to vomit.

And then the voice follows.

"Citizens of Baltimore, Maryland. This city is now under the Dome. Do not resist orders from armed and armored officials. Anyone found violating the rules of the Dome will be prosecuted to the highest extent of the law. You will receive more information in one hour."

The voice drifts off with an echo, like it's lingering to remind me and everyone else who heard it that whoever said those words is watching us. Closely. It rings in my head and clamps around my nerves like a vice, keeping me from moving.

Marco doesn't hesitate, though.

He pulls back and holds me at arm's length, his eyes wide with fear. He says one word—the only word I need to hear.

"Run."

Marco's voice cuts deep into my flesh, past the ligaments and bones, and finds its way into the soft parts of my body.

It's the look in his eyes that does it, the way I can tell that deep behind them, the poison of fear has taken hold of him too.

And then we're running.

My feet hit the pavement with heavy thumps, like a rhythmic drumbeat. How much longer do we have? Can we outrun the ominous warning of that wizardlike voice from on high? Is the threat even real? Does it matter?

A woman bumps into me. A man bumps into her. About five feet away, I see a girl no older than me get knocked down to the ground. She screams, her voice swallowed up by the confusion.

I stop for a fraction of a second. I should help her. *We* should help her. That's the right thing to do. But is there such a thing as right and wrong when survival is on the line? Right now, survival is the only thing that matters.

Stopping, though, is the kiss of death. When I was traveling with the crowd, I was part of the inertia. When I stop, I'm like a capsized rower in white rapids.

I feel like a pinball as bodies hit me. I don't take it personally, though each clip stings, and I know they will leave bruises. Everyone is trying to get to safety. Everyone simply wants to make it out alive.

I stumble once, twice, three times before I lose my footing. I'm prepared to hit the ground hard, ready to curl my body protectively around my vital organs. But someone catches me and pulls me close to their body.

Marco.

"Stay close to me, I got you," he promises. "Take my hand and don't let go."

I don't need to be told twice. I grip his hand so hard that I make a mental note to apologize for any bruising later. The world may be raging around us, completely devolving in a matter of seconds. But with my hand in Marco's, I feel safe. I feel like we'll make it out alive. I feel…okay.

For a moment.

The boom that follows, much louder than the first, is ear-shattering. The world suddenly looks like I'm trying to view a soiled watercolor painting through a filter of broken glass. Every nerve in my body hurts, and the sound—oh my *god*, the sound. It reminds me of what a dragon roar would sound like if you watched *Game of Thrones* in IMAX, except the IMAX speakers are inside my ear-drums. But the sound isn't the scariest thing. That's reserved for the light show in the sky.

A beam of pure white light shoots up from the antenna on top of the Transamerica Tower. The light extends more than thirty feet into the air before, like a pulse, it expands, milky-white see-through layers pooling outward like a dome, expanding as far as the eye can see before disappearing behind the buildings.

"What the hell," I whisper, squinting in bewilderment. The milky film moves like soap suspended on top of water. It's mostly translucent.

My camera is in my hand before I realize it. My body goes on autopilot. I'm a journalist; proof and evidence are our lifeblood. I snap a few quick photos of the beam of light, of the milky dome, of the way it illuminates the sky, all of it.

"Come on," Marco hisses. One block away, officers in black-and-blue uniforms line the streets, two on the left and two on the right. They're not dressed in riot gear but skin-tight suits like divers wear. I want to make a joke about how if they are considering taking a swim in the Baltimore harbor, they might want to make sure they aren't growing a third eye in a month or two. Instead, I raise my camera to snap a photo of them, but Marco yanks me hard, so hard it feels like my shoulder is being pulled out of the socket.

Marco tugs me to the right. I think we're going into an alleyway, but we stop behind a large, nondescript black truck. We press our backs firmly against one of the oversize tires.

"What—"

He covers my mouth so tightly with his right hand, I feel like I'm losing my ability to breath. But the panic in his eyes tells me not to fight back.

Keep quiet, he mouths.

And so I do. I put two and two together pretty easily. The shortest path between two points is a line. If we need to walk a quarter of a mile north, the cops are in our way. Sure, maybe we could go around them—and we might have to—but the more we walk, the longer we're out here, the higher our chances of getting caught.

And that's something Marco and I can agree is not a good idea.

I can see everything through the space under the truck. The heavy thump of rubber boots. The refraction of light as the sun catches the metal on their suits.

The advancing officers stop, the row of them perpendicular to Marco and me. My breath catches in the back of my throat. We're close enough that they could see if us they wanted to. The only thing protecting us is this four-foot width of metal.

They cock their guns, a familiar, metallic double-click. The crowd ahead of them screams. I feel their panic flood over me. Marco's free hand grabs mine. One squeeze. Two squeezes. Three squeezes.

Focus on me, his eyes say. *Only focus on me.*

We stay as quiet as possible, Marco and I both balancing on the balls of our feet. I let myself dissociate from the world around me as much as possible, focusing only on his brown skin, his shaggy hair, the minor scuff marks here and there that paint his skin with dried blood. He's the only thing that matters.

Even as I hear the screams of people and the firing of guns, the sounds of bodies hitting bodies, the noises of officers using what sound like heavier-than-normal batons against the protesters. Even as I hear the sound of metal folding over itself, like heavy Legos clicking into place, I don't focus on anything else. I only focus on him.

And the fabric my mother gave me in my pocket.

And the hot tears rolling down my face.

And how Marco keeps squeezing my hand like a pulse as the seconds pass. Knowing that eventually, one way or another, this will all be over.

FOUR

I don't know how long Marco and I stay hidden, but by the time he says it's safe to move, my legs feel like jelly.

It takes a moment for me to regain my footing, a moment longer than he is willing to give. By the time I'm standing, his arm is on my shoulder, attempting to pull me toward the alley. My body doesn't move in response, and he just looks at me sternly.

"We need to get moving. There's nothing for us here."

"There are people," I argue.

"You heard the same thing I did, right? The rubber bullets? The batons? The paddy wagons?"

"I'm not leaving," I sternly reply. "There could be someone who needs our help. You go if you need to; just tell me where to go, and I'll meet you."

Marco's defined jaw becomes more blockish as he clenches it. It's like I can hear his teeth cracking under the pressure.

"Fine," he spits, "but we have to be quick."

"I know."

"I'm serious," he says. "It won't be long until they circle back or more come, and we're lucky they didn't see us."

"You seem to know a lot for someone—"

"I'm street-smart," he interrupts. "Just a hunch. Let's do this already."

Marco walks ahead of me, ending the conversation. I turn to follow him but stop in my tracks. Just moments ago, these roads were lined with protesters, and most of them looked like me. Now there is broken glass. Blood smears. Ripped pieces of clothing. Forgotten purses, abandoned shoes, phones, and toys. There are a few people there too, maybe unconscious, maybe dead. I don't stop to check which ones are which. All I know is that the ones that are left are motionless bodies.

"Jesus," Marco whispers.

I can't move. No matter how much I will myself to, the command doesn't reach my legs. I'm stuck here in an endless loop, the video of what happened playing over and over again in my head. All those sounds, the noises of the cops beating people, dragging them… Marco didn't let me look.

Marco bridges the space between us. "You wait here, yeah? I'll check out the area. Keep out of sight, I'll just be a minute, two tops. Can you handle that?"

I nod.

"I need to hear you say it. Can you do that for me, Jamal?"

"I'll be here."

He smiles. "Good. Two minutes—you can count if you want."

I listen to Marco's footsteps disappearing as I slide back down to sitting, keeping my back against the wall. I count, each second punctuated with a word to make it feel real. *He'll be back once I repeat this thirty-ish times*, I think. *You won't be alone. You'll be okay.*

My mind begins to wander. What the hell is going on? Has Mom called anyone? Is anyone besides her worried about me? I look up at the sky; the milky-white layer is still draped over the city. It moves like it's alive, flowing and rippling, pulsing and dancing.

What are you? I think, studying it, hoping it'll tell me something I don't know, help me make sense of the world around me. But I know deep down that if I want to understand, there's only one person I can ask.

"Hey," Marco's familiar voice says. I look up, and he gives me a half wave, gesturing for me to walk over to him. A young girl, no older than thirteen, with her hair in braids clings to his side. Her shirt is black with bold white letters that read: I CAN'T BREATHE.

"Jamal, this is my new friend. New friend, this is Jamal; he's also my new friend. Guess I'm just making a whole bunch of new friends today."

The girl doesn't speak to me. Judging by the look in her eyes, I'm not sure she can speak. But the marks on her face, the scuffs, a little bits of dried blood and dirt, tell the whole story.

"Hey, nice to meet you," I say, putting on my bravest face. She doesn't need to see any more pain.

"Jamal and I are heading somewhere safe," Marco says. "There's food and a place to sleep. Do you want to come with us?"

She doesn't say anything. She's alone. She's too young to be out here by herself. Someone was here with her, and someone loved—*loves* her. And that person might be one of the motionless bodies in the streets.

No one should be alone.

I kneel down, keeping a little distance from her. "Hey," I whisper, "it's okay. You can trust us. I don't know if you were here with your mom or your dad, but I promise you, they'd want you to be safe. And once we take care of you, Marco and I will find your parents."

"Jamal…"

I don't look at him, keeping my eyes on her. "But you have to come with me, okay? That's the deal."

Five seconds. Ten seconds. Fifteen seconds pass before she finally agrees, nodding curtly and quickly. I nod back.

"Let's go," I tell Marco. "Lead the way."

Marco, the girl, and I walk through back alleys for what feels like forty-five minutes just to progress a few blocks. More than twice, we have to double back, hiding in places that smell like moldy trash, and pray to any god that the officers less than ten feet away don't see us.

An hour later, I breathe my first sigh of relief as we approach an alleyway that butts up against the house Marco claims is safe refuge.

"Who exactly lives here?" I ask while I watch Marco pick the lock on the back gate. The girl has found safety at my side and has been clinging to me the whole time. I wonder what she saw that made her lose her voice. Part of me wants to know. A larger part doesn't.

"Someone I can trust. I think," he says while diligently working.

"You think?" I don't feel comfortable wagering my life, and the life of this girl, on an *I think*.

"She and I go way back."

"How far back can you go? You're only, like, what? Eighteen?"

"Nineteen," he corrects. The lock finally opens. Marco smirks and pockets the lock pick. He turns to face us both. "Now, before we enter, a few things."

"I knew it."

He arches his brow.

"I knew this was too good to be true. What are you keeping from me about you and this woman?"

"Nothing bad," he promises, holding his hands up defensively. "I just…know her."

"How well?"

He shrugs. "We've crossed paths a few times."

"That's ominous."

"Look, I promised you I'd tell you the truth, and I intend to keep that promise," he swears, pushing the wooden door open. I step inside without another word, pulling the girl along with me.

The yard is a decent size, large enough to have a small pool big enough for two or three people. It's adorned with weeds and a few neglected flower beds, a firepit that looks like it hasn't been used in years, and old lawn chairs weathered down by the rainstorms of the past year. The back of the house shows few signs of life, the paint peeling off and the wood warped.

For a moment, I wonder if following Marco so blindly might have been a bad idea. What do I really know about him? Nothing! And I'm here listening to him just because he seems like he has his head on straight? I only met him by chance. And how come he always has an answer and seems to know just what to do?

But I guess I've made my choice. With a sigh, I turn my attention back to Marco, who is still knocking at the door. Slowly, after the fifth knock, the door creaks open. Warm light spills out, and the scent of—what is that, candied yams?—makes my stomach growl. I didn't eat dinner before I came, and I was too busy getting ready to have lunch earlier in the day; that lack of planning is catching up to me now. I think about the food in my bag, but something tells me I should save it.

A woman older than my mother pokes her head out the door. Strands of black-and-silver hair are pulled out of her braids, braids someone put together with care and love. She looks at Marco, then me, then the girl, then back at Marco.

"What are you doing here?"

Marco hesitates, and his pause makes my chest go tight. Instinctively, the girl pulls closer to my side. I grip her tightly.

"I wouldn't be here unless it's an emergency."

"And whenever it's an emergency, it always comes back to something you did," she snaps.

Marco opens his mouth, then shuts it and takes a deep breath. He pinches his brow, takes a moment, and speaks again.

"Look, I know we…ended things on the wrong foot."

"The wrong foot?" She laughs. "That's what you call it? Tell me, and don't you lie to me, did you have anything to do with this?"

"What's *this*?"

"Keep playing dumb, and I'll slam the door in your face. Don't try me."

Another tense beat passes. I look over at Marco, see a tightness in his face. This isn't good. What is she talking about? This whole interaction makes me want to pick the girl up and run in the opposite direction.

But where would we go? The streets are still crawling with cops, and I don't want to find out what's happening to the people they are carting away.

"I have nothing to do with this, Janna," Marco says firmly. "I promise."

She arches her right brow.

Marco sighs and corrects. "Mom. I have nothing to do with this, Mom."

"*Mom?*"

I didn't mean to say that out loud, but seriously? She doesn't look anything like Marco. Maybe he's adopted, which is probably the case, or maybe Janna's his biological mother—genes are weird. But she's an older Black woman who stares at him in that way that reminds me of my grandmother when I lied to her five years ago about not cleaning the porch. Black grandmothers have a way of yanking information out of your soul.

Janna turns her gaze to us. "Is that so hard to believe?"

"Not at all, Miss." I know my manners.

That seems to win me a little grace. Janna looks us up and down. "Who are you two?"

"I'm Jamal. And this is…" I don't know how to introduce the girl. "My friend."

"Your friend doesn't have a name?"

"She was on Main Street when the…" Marco points up at the

sky. The awning, made of warped and rotten wood, hides what he's pointing to, but we all know. "Her parents got arrested, I think."

"You think?" she asks.

"The alternative is worse, isn't it?"

Janna doesn't answer. She keeps quiet, and judging by her face, she isn't fully convinced. Or she doesn't care. But if we don't get into this house, we'll be on the streets again with the police officers, and Marco's luck is eventually going to run out.

"Look," I say, taking a step forward, putting myself in front of her. "I know you don't know us, and it's obvious you and Marco have some history to catch up on or correct."

"Ain't no correcting what he did."

"But I need your help. *We* need your help. We can't stay out here. If you're not going to help us…at least take her."

A part of me feels sick for using the girl like this, almost like I'm pimping her out for a warm place to stay for the night. But a good deed for her that also benefits me doesn't make the deed any less good. And besides, I don't want to die—or end up spirited away by the cops, like in Portland last year. If I knew what was going on, maybe I'd feel better about my chances of surviving in the streets tonight. But there is no handbook for this, no speech Mom could've given me on how to stay alive. This is new territory, and I need every advantage.

Finally, Janna reacts, stepping aside to let us in. "Come on," she says. "Quickly. But you"—she points to Marco—"I'm watching you."

FIVE

There are three things I notice right away about Janna's home.

One, it reminds me—almost to a tee—of my grandmother's home. Not so much in how it looks as how it feels. Grandma's house was a one-story rambler in Virginia that didn't have Wi-Fi, cell phone service, or cable. She owned a lot of land, though, and lived off it. Not in a doomsday survivalist way—in a smart, self-sufficient way. It's why Mom sent me there for a summer to build character.

Janna's home is modern and sleek, with that same protective feel. It doesn't feel tight or oppressive; it feels like somewhere you might visit when your philosophy professor holds a class at her house.

Number two: the house is quiet. I didn't notice how loud the rest of the world was until I walked inside. In here, there's a stillness, almost as if the outside world isn't trying to claw its way inside and rip us to shreds.

Almost.

And number three: we're not alone. Not by a long shot.

I count about twelve other people in the house. All of them are teens or college students; some of them are faces I saw at the protest.

"Go and get some food, baby," Janna says, gesturing to the girl we brought with us. "You must be starving."

The girl doesn't hesitate, running over to a table that has macaroni, greens, and some potato salad.

Soul food. Seeing it makes my shoulders relax. It feels like home, and I can tell Janna is doing everything in her power to make this a safe space.

"You two should get changed," Janna suggests. "I have some clothes that should fit you in the other room. Then you can eat."

"Mom?" Marco says, reaching out to grab her arm and giving it a small squeeze. "Thank you."

She looks at him, steel in her eyes, but her expression is softening. Her hand clasps his, gives it a squeeze, and then she pulls away, heading into the kitchen.

My body moves on autopilot. I'm not sure if it's the exhaustion, the adrenaline, or both. Probably both. The adrenaline is keeping me going, but the exhaustion is making me go through the motions without being fully in control of my body. I follow Marco into a study filled with clothes that Janna must have instructed us to pick from. I'm thankful for that; my own clothes are covered with dirt, grime, mud, and some smell I can't place.

I realize Marco has asked me something. "Sorry, what did you say?"

"Do you think this will fit you?" he repeats, pushing a shirt toward me. It's ratty, old, and gray, one of those Henleys with holes in the sleeves to put your thumbs through. I take it, examine it, then pause.

Marco is shirtless. When did that happen?

I should probably be focusing on the shirt, not on him, but that's…impossible. He's got an appealing sinewy form with a chest that's defined, but not overly so. He has a few scars here and there, more than most people, but not so many that I feel inclined to ask about them. The most unique thing about him, though? The tattoo on his right bicep.

There are rings—a thin one, a thick one, and another thin one—with small circles on them like planets. In the center, there is a triskelion.

I've seen that mark before… Where have I seen that mark before?

Marco catches me staring and quickly pulls a shirt over his head, a faded AC/DC tee that doesn't fully fit but works well enough.

"It was a stupid mistake," he says, referring to the ink on his arm. "I'm going to take a shower."

Before I can ask him about the tattoo or make him tell me what he knows about the Dome, he disappears, closing the door behind him. My stomach growls, and not just any type of growl—the kind that's actually painful.

"All right, all right," I mutter. Food first, answers later.

The shirt feels scratchy against my skin. It's irksome but refreshing in that it distracts me a little. It keeps me from thinking about all the terrifying *what if*s that are knocking at the door of my brain.

Food will help with that.

The dining room, converted into a makeshift buffet with tables pushed against the far wall and drinks of different colors on either side, is packed with about half the kids. They're all ages, but most of them are teens slightly younger than me. I'm guessing they lost their parents like the girl, separated from them when Baltimore went to hell.

But the common factor? They're all children of color, except for maybe…

"Three," Janna says, coming up behind me with a plate of rolls. "You're counting how many white kids are here, aren't you?"

Before I can deny it, Janna walks past me toward the kitchen.

"Help me with these ears of corn, will you? You look like someone who knows how to shuck them."

"Because I'm Black?"

"Because you look like someone raised you right."

Obediently, I follow her into the kitchen. I expect it to be hotter in there—most kitchens are, when they're alive and functioning—but the air is cooler than in the living room because there are fewer people.

"Corn's over there," she says, pointing to a table with a checkered cloth, where more than four dozen ears sit in bowls. Without hesitation, I sit down, and the unique sound of corn husks ripping fills the air.

Janna and I stay in our respective areas—me at the table, and her at the counter and the stove. I appreciate the silence, which allows my muscles to relax. We might not be safe with a capital *s*, but we're safer than we were twenty minutes ago. How long that safety will last, I have no idea, and I don't want to think about it.

But Janna seems to read my mind again.

"They won't break in, I promise," she says, her back still to me as she turns on another burner. "The police are too busy rounding up people in the streets. As long as we don't give them a reason to, they won't come here."

"How do you know? How do you know about anything that's going on? You seem…prepared and strangely calm."

A beat passes. "I have friends, just like Marco does." She leaves it at that.

"Not good enough."

Janna pause. "Excuse me?"

"You have to give me more than that," I say. "I mean, normally when children are in trouble, they return home to their parents. But Marco didn't come here just because you're his mom. There's more to it. You know something…more than you're letting on. Giving half-truths seems to run in your family."

Janna studies me, holding boxes of macaroni in her hands. Her eyes narrow, and for a moment, I think she's going to snap—literally snap my head off.

"You're right. You need every tool you can to survive." She adds the contents of the boxes to a pot of water and stirs slowly. She gestures with her head for me to join her at the stove.

"Pay attention, Jamal. I'm only going to say this once. That out there"—she points through the window—"is the Dome. Does exactly what the name says it does: keeps people in and people out. But not just people. Electrical systems. Voicemails. Emails. Nothing, and I mean *nothing*, is getting through that."

"Wait," I interrupt. "Hold on. That doesn't make any sense. That can't be real. It sounds like something out of—"

"Science fiction? That's what billions of dollars in government contracts will get you."

"No one would allow that. No government—"

"Really? A government that has allowed slavery, the internment of Asian Americans, and the unlawful search of Muslims? A country that repeatedly lets Black people die and puts brown children in cages? You think it wouldn't turn a blind eye to something like this?

"The Dome isn't just for us, Jamal. This is a test. A trial to see how it works—and if it works. Can something as simple as impenetrable light actually keep violence at bay? Can we isolate a problem area like it's in quarantine? And if so, what are the limitations? What are the possibilities? If there's one thing our government likes to do, it's find solutions that benefit them, not society. The Dome is a perfect example of that."

My head is spinning. Like any teen, especially any teen journalist, I've scrolled through message boards and seen conspiracy theories about everything under the sun. But an actual dome that keeps people inside? I've never seen anything like that.

Janna snaps in front of my face to get my attention.

"Jamal, I'm going to be honest with you. Nothing I can say will make any of it make sense. I can tell you're someone who has questions and likes to hunt for answers. There isn't an answer here. Some people are naturally bad and will try to one-up others when they get a chance by any means necessary. You're getting a crash course in a harsh reality of life. And I wish you and Marco had the time to sit with that, but you don't. None of us do. You don't have the luxury of taking as much time as you need to understand. I wish you did. So before I continue, are you going to be able to handle what I need to tell you, or are you going to panic on me?"

When we had to take a career aptitude test for my AP Psychology class last year, the top career that came up for me was journalist. Inquisitive mind, people skills, quick thinker: those were my top three traits. I wasn't surprised.

But I never thought I'd have a groundbreaking, newsworthy experience like this until I was at least a senior reporter for the *Washington Post*. But right here in front of me, there's a story. Hell, I'm a part of the narrative. I just have to be brave enough to take charge.

"Tell me everything. If I'm going to survive, I need to know as much as I can. As much as you know."

Janna grins. "Right answer."

SIX

An impenetrable dome. Militarized police. Technology dead zones. That's what Janna tries to convince me is happening right now in Baltimore.

She's speaking as if it's all perfectly straightforward, like none of it sounds as though it came out of a science fiction movie starring Ryan Gosling as the handsome, combative lead. But this is reality. Janna doesn't hesitate as she explains that no one can enter or leave Baltimore. She doesn't bat an eyelid as she says the police have suits of armor that cost billions of dollars, and she doesn't stutter as she demonstrates with her own phone that no information can leave the city.

"Essentially, we're stuck here," she says before passing out the food. "All we can do is sit tight and hope this blows over."

That last sentence is the one that continues to ring in my head later as I'm lying on an air mattress in the living room. *Blows over.* Does she expect everything to suddenly be fine one day? What makes her think the people who would create such a weapon are going to just…stop using it?

"Listen up," Janna said to all of us only a few hours ago. "You can stay here as long as you need to. I'm not going to make you leave, but while you're here, you have to follow my rules, got it?

"The rules are simple. One: at night, you stay inside, no exceptions. Two: no fighting. You fight, you cause a mess, and you're out. And third? We are all in this together. This is your family. Treat each other as such. We'll get through this *together*. That much I can promise you."

I can't even think about sleeping when those words are bouncing around in my head. I take two fingers on my right hand, put them against the pulse point on my left, and count to fifteen. My heart beats about twenty-five times, making my pulse one hundred beats per minute—significantly higher than my usual eighty.

Great.

"Count sheep," I whisper to myself, trying to ignore the chorus of snores from two other kids not far from me. "That'll help."

It doesn't. My mind wanders, my imagination shaping the lines of the warped wood on the ceiling into grotesque battle scenes.

I can't get the vision of those people in the streets out of my head, no matter how much I try. I attempt to use logic to get me through the downward spiral. A large portion of the people who were in the streets were probably arrested. Most of them are alive and in custody. They weren't all brutally murdered in the street. They won't just be names on a list. They won't be lifeless bodies, their souls taken from them and their murderers excused with *they charged at me* or *they were carrying something that looked like a weapon.*

But is being in custody really better? What happens behind closed doors when the police have absolute power?

I guess I'll soon find out. If there's no way to get information out and no one has the power to stand up to those with absolute control, what's to stop them from doing whatever they want whenever they want? What's to stop them from capturing me? Or Marco? Or Janna? Or the girl?

Nothing.

A creak of floorboards to my right breaks my train of thought. I sit up faster than I intended, the rustle of the worn plastic air mattress threatening to wake one of the younger children closest to me. Standing in the alcove is a shadowy figure wearing a ski mask.

My body freezes, and my pulse skyrockets so high I feel dizzy and sick. Did someone break into the house? How did no one hear? Is Janna so exhausted that she's upstairs, immune to sound of intruders? Does it fall to me to protect everyone?

The person and I lock eyes, neither of us moving. A scenario plays out in my head in a matter of moments. We outnumber him. If I attack first, the others will join in once the noise wakes them. But what if he has a gun? What if he's a scout for the cops? They'd send someone like that, wouldn't they? It makes logical sense! If they did—

"Jamal, if you're going to stare at me, at least get up and come over here," a familiar voice hisses.

It takes a second for the gears to click into place. "Marco?"

A child shifts in his sleep, muttering about Oreos chasing him.

"I'm coming."

Stepping over the sleeping bodies like land mines, I zigzag until I reach him. Marco jerks his head toward the kitchen, where plates and containers of food are stacked in makeshift towers. It's far from any sleeping people, and the door that separates it from the living room slides closed, giving us more privacy.

I cross my arms over my chest. "Are you going to rob someone or something?" I ask, gesturing to the mask he's wearing.

"Do I look that stupid?" He pulls the mask up above his mouth, taking in a deep breath of air. "I hate this thing."

"Then don't wear it?"

He doesn't reply to that, changing the subject entirely. "Why are you up?" he asks. "You should be asleep."

"Same for you."

"I have something to do."

"I can tell. Does it have something to do with the tattoo on your arm?"

Marco visibly tenses up, which tells me everything I need to know.

"What is that tattoo, Marco?" I ask. "You were acting really skittish about it before."

"We're stuck in a lockdown, and you're worried about my tattoo?"

"Color me interested. Journalists often ask questions to get to the truth."

"Yeah, but you're not a journalist."

"And you're not some savior, yet you sure act like it. And if that tattoo didn't mean something, you wouldn't be so defensive about it. So I'm going to ask again: What does the tattoo mean?"

He sighs, annoyed, leaning against the counter. He crosses his legs at the ankles and his arms across his chest. "You're really not going to let me leave here without telling you, are you?"

"Absolutely not," I promise. "I'm sure Janna would like to know you're trying to sneak out."

"You'd rat me out?"

"In a heartbeat. Janna said if any of us leaves after dark—"

"I know what she said."

Marco stares me down, as if keeping his gaze on me will make me change my mind, as if his eyes are some sort of lock pick. But I'm tough. I'm a journalist. It's our job to keep our emotions in check and give away nothing to a source. Marco's going to have to do better if he thinks he's going to break me.

Finally, he sighs. Not an exhausted sigh, but a defeated one. "I can see why you and Janna get along," he mutters, running his hands through his curls. "Fuck it, it would be better if I showed you. You ready to break the law?"

"I was pretty sure there was no direction this could go besides that."

Marco's lips curl into a lopsided, sly grin. "If Janna finds out…"

"We're kicked out. I know."

"And you're okay with that?"

"Again, I'm a journalist; I feel safest when I have knowledge, and something tells me you're going to give me that."

"You're a strange one—you know that, right?"

"Strange people will inherit the earth…or something like that."

Marco opens his mouth to tell me that's not the right biblical phrase but instead shakes his head and gestures for me to follow him.

"Hold on," I mutter. I carefully tiptoe back into the room, reaching where I was sleeping before.. My bag is in the corner. Carefully, I unzip it, revealing my camera, not a scratch on it.

Pulling it out, I grin. I know every curve, every edge of it. Even in the faint glow of the night-light in the corner, I could disassemble and reassemble this camera without making a single mistake. Right now, it's the most valuable possession I have, and its going to take me places.

"Leave it," Marco hisses as I stand up, his voice cutting through the silence.

"What?"

"Leave. It."

He must see the hesitation and indignation on my face, because he continues, "Where we're going...they're not going to allow that."

"I'm not going anywhere without it."

"You're going to have to trust me. Do you trust me, Jamal?"

Again, the answer is no, but I'm not stupid. If I don't leave it, he won't take me with him. This is what Mark Felt had to deal with, I imagine. One choice about who to trust changed history.

I put the camera back, placing it in its case and tucking it into the bottom of my bag, under my grandma's shawl. I step over sleeping children and return to the other side of the room, then turn to give them one last look...and lock eyes with the girl we brought with us, staring at me, clutching the worn stuffed bear Janna gave her.

SEVEN

Baltimore doesn't feel like the city I remember when we step out of Janna's home.

It's still, but not quiet. Fire and light illuminate the buildings in the distance, giving them an eerie, almost ominous glow. I don't know why my mind goes straight to Disney movies, but I feel like I'm in a painting that personifies "Hellfire" from *Hunchback of Notre Dame*. I can hear the sounds of constant rumbling, the metropolis inhaling and exhaling with excitement. But not a good type of excitement. It's a kind of heavy breathing that comes from fear.

That's the word I've been looking for: *fear*. It's low-grade, bubbling under the surface, but I haven't stopped being afraid since this all started.

"Jamal," Marco says, nudging my arm. "Come on, we can't stay still. Keep your hood up and stay close."

I follow, pulling the hood of my dark gray hoodie as tight as possible. My pulse vibrates through my body. Boys—Black boys like me—have been shot for wearing hoodies. Now seems like the *worst* possible time to be wearing one. But blending in with the night and sticking to the shadows is the best chance we have to make it to… wherever Marco is taking us.

I should have asked, I think. I shouldn't be following him blindly. But Marco has a certain allure about him. A certain hook-line-and-sinker aspect to his personality that makes him easy to follow into the belly of the beast—literally.

After all, it takes me only a few blocks to realize where we're heading.

"We're going *toward* the city center?"

Marco doesn't turn around, but he nods. "Not far, I promise. Just a few more blocks."

"Is this one of those 'few block' distances that's actually way more and you're just saying that to keep me quiet?"

He pauses, because he knows I know the answer. "You didn't have to come along."

"I know."

"You could have stayed back."

"I know."

"But—"

"You wish I had?" I interrupt.

He glances over his shoulder, and one of the streetlamps catches his eyes, glinting off them. "No, I'm glad you're here."

"Really?"

"Really."

His deep baritone voice is laced with honesty. Marco, from what I gather, isn't a good liar. He's a master at keeping information just out of reach, but when it comes to completely diverting someone's attention and focus? Using his words like sleight of hand? That's not his talent. And I'm not sure if I should be thankful for that, or worried for both of us.

"No matter what assumptions you have about me, I am a good person, you know."

"I never said you weren't."

"But you were thinking it, weren't you? When I said we should leave, before? When you insisted we stay and try and find survivors?"

That feels like years ago, but it was only a few hours. Time is like an elastic piece of warm bubble gum, stretchable and malleable.

"I think you were being pragmatic," I say as we turn a corner.

Marco quickly grabs me by the shirt and yanks me back, slamming both of our spines against the nearest wall. Before I can shove him off, a patrol car lazily rolls by, its bright lights painting the streets. The light never gets close to us, but five feet away from being exposed is still too close.

We stay as flat as possible for three minutes, as if we can become two-dimensional if we wish it hard enough. Long enough for the soft sounds of the engine to be swallowed by the darkness.

"What were you saying? Sounded like you were about to praise me?" he asks with a grin.

There's more behind that grin, though. There is hesitation and self-doubt and so much more that I can't even unpack. It's almost as if his grin is telling me to keep going, keep pushing, but at the same time, don't go any deeper.

"It's really not far," Marco promises me.

We take a right down an alleyway, turning our bodies to slip through a torn fence. Marco moves through it easily, like he's done this a thousand times.

I, on the other hand, do not.

A jagged metal edge catches my arm. I bite back a yelp, feeling warm blood drip down my forearm and smear my palm.

"Here," Marco says. He rips off the edge of his right sleeve, which was already coming off. He uses the rag to clean the blood off my skin in one, two, three swipes, then wraps it twice around the cut. "This is going to hurt."

Hurt isn't the right word, but I do wince. The added pressure makes the throbbing of the wound more apparent. He ties it a second time and tucks the loose ends in. "We'll get that cleaned up when we're done here."

"It's just a scratch."

He raises his brows.

"Metal—rusty metal, at that—can lead to tetanus. Which can easily lead to lockjaw, which can—"

"—lead to death, I know," I finish for him. "Let's just focus on one thing at a time, yeah?"

"Isn't focusing on your health important? Don't tell me you're one of those people who thinks the truth or whatever is more important than anything else."

"Aren't you?" I ask, verbally pushing him into a corner. "I don't know where we're going or why we're out here, but I'm pretty sure it's one of three reasons."

Marco puffs out his chest in that defensive way people and

birds do to make themselves look bigger and more threatening. He crosses his arms over his chest, accentuating his biceps. The one that's exposed, thanks to the ripped sleeve, flexes a bit in the process.

He really is attractive.

"Go on," he says, "enlighten me."

Challenging me isn't a good idea. Everyone in my school knows that. I make it my job to know as much as I can, to be able to put pieces of the puzzle together. I can do that with Marco. There's nothing stopping me.

"You've been cagey since I met you," I begin. "You know more than you should about things no one else knows. You're always two or three steps ahead."

"Maybe that's called being prepared."

I shake my head. "And maybe having insider information isn't actually an act of treason."

"Wait." He holds up his hand. "Do you think I'm a terrorist or something?"

"Didn't say that."

"But you did say *treason*."

"I also didn't finish. There are three options here. Terrorist is one of them."

"I'm not a freakin' terrorist."

"The other two are probably more plausible. One, you're somehow involved with this"—I gesture to the milky white sky—"and you're working for the government."

"Okay, so you went from—"

"*Or*," I interrupt, "you know how to make it go away."

That shuts him up quick. His mouth closes into a thin line. He's thinking, trying to keep his face as still as possible so as not to give away too much information.

That's the opening I'm looking for. Marco knows how to stop this, somehow. This makes him interesting.

I'd be lying if I said I wasn't thrilled to be here. The Dome, as Janna called it, that keeps everyone inside and prevents anything from leaving, is a work of genius. Evil genius, sure, but it's a tool that's never been seen before. Are there any journalists inside? I'm sure there are. But I'm also sure the police are doing everything they can to keep people from recording. Bloggers, reporters, photographers—they're probably all being silenced. If I were trying to keep a city under my heel, that's what I would do.

But to them, I'm just a teen. I'm nobody. They don't know why I'm here; they might think I live here. No one knows I have a platform, that I intend to gather information and put together an article. Forget Brown or Dartmouth or Penn—this could get me on a direct track to NBC or the *Washington Post* without even having to go to college.

And of course, if I survive this—and I intend to—I can show the world really what's going on. Show them that everything people of color have said about the police—that they're the real fourth estate, that they have too much power and money—is true. I can maybe stop this from happening again.

This is the chance of a lifetime. I can change the world *and* change my life. I just have to be brave. I can do this.

Finally, Marco speaks. "It's not what you think," he says quietly. "You're wrong."

"I am?"

"Well, not wrong. Just not right either."

"That's close enough for me. I'm not asking you to tell me everything. You've confirmed enough. But don't think for a second that I don't know you're hiding something important. I'll let it go for now, but soon I'm going to demand that you're honest with me. And I want to know that if I support you, you'll support me when I need you."

Marco falls silent again as a siren blares through the air, bouncing off the walls. Without hesitation, we push ourselves flat against the concrete to blend in. A police car zooms by, but no one sees us. Still, it was too close for comfort.

"Deal," he says. "But once you know what I know, you can't go back. You're going to be a target too. Especially if they think you're with me. If they think you're with who I work for."

"I'm a Black gay man in America, Marco. I'm already a target."

"Point taken. Come on, just another block."

"Until?"

"Until you meet some people."

"Some people?"

He jumps on top of a stack of precariously piled boxes, hoisting himself up the wall. Standing there with his boots digging into the concrete, he extends his hand to me. I grab it, gripping his forearm, and with a surprising strength that doesn't match his sinewy form, he hoists me up.

"Yep. The Maryland branch of Nemesis."

EIGHT

"Wait, I'm sorry, did you just say Nemesis?"

The words feel heavy as they root themselves into my brain. He really did just say what I think he said?

"Mm-hmm."

"The—"

"If you say *terrorists*, I'm going to have some words with you."

"I wasn't going to say that."

But many people would. They aren't just some happy-go-lucky kids who like to play with computers. They're the second version of Anonymous. Every movement—the LGBTQ+ movement, racial advocacy groups, feminism—has its second wave, one that learns from the first and pushes the boundaries more. That's what Nemesis is. They're ruthless. They scrap, kick, and scream, and they aren't afraid to stab you in the back, all under the guise of helping the world and making it a better place.

People have a lot of mixed feelings about them, obviously.

"Are you working for them?" I ask.

Marco and I wait for a group of cops to turn their backs before quickly darting across the lot. I'd be lying if I said there wasn't a bit of a thrill in all this. It reminds me of playing *Tomb Raider* and having to sneak around. But in the game you can always restart, or hide behind a wall when you're low on health. There's none of that here. But it answers the age-old question: What would you *really* do if you were put in a situation like the game you're playing?

Seems that with some help, I wouldn't do half bad.

Marco doesn't answer me until we've walked another block. "It's complicated."

Another half answer. I want to ask more—I deserve to know more—but everything goes out the window when we approach a derelict building, one I know well.

"What are we doing at the Red Lion?"

The Red Lion is a nondescript hotel. There's nothing special about it at all, except for the fact that it's a closed building. Which, again, isn't new. Baltimore has a vacant building problem. For each one that's knocked down, another one appears, so over the past decade, the number hasn't gone down. People move away, and not enough money comes into the city. It's a growing blight, and it makes the income gap even worse.

The Red Lion Hotel was also hit hard. With not as much money coming into the city, many hotels closed. Why do you need hotels if people aren't visiting?

A few industries have tried to take over the space the Red Lion occupied over the past three years, but nothing has worked. It's like the land is cursed. As such, it's just a broken, fractured shell of its previous self. The building looks like a skull with all its flesh, muscles and ligaments torn away, even the bone beginning to flake.

"You wanted to meet Nemesis, yeah?"

"I said I wanted to know where we're going. I didn't say I wanted to walk into a death trap. Do you see those signs?" I gesture to ones that say CAUTION and DO NOT ENTER. "This place is going to collapse on top of us."

Marco chuckles—and not an actual *this is funny* chuckle, but one of those patronizing ones that makes your blood boil. Well, at least it makes *my* blood boil.

"Sorry," he says, raising his hand in defense, like that'll keep me from volleying a string of sharp words at him. "We've narrowly escaped cops, you're about to wander into the viper's den, and you're worried about a building collapsing on you? Just…funny to see your priorities."

"Look, I have my priorities in order. Did you know that thirty-seven thousand people have died from collapsing buildings in the last fifteen years?"

Marco blinks me at me owlishly. "Sorry, I have a few questions. One, did you just pull that information out of your ass?"

I nod.

"Two, you *do* know that means that every year, only about—"

"—twenty-five hundred people die," I finish for him. "That's roughly seven people a day."

"Across the world?"

"Mm-hmm. I'm not going to be one of those seven."

Marco nods slowly. "Okay, I'm following. And how many people do you think die from police violence every day?"

"About one thousand people per year."

"Which is about three people per day, and if you take into consideration race and, you know, bubbles of influence such as"—he gestures widely—"don't you think that number is more likely to go up?"

"I see what you're saying."

He puts his hands on my shoulders, giving them a squeeze. "So how about we focus on what we can control and not on what we can't?"

"That makes logical sense."

"Mm-hmm." He pats my shoulder. "You're not the only logical one."

Marco turns and looks around twice before pushing the DO NOT ENTER gate aside enough to slide through. He holds it open for me, ensuring that this time, I don't get cut on the metal.

The air inside the abandoned hotel stinks of death, old plastic, and rot. I do my best to fight the gagging feeling galloping up my esophagus, swallowing it down with several gulps. I look over at Marco, who seems unfazed, walking with purpose toward a room at the far end of the ground floor.

"They're in the basement," he says. "They always meet in the basement."

Great, I think. So if the building does collapse, it will most certainly crush us.

Tingles of nervousness start to prickle at my skin. Claustrophobia is a bitch, and she'll cripple me if I'm not careful. The only thing that helps? Talking.

"So, you're a hacker?" I ask quietly. Any louder, and the emptiness of the ground floor will bounce my voice around.

"Not exactly."

"Sounds like there's a story there."

Marco shrugs. "Yes and no, then."

"Still not a good answer."

He sighs. "I hate journalists."

"Me too. So, hacker?"

The light in the hotel comes in shudders. I catch glimpses of his tight face and tense muscles.

"Yeah, I am."

"With Nemesis?"

"Do you really want to be talking about this here?" he asks. "I brought you with me, didn't I? That should be answer enough."

"Is there a *better* time to talk about it?"

"I dunno, maybe after?"

"After *what*?"

We take the steps two at a time, steps that creak and groan under our weight, making it impossible for us to enter the basement silently. At the bottom, a pool of light expands, and a chorus of rapidly talking voices starts to fill my ears.

"Just...stay close to me and be quiet, okay?" Marco whispers. "Please? Just this once?"

There's urgency in his voice. This isn't a game to him; it's personal.

To show him I can be quiet, I nod instead of speaking.

He smiles. "Good boy."

That shouldn't make me shiver as much as it does.

When we get to the bottom of the steps, my feet touch down on something soft. At first it feels like moss, but as my shoes sink into it, I realize it's a mixture of grit, mud, and water. It's colder down here; there's a draft somewhere, and the walls are silvery with dripping moisture. I remember it rained earlier this week. But the fact that it's all pooling in the basement makes my mind race with thoughts of mold of all different colors, shades, and toxicities.

Marco doesn't seem to notice—or maybe he doesn't care—and he trudges forward toward the source of the pooling light, each footstep heavy with determination and conviction. He looks like he belongs here. Is that confidence fake, I wonder? Or is he one of those people who uses confidence like adrenaline to charge his body?

The light is coming from the far side of the massive, mostly unfinished basement. The only thing separating us from the voices is a single door, a sliding metal one that is partially opened by a brutish man with far too many tattoos to count on his arms, exposed chest through his tank top, and neck. As if that isn't intimidating enough, he has a gun in a holster, a shotgun on his back, and what I can only guess is a police baton on his left hip.

He barely looks at Marco, barely looks at me, and opens his mouth to say something, probably along the lines of *Get the fuck out* or *What are you doing here?* Something tells me this will be our only chance to prove ourselves. There's a reason few people know anything about Nemesis, besides they only let you know as much as they want you to know.

"Calm down, big guy," Marco says before the man can speak. "I was invited."

"By who?"

"Whom," I whisper under my breath. But not quietly enough, it seems.

The brute's eyes snap up to lock on me. "What the fuck did you say?" His thick hands move, surprisingly fluid, to the gun on his hip.

"Nothing!" Marco says quickly, standing between us. He glares back at me before turning to the masculine sphinx. "He said nothing. And I was invited by Karma."

That gets the man's attention. He stops, as if the name is some sort of Bucky Barnes–like activation code. He narrows his eyes suspiciously. "You know Karma?"

"Mm-hmm."

"You?"

Marco puts his hand on his chest. "Your lack of trust—I'm hurt," he says. "Yes, I know her. Do you think I just pulled that name out of a hat?"

The man seems to believe him, but he juts his head toward me. "And what about him?"

"He's with me," Marco says.

"No shit."

"He's my boyfriend. He's down with the cause."

I'm sure Marco says more after that, because the brute doesn't ask me any more questions, but the words *my boyfriend* are rattling around in my head. Am I upset that he just assumed he's my type?

Or am I pissed that he has forced me into a lie that I'm going to have to keep up while we're with Nemesis?

Or am I just aflutter because he said I'm his boyfriend? Because he's the first guy to say those words about me...ever?

The man steps aside. Marco doesn't give me time to open my mouth and say something stupid—which, let's be honest, I probably would—before pulling me into the room filled with light, people, and a very strong stench of alcohol.

"You made it just in time," the man says as we step through. "The meeting is about to start."

"Thanks," Marco says, giving him a salute I've never seen before.

The man returns the gesture—must be some Nemesis thing—then slides the door shut and locks it.

There's no turning back now.

NINE

"You're a goddamn idiot, you know that?"

Marco doesn't hold back once we're past the guard. His shoulders haven't fully relaxed, but they are an inch or so lower. He doesn't let go of my wrist, though, and heads straight for a table at the side of the room, lined with bottles of different colors of liquid, mostly alcohol. Okay, all alcohol.

"I get that a lot," I say, trying to lighten the mood.

It doesn't work.

"I told you to be quiet," he hisses, grabbing what I think is whiskey and pouring himself a cup. "That's it. One task."

"Sorry! It just came out."

"And of all things to just 'come out,' it had to be correcting his grammar?"

I shrug. I have no excuse.

After hastily downing the first drink, filled with only about a shot of whiskey, Marco messily pours himself another cup, splashing the liquid on the table. He refills it again, only a quarter full this time, and hands it to me.

"Here," he says. "I'm wary of giving you alcohol, but maybe you'll relax a bit more."

"I don't drink."

"Don't drink, or haven't before?"

"Yes."

He urges me to take it. "Look around; everyone has a cup in their hands. You're going to stand out if you don't, and you don't want to stand out here."

I don't need to ask why. My mind flashes to the guard and his plethora of weapons. I'm sure he has more hidden.

Begrudgingly, I take the drink from him, intending to just hold it. Blending in is good. Blending in is important. The less people look at me, the more time I can spend focusing on committing details to memory. They'll be important for the article I want to write later.

There are more than thirty—no, forty—people here. They're all ages and from all different walks of life. Seems like about a sixty-forty female-male split—I thought most hackers were men? Some of them are even younger than me. The most interesting thing is that none of them *look* like hackers, or at least, what the media wants us to think they look like.

Most of them look like people I'd see at Barnes and Noble or the local Target. One, I think, might be a teacher I had in middle school? These are people who live normal lives, have dreams and hopes, pay taxes, go to movies, host block parties.

But what exactly is a hacker supposed to look like?

I glance over at Marco, comparing him to my idea of a hacker. His unruly brown hair, a mix of tangled curls and bangs, gives him a boyish look. His body is not exceptionally muscular, but he's not super thin either, just a good middle-of-the-road amount of tone, like a normal teenager I'd see in Baltimore at the aquarium or a museum or a concert.

But there's something more about him, a gravity that pulls you in. I'm not sure if the right word is charming, enigmatic, or persuasive, but I feel like a spaceship being dragged into his orbit. Even if I wanted to pull away—even if I wanted to explore the room and get a feel for who's at this Nemesis meeting—if it meant leaving Marco's side… I can't exactly pinpoint why, but the idea sends a chill through my stomach and generates a wave of nausea.

"This way," he says, gently nudging me with one arm. He leads me through the crowd, turning his body to the side and moving effortlessly to the front of the room. The crowd gets tighter, and when we find a place to stand about six feet from a stage, we're shoulder to shoulder with the others.

Marco gives them a nod and the same hand signal he gave the guard. They return it and nod back.

"What is that?" I ask, mimicking it.

Marco hisses, grabbing my hand and pulling it down, snapping my wrist to my side like a magnetic toy being locked into position. "Don't," he warns quietly. "Just…don't. You're not one of us. You're a guest here. Remember that."

"All right, all right. Jesus." I yank my hand back. Time to change the subject. "Can you at least tell me who Karma is?"

"The leader of the eastern Nemesis branch," he says under his breath without moving his head.

"Does she have information about the Dome?"

A shrug.

"Does she live in Baltimore?"

He shrugs again. "Does it matter?"

I want to tell him yes, it does. It would explain how she knew this was about to happen. The Dome keeps everything inside. Nothing can leave or enter. It's not like she put out a Bat-Signal when it went up and smuggled dozens of people from other cities inside.

But Nemesis is a top-tier hacktivist group. If anyone had information, it would be her.

And then it all clicks.

"That's why you're here," I say. "In Baltimore, I mean. You knew. You all knew they were going to use the Dome. That's why you planned the protest."

"Bingo."

"The protest was just a mask."

Marco glances at me sideways. "Do you think less of me now?" he asks. "You know it's all connected, right? Police brutality, the Dome…it all stems from the same thing."

He doesn't explain, giving me a moment to put two and two together. A moment's all I need.

"Power."

He nods. "Who has it, who doesn't, and who is willing to use it to remind those who don't that they never will. If you want to understand what's going on with the police in Baltimore, you have to go one step further; you have to know who's giving them power, and the Dome is a one-way express road to the source."

"Wait, go back. You're saying you think this goes up to, what? The police chief?"

"Higher."

"The mayor?"

He points up.

"You're not serious. The governor?"

He shrugs. "Why not?"

"*Why not?* What's your proof?"

Marco chuckles. "That's the problem with you journalists. You always need proof."

"Because wrong information can result in people getting hurt. Have you ever seen *The Newsroom*?"

"The what?"

"Never mind."

"Anyway…" Another shrug. "Sometimes that's worth it. The ends justify the means. And besides, people are already getting hurt. You're fighting by the old rules, Jamal, assuming the opposite side is going to have honor and valor, and treat you like a person. If you're going to survive this, you need to remember that they don't care about you, so you can stop caring about them."

My shoulders tighten. "Because no one is without sin, right? Everyone has done something worth being punished for?"

Marco gives me finger guns. "Bingo."

"Then what's your sin?" I ask. "You're not immune."

He turns his head back toward the stage, ignoring my question. "She's coming. Pay attention."

"That doesn't—"

"Pay. Attention."

I want to tell Marco he can't talk to me like that. Just because he feels like he's in charge or that he's in his element doesn't mean he gets to boss me around. That's not how this *relationship* works, if you can call it that—*friendship* is probably a better word. But the air in the room changes before I have time to *firmly* remind him of this.

Two men dressed in black quickly walk in through one of the side doors. Instinctively, everyone in the first three rows in front of the stage moves back. The men stand on either side, guns in their hands, fingers on the triggers. They're not police officers; they're dressed more like military, or maybe SWAT or some type of black ops team, but no one seems particularly afraid of them. Even with their guns—I think they're AK-47s—primed and ready to shoot.

And then I see it. One of the men has it on the back of his right hand. Another has it on his right cheek, and another man, the farthest away from me, has it on his neck: the same tattoo Marco has on his bicep. They work for Nemesis.

Moments later, the heavy, sharp echo of boots clicking rhythmically against the cold floor fills the room. A woman walks briskly onto the stage, dressed in a black halter top, fingerless gloves, and a pair of tight cigarette pants tucked into chunky boots. Her short black hair is streaked with purple. She looks around, slowly at first, then quickly locks eyes with everyone in the room, one by one. When she looks at me, I feel like she's peering into my soul, like she can see every bit of me that I hide from myself and others, as if her eyes have the ability to hack into my deepest and darkest desires.

As if she knows I don't belong.

As quickly as her eyes landed on me, they move on to someone else. And then she speaks.

"Brothers and sisters," she says, her voice warmer and more inviting than I imagined, "thank you for coming. I'll keep this quick, because as many of you know, we don't have much time. With the creation of this Dome, the police have become even more virulent and quick with their weapons. Let me be clear: I want no one here to be caught by the police. Not because of the information each one of you holds, but because I consider you my children, my brothers, my sisters, my lovers, my friends, my family, and I will let no one be harmed because of me."

The crowd cheers, Marco included. They clap in unison, chanting in hushed voices to keep the noise from rising above the basement. *Kar-ma. Kar-ma. Kar-ma.*

She raises both her hands and lowers them slowly, the bubbling of the crowd simmering down until her hands reach waist height and silence returns to the room. This feels more like a cult than an activist meeting.

"We knew this day was coming. The Dome is not a new invention; it is just new to those stuck inside of it. Many of you have trained for this, for the one action that will make every hardship, every bout of suffering worth the sacrifice. We are the knights that protect this planet from harm. We fight a thankless fight, but we rage on.

"Today is the day, my brothers and sisters, that we prove ourselves."

Karma flicks the pointer finger of her right hand. Her guards wheel out a set of TVs and place them so that no matter where you are in the room, you can see a screen.

"This is what we're up against."

The screens click on all at once. It takes me only a second to understand that the shaky footage is video recorded on a phone. The time stamp on the bottom is only an hour ago, about two hours after the Dome kicked in.

The person filming doesn't say his name, but I can tell it's a man when he lets out a curse after tripping and almost dropping the camera. I hear his broken, panting breath, and I can tell, based on the chain-link fence and the forest surrounding him, that he's somewhere on the outskirts of town. But even though this was recorded at night, the screen is fully bright, like it's the middle of a summer day. Overexposure, perhaps?

And then, when the man pushes his right hand through the thicket, I see why it's so bright. He's no more than fifteen feet from the edge of the Dome.

"This is one of our brothers. He goes by the name Savage. Remember him. Honor him."

Savage stumbles toward the Dome, almost dropping the camera. Is he wounded? Or drunk? Either way, he walks like it. I push my concern for Savage back down, instead taking in every bit of information I can. The Dome looks exactly like it did outside. The milky whiteness of it distorts the image on the other side of it, but I can make out the continuation of the forest. Savage pauses at the barrier, turning the camera around to show his heavily tattooed face.

"This is Savage, part of the Nemesis East Coast branch," he says, his voice surprisingly deep. "I'm going to upload this as soon as I can, but in case I don't make it…in case you're the only one who sees this…" He turns the camera back to the Dome and presses his free hand against it.

I wince, expecting something—a shock, a burning. But there's nothing. Savage pushes his hand forward, adding more pressure. The Dome ripples against this force.

"Nothing. It doesn't move. This isn't the first point I've tried. The Dome doesn't move. It—"

Behind him, a twig snaps. Savage curses and pockets the camera, turning it off seconds later.

"Savage outran the cops to get this to us. He was taken into custody, and we haven't heard from him since. He most likely sacrificed his life so we could have this information. So we could see the truth," Karma says, as the screens turn off and the TVs are wheeled out. "The chief of police and his renegade forces have been acting without oversight for too long. Let me be clear: this Dome is not a sign of strength. It is a sign of weakness. They know they are losing their power. They know people are taking that power. And they will do anything and everything to hold on to it.

"They want to stay in the past, hold on to the days when white men, straight men, rich men, and men of the old guard controlled the fates of the many. But what do we say to that?"

"No more!" the crowd cheers, louder than before.

"What do we do about that?"

"Tear them down!"

"And how do we do that?" Karma points to the left side of the room.

"Quickly!" that side says.

She points to the right side of the room.

"Silently!"

Finally, she points to the middle, where Marco and I stand.

"Mercilessly!" they cheer, Marco included. He hoots and hollers, clapping loudly and nudging me. There's a fire in his eyes that looks like valor, but if you look a little closer, there's something else there too. It's the warm glow of an infection, and Karma is patient zero.

I smile nervously at him and holler too—not as loudly, of course, but enough to blend in.

"How do we do it?" a man in the left group says. "Have you seen the weapons the police have now?"

"I have." Karma nods, walking over to stand in front of him. "We are outgunned, outmanned—"

"And womanned!" someone in the right group says. The whole crowd cheers.

Karma smiles a wolfish grin. "But we have one key thing those pigs don't have: brains. Some of the greatest hackers from across the country are here with us. Lynes Flare, who shut down the San Francisco power grid last year. Shadow, who crippled predatory banks in New Mexico who were preying on indigenous people. And we can't forget Macabre, who hacked into the New York hospital system during the pandemic a few years ago."

"Wait, seriously?" I whisper.

Marco nods. "You're in the presence of hacktivism royalty, Jamal. And you decided to wear *that*?" He smirks. "*Tsk, tsk*. Let's hope you do better next time."

I roll my eyes and turn my attention back to Karma. Like Marco, she has the power to draw my gaze and focus, making everything around me disappear. Are all hackers like this?

"We might not have the numbers they do, but we have the resolve. We have the power. We have the drive, and that's something they can't take away!" she yells. The crowd cheers louder, stomping their feet in unison. The whole building feels like it's vibrating with energy. "And we're going to remind them what the full force of Nemesis can do. We're going to remind them who we are. And we're going to take their precious fucking Dome down, one byte at a fucking time!"

More cheers. More hollering. More infectious energy like a live wire, bouncing from one person to the next, flooding them with resolve. I can't help but cheer along with Marco. It feels like I'm part of something. My mom was—is—a Delta. I wonder if this is what she means when she talks about what belonging to a group feels like.

And that's when everything goes to hell.

TEN

Everything happens so quickly I'm barely able to piece it together, but my mind, used to combining a lot of information in a short period of time, kicks into gear.

First, the main door bursts open. The guard is thrown—no, that's not the right word—*launched* through it. His large body slams like a bowling ball into a half a dozen people, knocking them to the ground.

Second, three small metallic orbs soar into the room, each no bigger than a volleyball with smooth sides, no seams, and a red diamond-shaped eye in its center. They fly like drones, moving so quickly they look like blurs, and space themselves throughout the room.

And third…we're going to die here.

Side panels open on the seemingly smooth floating orbs. Thick plumes of white smoke pool out. In a matter of seconds, the room is filled with smoke, and my vision becomes hazy.

But that's not the worst part. I can deal with temporary blindness.

It's the burning that follows.

"Get down!" Marco yells. He doesn't wait for me to reply. Instead, he tackles me to the ground and practically drags me behind the makeshift stage where Karma stood. Some of the other hackers have the same idea, getting as low as possible as quickly as possible. Many of them are coughing too hard or were too close to the orbs to care about anything except their burning eyes.

Most of them aren't ready for the second wave.

After the smoke has filled the room so that all I can see is shadowy figures, the orbs begin their second assault. The lights at their centers shift, changing from deep bloodred to a blinding white. Those small circles, no bigger than two inches in diameter, produce enough light to burn through the smoke, enough of a glow that even looking in that general direction makes my eyes burn.

"Cover your ears," Marco says, moving my hands into position, but not taking his own advice. His eyes are bloodshot, tears running down his cheeks. I see that his teeth are gritted as he fights through the pain, but he keeps pushing through. "Hold on."

Nothing about that sounds good.

I don't see the orbs' next shift in form, but I *hear* it. The sound is so high-pitched, it's almost inaudible, such a horrific banshee blare that I can feel it in my bones. The few hacktivists who were left standing, immobilized by the smoke or the light, collapse to the floor.

Marco and I are lucky—his quick thinking helps. The stage blocks most of the smoke and absorbs a large portion of the sound and light. We're far enough away that the attacks don't hit us straight on. But the few people standing right underneath the orbs? I imagine they just lost their hearing, and maybe their eyesight too.

"We have to move," Marco yells, standing up and pulling me with him. He might be right next to me, but his voice sounds thousands of miles of away. He taps my shoulder with two fingers, pointing to the door Karma came through. We can move along the wall, using the stage as cover, and then the door will only be about six feet away. We can easily make that.

"You ready?"

I want to say no, but I know that's not an option.

"Three…two…one…go!"

I'm good at following orders. I'm good at pushing through pain, fear, and anger and focusing on one singular goal. Right now, that goal is getting out of here alive and in one piece.

Marco and I stand, and my legs move within me having to think. One foot in front of the other. The door isn't far, maybe fifteen paces away. We'll be there in seconds, if nothing goes wrong. If nothing changes. We've got this.

Of course, something changes.

One of the orbs zooms in front of us, floating at eye level.

"Halt," the drone says in a mechanical voice. "You are in violation of Dome laws two and four: out after curfew and with the intent to incite violent. As such, you will be detained for questioning. Please wait for—"

Marco slams his fist into the side of the drone. It sputters and spins, dipping down low as it tries to right itself. Before it can, he digs the heel of his boot into the drone's eye.

One stomp.

"Halt, you are destroying government property."

Two stomps.

"Halt, you are destroying—"

Three stomps.

"Halt..."

On the fourth stomp, the drone goes quiet, the light flickers out, and it returns to being just a hunk of cleverly constructed metal instead of a weapon.

"Shut the hell up," Marco growls, looking up at me. He raises his arm to cover his mouth, coughing into his sleeve. The smoke has mostly dissipated—it burned hot and fast. The other drones hover around the room like sentinels, keeping watch over the writhing, squirming hacktivists who were unlucky enough to be close to the main fallout zone.

"Are you okay?" I ask, my hearing slowly returning. I keep an eye on the drones. They don't seem to be linked in any way. They don't come and check on their dead friend. Each must have its own instructions, independent of the others.

"I'm fine," Marco says, wiping his eyes quickly. "Come on, let's—"

"STOP!"

The voice is new. Three men appear through the main door, dressed in black military garb. But they're not like any outfits I've seen before. The angles are sharp. The plates of metal adorning their bodies look heavy, and the helmets look like something you'd see in a Marvel movie. Hell, the whole outfit looks like something you'd see in a Marvel movie.

"You're all under arrest," the first man says, cocking his gun. "Any of you move even an inch, and I swear to god…"

The good news? Marco and I dip behind the stage fast enough that they don't see us. There's so much going on in the room right now, and that's our only saving grace. The bad news? There's no place to run, and eventually, they'll find us.

It's just a matter of time. My legs are cinder blocks, and every thought goes out of my head except one:

I'm going to die.

"Round them up," the first man says to the other two. "All of them. Tag them, bag them, and take them to base."

Funny, you only tag and bag things, not people.

They'll find us eventually. The stage isn't enough cover to keep us hidden forever. Marco peeks around the corner, then pulls his head back quickly, wiping the snot from his nose.

"All right, all right, all right," he whispers. "This is what you're going to do."

"Me?" I whisper back. "You mean *we*?"

"No. You," he says firmly. "You can make it to the door. It's the same distance as it was before. Just don't stop running. I'm going to head the other way." He points.

"Toward them?"

He nods. "I have a record. You're clean, so you're not a high-value target. They'll want to go after me, not you."

Again, Marco has more information than I do, but this time, I don't have the time to ask what he knows or how. In two minutes or less, they'll find us.

"Go back to Janna's. Don't stop for anyone or anything. You can do it. You remember the cross streets, right?"

I nod.

"I'll meet you there as soon as I can. Tell her everything you saw here, and I mean *everything*, okay? She needs to know."

Marco makes it sound like I'm not going to see him again. These are the words of someone who is saying goodbye. There's a sinking feeling in the center of my chest, but I don't have time to address it. The cops are getting closer, based on the sound of their heavy boots. I have to think fast.

I nod, not risking attracting their attention with my voice. Marco nods back. He raises his right hand, showing three fingers and counting them down one at a time.

Three.

Two.

One.

He makes a fist: the sign to run.

Marco and I move, almost in sync, in opposite directions, me toward the door and him toward the cops.

"HEY! FUCKOS!" he yells, making himself bigger. He pounds his chest, another universal symbol of *What's up?*

I don't look back to see what happens. I don't focus on what Marco does to distract them. He's doing it for me, so I can get out of here safely. So I can let everyone know what happened.

My body moves on autopilot, running through the hallway. One step at a time. Faster, faster, faster. Can't stop. Won't stop. Doesn't matter that my lungs burn. Doesn't matter that my head is throbbing. Doesn't matter that I want to turn back and help him.

Making it out of here *is* helping him.

Voices behind me echo through the hallway. I think they're telling me to stop. I push off the ground harder. No slowing down. No pausing. Because who knows what might happen if I do?

I turn the corner, sneaker slipping on something wet. I lose my footing, cursing as I hit the ground. Pain rockets through my right knee. A wet feeling of lukewarm warmth spreads across my jeans. I struggle to stand, but my foot slips again. My hands scramble for something, anything, to hoist me up.

No such luck.

When I finally get to my feet, the light from a police officer's helmet fills the hallway. I wince, having adjusted to the darkness of the abandoned hotel's underground tunnels. He's not far behind me, but maybe, just maybe, if I keep going, I can get to the exit. I hear muffled sounds and rumbles I couldn't hear before, so I can't be far from the street. I can lose him aboveground.

A glint of light catches my eye, bouncing off something silver. I glance over, and behind a pile of timeworn and water-warped boxes, I see the face of a boy. He's no older than me, probably younger. I remember seeing him in the meeting room.

If I keep running, there's a chance the cop will find this boy. If I were the cop, I'd look here too. But if I stay, if I turn myself in… can I save him?

My stomach turns violently. I touch the piece of shawl in my pocket. I only have a few moments to decide. The answer's simple.

"Stay quiet," I whisper. "Don't leave until you're absolutely sure there isn't anyone around."

The boy doesn't nod or give me any indication he understands what I've said. I hope he does, or this will all be for nothing.

"And turn your head," I quickly add. Interactions with the cops are never, *ever* good.

That he does listen to, turning his face down. His messy mop of black curls blends into the darkness, making him almost impossible to see.

I don't have time to think about how our hair is almost the same. How in another life, this Black boy might have been me. I don't have time to say a silent prayer to ensure the boy's safety, though I haven't been to church in years and I'm not sure God would answer me even if I did. Because before I can take a full breath to steel myself, the cop rounds the corner, weapons raised.

"Freeze," the officer growls.

I do what I'm told. I'm not sure if I'm proud of that, but I don't want to die. Not here.

The cop slowly approaches me, and I get a better look at his suit. The sharp, threatening angles aren't the most intimidating part—it's all the add-ons. His helmet is ringed with six flashlights, and his boots look like they could wade through lava. It looks like an advanced SWAT uniform, but more flexible. The darkness of the visor, obscuring the top half of his face, is a scare tactic, I know.

Doesn't make it any less terrifying.

From one of his many, many pockets, he pulls out a black rope with a thick handle. It uncoils, skimming the ground. The coil glows in the middle like there's a power core running through its center.

"Turn around," he says, grabbing the end of the rope and snapping it. It makes an electric hiss that echoes off the cold stone walls. I wince, not even attempting to hide my fear.

"I'm not resisting!"

A sharp pain ripples upward from my legs, and my knees buckle, thanks to the force of him kicking me. I wince but don't scream as my knees hit the hard ground.

"Shut up," he growls. He slaps the rope against the ground, and the crackle of a whip with an added electric hum fills the air.

I shut my mouth as tightly as possible. There's no advantage to fighting him. Not only could that tip this cop over the edge and make him hurt me more, but I have someone else to think about. The boy, not far from me, is still cowering behind the boxes.

What will they do if they find him? He's probably just a kid who was brought here against his will because his parents wanted him to tag along.

I grit my teeth as my arms are wrenched behind my back and tied tightly. The cop pulls so hard, so roughly, it feels like my arms about to come out of their joins. He wraps the rope around my wrists twice and uses some fancy knot to secure them to my ankles.

"Stand."

Easier said than done. If I try to stand up straight, the knots around my wrists and ankles will become so tight it'll be impossible to move my legs. The cop shoves me forward, the blunt end of his gun jabbing between my muscles.

"Walk."

Each step we take away from the boy is a good thing. With each foot of distance I put between us, I feel myself breathing a little easier.

What's going to happen to me, though...that's Future Jamal's problem.

ELEVEN

The ride in the paddy wagon is quiet. It's just me, the cop who brought me in, and two drivers up front.

"Can't believe they actually thought they'd get away with it," the cop in the passenger seat says.

The cop who arrested me shrugs. "Probably thought they were well prepared. I mean, they are 'hackers,' after all," he says, mocking the title like it's something to be ashamed of.

The ropes are cutting into my wrists. I can feel warm blood pooling around them. I do my best not to move, not to fidget too much.

They dragged me out of the hotel and threw me into the car with no hesitation. I saw three other cars just like this one, packed with people from the rally. I didn't see Marco, but that doesn't mean he wasn't there.

We've been driving for about ten minutes. The streets are empty, and the cops don't seem to care about traffic rules. I don't think we've slowed down once, not even to take a corner.

"Look, it's not that I agree with them…" the driver says.

"Here we go again." The cop across from me groans. "Holland always takes the devil's advocate approach."

"Shut up, Lewis," Holland growls, looking in the rearview mirror at the other cop. His eyes flicker over to me. I quickly look away.

"All I'm saying is, I can understand being pissed and wanting to fight back."

"You sound like a sympathizer," Lewis says.

"Understanding your enemy doesn't make you a sympathizer; it makes you smart."

The paddy wagon jerks to a halt, causing both cops to fly forward. My body lurches to the right, the ropes digging into my wrists even more. I wince but don't give them the satisfaction of hearing me scream.

"Say that shit again, and I'll make sure you fly through the window," Holland warns. Something tells me that's something he'd actually do.

I study Lewis carefully. He's not much older than me, maybe five or six years. It takes so little experience to become a cop. But that's the trick, isn't it? Most cops aren't old enough to hold other people's lives in their hands, and yet we trust them with exactly that.

How many months of training does it take to be able to use a gun? Six? Nine? Twelve? A lawyer has to go through three years of training. A doctor? Four, and that's the bare minimum. How can they expect someone Lewis's age to make life-or-death decisions correctly?

They know the answer. They just don't care.

The truck comes to a halt as we round a corner, the wheels and axles grinding. The two cops in front get out first. Lewis leans over, his face close to mine.

"Don't do anything stupid, all right?" he growls.

I nod, keeping as still as I possibly can. He undoes the restraints around my arms, unhooks my legs, and grabs my shoulders.

"Move."

He practically pushes me out of the car, so hard I almost fall, but I regain my footing. I do a quick survey of my surroundings. I'm not from Baltimore, so the city, especially at night, looks eerily unfamiliar. It's too quiet to be a metropolis, but the lack of noise also makes it feel bigger than it actually is, like it's looming over me, judging me.

But the police station is lit up like the White House every day of the year. The station has more than two dozen cops standing in front of it. Floodlights burn away the darkness on the whole block, like it's some sort of light center that darkness can't touch.

"Put him in the back," Holland says. He and the other cop walk forward, the sea of fellow cops parting for them.

"Come on," Lewis orders. He forces me down an alley to the right.

"Where's Marco?" I finally find the courage to ask.

"Who?"

"The kid with me. Shaggy black hair. Hispanic."

"I don't know," Lewis says. "There were a lot of you people there."

You people. What doe he mean by that? Hackers? Rebels? Minorities? Fags? What is he insinuating? I don't have the courage to ask.

"Where are you taking me?"

"Shut up."

"I need to call someone. I still have that right."

"I said, shut up."

"You can't just—"

It happens so fast, I barely have the chance to gasp. Lewis shoves me hard against the brick wall, so hard the colors in front of my eyes blend together into a watercolor tapestry. The world around me blurs, and a ringing in my ears takes over, muffling his voice. I can make out his words, though.

Shut up.

Keep talking, and you'll regret it.

If you're smart, you'll do what we tell you to do, and this will all be over.

Sounds like there should be an *or else* somewhere, but I don't push my luck and point that out.

Lewis opens the side door of the station, a heavy metal sliding thing that whines when his biceps flex. He pushes me inside, closing the door behind him. The darkness is welcome after the obnoxious light outside, but it lasts for only a moment before he flips a switch. Overhead lights flicker on one at a time, leading down the hallway.

He doesn't have to tell me to walk.

Each step feels like I'm walking deeper and deeper into darkness, literally and figuratively. Will anyone be able to find me now that I'm down here? Will anyone care enough to look?

Someone will care, I tell myself. Someone has to care. American citizens don't just go missing without someone asking questions.

You're a journalist, Jamal. You've read all the stories about people who have championed a missing person's report for months—even years—to get the answer. Trust the system.

Yeah, but here's a counterpoint: that same system let this happen. That same system lets Black girls go missing all the time, and no one cares. That same system keeps reporting Black-on-Black crime like it's the most horrible thing our society has to face.

There's no reason to trust anyone, because there's no one *here* to trust. Only myself. And Marco.

Where the hell is he?

When we reach the bottom of the steps, I realize exactly where we are.

Back in middle school, we took a trip to Baltimore. Our history teacher talked about how some of the buildings were used in the Revolutionary War and never refitted; the city just built on top of them. Some of those buildings once held prisoners. Rumor has it some of those prisoners witnessed the bombardment of Fort McHenry by British naval ships in Baltimore harbor during the Battle of Baltimore in the War of 1812. Supposedly, some of them helped write "The Star-Spangled Banner."

Sure, history is important, but what's more important is the reality that this is a prison. An old, abandoned prison where no one will find me unless the police want me to be found.

Lewis doesn't stop at the first, second, or third cell. No, he walks all the way to the end of the hall, the coldest part of the basement, and opens a heavy door. My feet walk obediently forward, but I can't feel them touching the ground. All sensation in my body is gone, and my heart is pounding so hard I think it's going to claw its way out of my chest.

I don't do well in closed spaces. A prison is one thing, but a prison under a police station? That's the epitome of closed space. I feel my throat tightening and my skin turning clammy. My vision is turning black at the corners, and that blackness is spreading.

"Get in," Lewis orders.

At first I don't move, planting my feet as firmly as I can. Maybe if I root myself, I can stop this. Maybe I can buy a few more seconds for something to happen in my favor.

"Goddamn it," Lewis growls. His boot collides with the small of my back, shoving me forward. My legs are still bound, so I can't walk too quickly. My ankles tangle with the ropes, and I stumble forward, knees hitting hard against the cold, rough concrete.

Pain. That's all I feel. White-hot searing pulses from my bones. I want to cry; I should cry. Who would fault me if I did? But I don't want to give Lewis that satisfaction. I won't give them that satisfaction.

"You're fine," he gruffly responds. "Sit there and don't make any fucking noise."

With that, the door closes, and I'm left in darkness. Just me, darkness, and pain.

I'm not sure how long I lie on the cold floor. Long enough for my eyes to adjust to the faint white light coming from the overhead bulbs in the hallway, and long enough to find the warmest parts of the concrete. The pain in my legs is gone; it's nothing more than a dull, annoying throb now.

My fingers have memorized every inch of the room. It's not huge—six by six, maybe—but it's big enough for me to lie down and not feel squeezed in. The rocks are weak, probably from age, and there are signs of water—I hope it's water—dripping down the walls, staining the rocks and creating small grooves. Water can cut through anything. It's the strongest element out there.

I wish I was like water. Wish I could fit myself through the smallest holes and wiggle my way out of here. Wish I could be anywhere else.

The pain in my wrists is gone, which is a good thing. For now, I'm only thinking about what's going to happen next. How long has it been since the officers left me alone? Ten minutes? Thirty minutes? Two hours? I think closer to two hours. Layers of time start to fold over on themselves like sheets of metal.

What's my plan? Am I going to try and rush out of here when the door opens? Am I going to be obedient, follow their orders and do what they say? One path will keep my body alive. The other will keep my soul alive. There's no point of a body without a soul.

There's no point of a soul without a body.

My right cheek is flat against the cold stone when I feel vibrations pulse through the floor. Is someone coming for me? I frown and quickly sit up. Sitting turns to standing, and I do my best, in the dark, to clean myself up.

Stand tall, Jamal, I hear Mom whispering in my ear. *You have the blood of kings and queens running through you. You don't bow to anyone.* We *don't bow to anyone.*

Shadows pass by the strip of space under the door. One, two, three cops. Why so many?

The door opens heavily, and for the first time in what feels like forever, I feel my muscles relaxing.

It's Marco. And even though we're in this prison with cops who are eager to put bullets in the backs of our heads, I'm happy to see him. He's here. Beaten, bruised, exhausted, but *here*. The black bruises over his right eye tell me all I need to know. The welts on his exposed arm and cheek, the busted lip, and the way he limps and almost collapses when they shove him forward completes the story.

I catch him before he loses his footing.

"I'm all right," he whispers. His voice is thin like frayed, dried paper. He doesn't even believe that himself, does he? "You're not supposed to be here."

"I know."

"You were supposed go back to Janna's."

"I know."

"What happened?"

How do I answer that? Do I tell him he sacrificed himself so I could be safe, but then I sacrificed myself for a kid? Would he understand that?

I don't say what I want to say. I don't show any weakness. I hold him close and tight, letting him rest his weight against me. It's not the fact that they hurt him that makes something boil in the pit of stomach, something that feels like silvery, white-hot lava burning through my core.

It's the looks on their faces. The smirks. The confident smiles. Like this is something *funny*.

But none of the three cops move.

What are they waiting for? Do they think one of us will slip up and say something incriminating? They don't seem like the most… patient types. *Brutes* is the wrong word. That's insulting to the muscle-bound men who have defined generations of himbos. No, these cops are something else.

The hackers at Nemesis called them pigs, as have many others. That word has always felt sour in my mouth, like poking a sleeping bear and asking to get mauled. But right now? I get it. No other word slots so perfectly into the groove of my vernacular as the one-syllable, three-letter *pig*.

Thump, thump, thump.

My head snaps to the left. Footsteps—heavy, firm, and strong. They belong to a man—a large man.

Thump, thump, thump.

Closer and closer they get. As they do, the cops' demeanor changes. Their backs get straighter, they stand shoulder-width apart, and they salute—they actually *salute*.

The shadow on the ground grows larger, swallowing up the other cops' shadows like it's consuming them. Survival of the fittest applies even when it comes to the absence of light, it seems.

I steel myself, tightening my core and holding on to Marco tighter, as if holding him close can protect him from what's to come. There's a sinking feeling in my stomach as the steps get closer and closer. Cold trickles down my spine. I don't even know who this guy is, and I already know I'm going to regret meeting him.

It takes a moment, what with the shiny brass and surprisingly stiff suit the man is wearing, for me to recognize who he is, but once it clicks, my heart skips a beat. And then, sure enough, the familiar face of Police Chief Ian Coles appears.

"Hello there, Mr. Lawson and Mr. Gonzales," Chief Coles's deep and recognizable baritone voice says, sounding like absinthe sliding against smooth metal. "I'm glad we finally got to meet each other."

TWELVE

Depending on who you ask, Chief Ian Coles is a lot of things.

A war veteran. Exactly what Baltimore needs. Mediocre. The epitome of white privilege. A horrible chief. A loving husband. A soldier. So many different words to describe the man.

The chief of police was at the center of the murder of Jerome Thomas. He'd been chief for barely two years when he was assigned to head up a task force, suggested by the governor of Maryland, to help fix crime throughout Baltimore. Before that, he had served as a cop for twelve years, which most people would consider impressive. He'd created an atmosphere where you could shoot first and ask questions later. Sure, his wasn't the hand that pulled the trigger, but he was the one who'd made that cop feel like he was within his rights to kill Jerome. The whole system was responsible for Jerome's death, rotten from the top to the bottom.

The thing that stood out most was how Ian Coles jumped from job to job. He wasn't a Maryland native. In fact, he had only been in Maryland for a year before he was appointed chief. Before that, he worked in Indiana, Alabama, Kentucky, South Dakota, and, briefly, Kansas.

All of those states have one thing in common: they're red states.

But what makes Ian Coles so dangerous isn't his position or his title. It's his charm. He has that Southern hospitality that makes defenses fall. Even during press conferences and meetings, *charming* is the word that often follows *mediocre*.

That combination is a deadly one. Because charming people lower your defenses. Mediocre people stab you in the back when your defenses are low, step on your corpse, and use it to climb to the top.

"Follow me," Chief Coles demands.

Neither of us moves.

"I won't repeat myself, boys," he says, a faint Southern accent evident in his voice.

Another irritatingly condescending word. *Boys.* I instinctively squeeze Marco's waist.

"The chief said something to you," Lewis warns. His right hand moves to the taser at his waist.

Chief Coles raises a hand. "That's not how we treat our prisoners."

"At least you said it," I blurt out.

Chief Coles turns to me, raising one brow. Shit. I didn't mean to say that out loud. I push my lips together, hoping they'll fuse shut.

"Well, go on." He gestures. "You have the floor."

A moment of silence fills the room.

"Prisoners," I say. My voice cracks. "You called us prisoners. At least you're being honest."

"I've found that honesty is best when you're trying to get something done. Helps create an even playing field and set expectations."

"And what are you trying to get done?"

He turns on his heel and walks out the way he came. "Follow me to find out."

The cops don't move. Lewis keeps his blue eyes on me. He's like a beta in a wolf pack, always trying to impress the alpha. Thinking he's destined to take the throne someday. It's aggravating and makes the hairs stand up on the back of my neck.

Chief Coles wouldn't shoot me in cold blood. It would be Lewis. Because he thinks that's the right thing to do to people like me. People like *us*.

Or, more likely, because he doesn't think at all.

Marco stands, leaning against me, putting all his weight against my side. I grip him tighter, having no intention of letting him go. No matter what, we're in this together now. Our fates are tied.

There are pros and cons to going with Chief Coles, and when I do a quick mental analysis, the end result is the same. There's a pit in my stomach that's growing larger, expanding in such a way that it's hard for me to breathe. But I don't show Marco that. He has to know what's happening. He has to know what's to come, right?

"Come on," I said, giving his side a squeeze. "Let's go."

Together. That's how we'll face this—together.

We follow Chief Coles up the stairs, his three goons trailing behind us. They don't give us much breathing room, barely enough for us to move without the pointy ends of their guns pressing against our backs.

"You know you don't need those, right?" I ask quietly. "We're listening. We're following your orders. You don't have to—"

"Shut up," Lewis says, poking me in the back.

I grit my teeth to avoid the feeling of pain, not wanting to give them any advantage. When we reach the entryway at the top of the steps, Chief Coles leads us out the door, and I look around for a moment. We're in the open air, under an endless sky that extends upward until it hits the white film of the Dome. There aren't too many guards.

"It's not worth it," Chief Coles says before I can speak. "You're thinking of trying to run, right? Thinking you can make it that twenty or so to the open gate?"

I don't answer him, but he keeps going.

"Let's say you do make it—and I don't think you will, if I'm being honest, because I don't think your friend here has the strength, and my men have pretty good aim. But let's say you *do* make it. What are you going to do once you get out? Run home? Head somewhere you think is safe? You know you'll be enemy number one. A terrorist. We'll throw the full weight of the Baltimore police force at you, and it won't be pretty, Jamal."

Chief Coles's voice is so even. "Personally, I don't care if you live or die," he says calmly. "However, as the chief of police and a humble servant of this city, there's a part of me that hopes we can keep the bloodshed to a minimum."

"And the other part of you?"

He turns fully and takes three large steps toward me, bridging the gap. "That part of me hopes you and your criminal friend give me a reason to shoot you. Please, it would make my day."

I fall silent, taking in every bit of him. The wrinkles on his face, the smells of Irish Spring soap and alcohol, the small beads of sweat. The razor burn. You can learn a lot just by examining a man.

Nothing I learn about Chief Coles is good.

"That's what I thought," he says as he turns, and I don't reply. "Now, come on."

This time I listen, following him into another building. He holds the heavy door open for us and his three subordinates, then closes it behind him. Darkness fills the room, swallowing us whole. Chief Coles doesn't turn on the light before I hear a thump, along with grinding gears. A heavy *click* follows. I don't need to see to know what those sounds are—a very complex, very old door locking.

"Officer Lewis," Chief Coles says.

"On it."

A moment later, yellow light fills the room. No, *room* isn't the right word. It's more of a concrete box, no bigger than the dorms I've seen on college websites. There's a metal table with handcuffs attached to a bar in the middle. On the far end, there's another door leading out. To the left and the right, there are windows. Through the panes, I can see identical rooms to the one we're in right now.

Before I can ask any questions, Lewis's rough hands wrap around my throat, tight enough to make my whole body seize up.

"Hey!" Marco yells. "Get the hell off of—"

Marco falls silent as one of the other two guards grabs him and pulls his arms tightly behind his back, forcing him to walk past me while Lewis drags me effortlessly to a chair.

"Let him go!" I struggle, trying to make it harder for Lewis while at the same time not putting up too much of a fight. The club that dangles from his hip looks heavy. I don't need to see what it feels like against my head.

Marco kicks and screams, snarling like an animal, struggling to get free. It takes the third cop grabbing his legs to carry him out of the room.

"Jamal!" Marco yells, his voice growing quieter and quieter. "Jamal, it'll be okay! Don't tell them anything! I promise, it'll be—"

The heavy door slams shut, his voice disappearing with it.

Lewis turns his attention back to me, slamming me down in the rickety old metal chair—hard. He uses both hands, with little grace, to force my hands in front of me and cuff them to the table.

"Be a good boy," he whispers—no, *sneers*—in my ear.

I'm not worried about me. Maybe I should be. Maybe it's stupid not to be afraid, but I'm only focused on Marco. What are they going to do to him? Is he going to get medical help? I can't see any cameras in here. Why would there be any? I bet Chief Coles wants us to himself, to do whatever he can without having to answer for his crimes.

"Hey!" A loud snap brings me back to reality, focusing my attention. Chief Coles now sits directly in front of me, smiling wolfishly again. "Let's have a chat, shall we?"

THIRTEEN

"This isn't going to work."

I've been to therapy before. I hated it.

When my father died five years ago from diabetes complications, my mom thought it was a good idea for me to talk to someone. She wasn't wrong. I should've talked to someone—I just don't think *she* was the right therapist for me.

Dr. Kline was her name. She was too abrasive, always forcing me to talk. I agree that it's important to talk through your feelings, but I didn't want to do that with her. She wasn't happy with that, and she told my mom I was being stubborn. That I needed medication. It didn't take Mom long to realize she wasn't the right therapist. We didn't try anyone else after that.

I know what the silent treatment looks like. I know what it's supposed to accomplish. Dr. Kline tried that with me in the beginning. It didn't work.

"What's not going to work?" Chief Coles asks, the first thing he's said in the past ten minutes.

"You just sitting here." I try to gesture with my hands, but they're bound, the handcuffs looped through the metal bar, making it impossible for me to move more than a few inches. "You think that if you wait long enough, I'll give you what you want."

"I know you will. You need something from me."

"I don't need anything from you," I say carefully. "Why did you bring us here if you were just going to separate us?"

Chief Cole raises a finger with each word to accentuate his point. "Number one, you do need something—something from me: Safety. Absolution. Number two, I brought you two together to remind you, before we have our chat, what is at stake. And number three, the woman you stayed with…what was her name? Janna? Yes, that's it. She's been on our radar for a while."

"How do you know about her?"

"We're the police, Jamal. We know everything," he says matter-of-factly. "I'm sure it won't be hard to get a warrant for her arrest."

"She didn't do anything."

"Are you sure about that? I'm sure she's harbored a fugitive or two. She seems like the type. I don't think it would be hard to make that stick. And, of course, most importantly, if you work with me, I can promise your friend's safety."

There's more to Chief Coles's words than he knows. He thinks he's blustering, pushing out his chest and threatening me. Which he is, but he's doing something else too. He's reminding me who has the power here.

Safety. His way of saying that if I work with him, he'll make sure

I don't get hurt. Which also means there are people who *are* going to get hurt.

Absolution. That's a specific word choice. Biblical. I wouldn't be surprised if Chief Coles is Catholic. It tells me the police aren't going to stop targeting Black and brown people, even when this is over. I bet everyone arrested or identified is going to be put in some sort of database, labeled as criminals or deviants. If I give him what he wants, he'll make sure that doesn't happen to me.

Because I'm not like other Black people.

And finally, if I tell him what he wants to hear, he'll make sure Marco's safe. Janna too. Someone is going to suffer; why not protect those who are close to me as much as I can?

Chief Coles leans back in his chair. The old leather squeaks and hisses under his weight. His crosses strong arms over his chest, tapping his right middle finger on his left forearm. "So, start from the beginning," he says.

I bite my inner cheek hard until the taste of copper floods my mouth. This is a bad idea. This is a really bad idea. But what other choice do I have? Helping Chief Coles is the only thing that might keep us alive, even if it'll hurt other people.

"What do you want to know?" I ask.

He flourishes his hand. "Anything you're willing to give me. Every bit of information is important if we're going to protect our city from Nemesis, those agitators we found you with."

"That's what you call them? You know *you* people are the ones who did this." I gesture as much as I can with my hand. "They're just trying to make the work better. It wasn't *agitators* who put the city under lockdown. It's not *them* running around with weapons and whatever suits you all are wearing."

"We wouldn't have to do this if your people weren't threatening the sanctity of our city."

"We're not doing anything. We were *protesting.*"

"You were causing a ruckus."

"That is *not* what was happening," I object. I feel heat boiling in the center of my chest. I take a deep shaky breath. Being angry won't help anyone. I have to stay calm. I have to stay in control as much as I possibly can. "Protesting is a human right. The First Amendment allows it. Cops killed Jerome Thomas. We just want those who are guilty to be held accountable. That's all."

"That's what happened, Jamal," Chief Coles says with a tinge of annoyance. I wonder how long he can keep his cool. He's trying his best to stay calm, but the facade is cracking. Is that something I can use to my advantage? "The system did its job. The officer was tried and convicted. Justice was served."

I shake my head. "Your cop friends were put on probation."

"Without pay."

"That's not justice."

"Justice is whatever the courts decide."

"It's not justice when the courts play in favor of the accused."

Chief Coles's lips turn into a thin line. He sighs, running his fingers through his short hair. "I'm not here to debate the merits of our legal system with you," he says. "I'm here to offer you a way to protect yourself and your friend. And the only way for you to do that right now is by giving me the information I need."

Chief Coles leans over, pulling out a briefcase and setting it on the table. The heavy locks click open, and he tosses police reports in front of me. Marco's mug shot is there—not once, not twice, but four times, spanning years.

Last month.

Ten months ago.

A year and a half ago.

The earliest one is from three years ago, when he was fifteen.

"Marco is a criminal, Jamal," the chief says plainly. "Grand larceny. Hacking. Theft. Assault. He's done it all. Whether or not he's done it on behalf of Nemesis doesn't matter. Getting him off the streets is better than letting him walk free."

My eyes scan the papers quickly. Speed-reading is a skill every journalist has, and trying to understand what *types* of crimes Marco is guilty of is important. There's always some truth behind what's on the page, but there's always more than meets the eye too.

But the information here is damming.

Five months ago, Marco stole a car after beating up a guy in a bar.

Ten and a half months ago, he got into a fight that sent four people to the hospital.

A year and a half ago, he shut down power to a whole city block, which resulted in two hospitalizations because people lost access to their medical devices.

And the earliest one—he stole computer equipment from a mom-and-pop electronics store. I'm guessing that's what started all of this.

Chief Coles leans forward. "He is not a good man, Jamal," he says quietly. "None of these people are good people. You, on the other hand—I ran a search on you. There's no record. You're clean, an upstanding citizen. You're probably hoping to go to an Ivy League school, aren't you? I'm proud of you. You're one of those good people, the type of people we need. Not like this." He gestures to Marco's bloody face and confident smile. "And good people, good citizens, they help the police. They keep their city safe. They put their community over some criminal."

I've heard this song and dance before. *Your country above your party. Your country above your family. Your country above your well-being.* This mantra isn't new, and nothing, absolutely nothing Chief Coles says, will distract me from his first sentence.

You're one of those good people.

What does *good* mean to him? Does it mean I'm one of those people who will side with the police over other Black people? I'd call that a race traitor. Is that who he thinks I am? Is that what I'm going to become?

I'm not that. I can just imagine my mother seeing the news: Chief Coles and me standing side by side, him thanking me for helping, talking about how they couldn't have taken down the vagrants who are destroying our city without my help. That's going to be my legacy: helping the police. Betraying my people.

But that means I can live to fight another day. That means I can stay alive. That's something, right? I can fix what I do wrong if I'm still breathing.

I'm a journalist. That means I thrive best when I have as much information as possible. And Chief Coles is the holder of that information.

"If I don't tell you what you want to know, you're going to kill me, aren't you?"

Chief Coles barely hesitates. "The Baltimore Police Department doesn't kill people," he says. "Unless they deserve it."

There it is, I think, the quiet part loud.

Chief Coles stands up and walks over to the window on the western wall. He taps his knuckles three times on the glass before stepping out of the way.

Lewis appears in the window, holding Marco by his collar. His face is bloody, his hair matted with sticky red liquid. His lip is completely busted, his shirt torn, his black eye swollen worse than before, completely obscuring his vision. Lewis pushes Marco's body against the glass, holding him there so the blood and spit smears on it.

My heart beats so hard I can hear it thumping in my ears. It's nearly impossible to hear the heavy sounds of Chief Coles's boots as he walks to stand next to me. I feel his callused hand on my shoulder, feel the squeeze against my skin. I feel his hot breath against my ear as he whispers, "But, under the rules of the Dome, we are allowed to do what we must in order to retrieve the information we need. No matter what that entails. If some helpful citizen were willing to give us that information, then we might be able to—"

"I'll tell you what you want," I breathe before I can stop myself. "Whatever you need. I'll tell you."

I know Chief Coles is smiling, even as I keep my eyes locked on Jamal's swollen face. I don't care. I focus only on him.

Even if I know that look on his face is defeat.

I'm sure my face looks the same.

FOURTEEN

I spend the next two hours giving Chief Coles exactly what he wants. Information on Nemesis. The meeting we just had. The video. The guy named Savage. The woman named Karma. What they said about the Dome during the meeting. Every little bit of information about Nemesis that I've learned from Marco or gleaned from the internet and given to him seems to pique his interest.

He makes me repeat my story three times, interrupting me and challenging me on anything he deems a discrepancy. He shows me a map of Baltimore, forces me to recount the paths I took, what I saw along the way, how we got to the meeting site. There's a younger cop there, a girl who doesn't look much older than me, with sharp features and a high ponytail, rapidly taking notes on her iPad. She only locks eyes with me once, when she enters the room.

I wonder if the reason she avoids looking at me is because she feels ashamed that we have the same skin tone, yet she's helping the police so readily.

But I'm not any different. I'm sitting here giving them

information just to save my own hide. Deep down, she's doing the same thing.

Two and a half hours later—or at least that's what it feels like—Chief Coles nods.

"I think we have everything we need," he says with a grin. "This has been very helpful, Jamal. Truly. Your city and your state thank you."

Why do his words feel like poison burning through my stomach? Why does my whole body feel heavy? Throughout the whole interrogation, I kept glancing over at the window. I had Chief Coles's word that Marco would not be harmed. Lewis came in a few times, whispering things in the chief's ear before leaving. That at least told me he wasn't in the room with Marco, which meant Marco wasn't getting beaten up. That was something.

Chief Coles pauses at the door, then turns on his heel and walks back over to me. I tense up and instinctively pull away from him, trying but also *not* trying to put some space between us. Chief Coles's right hand rises like he's going to slap me, but then he lowers it and slips it into his pocket, pulling out a business card and tucking it into my own pocket.

"Call this number if you think of anything else or if you need anything. And I mean anything, Jamal," he whispers. "I like to take care of the people who help me. You could have a lucrative career helping the Baltimore police; keep that in mind. Come on, Lewis."

Almost an hour passes before I see anyone again. I'm still chained to the table, the metal wearing into my flesh and creating bloody, crusty divots in my skin.

The heavy metal door creaks open, and Officer Lewis wanders in. My body tenses. He hasn't hurt me yet, but that doesn't mean he won't. He leans closer to me, and I smell alcohol. Slowly, his meaty hands move to my wrists. A few sharp tugs later, I'm free.

"You can go," he says, stepping back.

"Wait, what?"

He doesn't seem interested in me, focusing on the dirt under his nails. With a lazy hand, he gestures to the door. "Pass through the door. Head down the hall, turn left, then straight down another hall, and you'll see the door. You can't miss it."

How am I just free to go? They're going to let me walk out as if nothing happened? That doesn't seem right. I mean, I understand that I just gave up not only my own soul but the souls and bodies of dozens of others to save Marco's and my hides…but was that really all I needed to do? The acid in my stomach is eating away at me. It feels like I'm devouring myself, like I'm going to slowly break apart until I'm only a heap of flesh, muscles, and bones on the floor, a mess for someone to scrape up and toss to the side.

"What's the matter?" Lewis asks impatiently. "Come on, we don't have all day. Can't you walk?"

The question is, *how* can I walk outside and face the world, knowing what I did in here? I think about Janna. I think about the people in her home. I think about the people on the street. I think about what the outside world does and doesn't know about what's going on in here, and now I've contributed to this mess of a world. Willingly.

How could I have been so stupid?

I take a deep breath and force myself to walk. There's nothing left for me here, just Officer Lewis, who barely acknowledges my existence, and the memories of what I did. If I want to change anything, if I want to stop what's happening, I have to leave; I have to face my mistakes and try and fix them as quickly and as efficiently as possible. I'm guessing the cops are going to head straight to Janna's to round up as many people as possible. I can't stop that from happening, but maybe I can save one or two people. Maybe I can find that little girl Marco and I rescued from the street and get her somewhere safe. I have to do *something*.

I pick up my pace, walking as quickly as I can without running, and follow Lewis's instructions. Down the hall, left, down another hall. With each step, my feet get faster and faster, my heart quickens, and my muscles lock into place. For a moment, it's like I've forgotten how to run, but I haven't forgotten how to care about someone and to make it my sole focus. I have to get out of here. I have to help.

At the end of the hall, I see the large door that Lewis was talking about. It's cracked open, enough for me to see yellow-and-orange light spilling from the alleyway. I push the door open faster and harder than necessary, trying to get out of this suffocating building as quickly as possible.

The plan is simple. Run as fast as I can down the street until my lungs give out and start burning. Find my way back to Janna's and apologize to her profusely. Somewhere along the way, as my legs turn to jelly and my chest begs me to stop, I'll swear I'll find a way to make this right.

I know what I'm doing.

I know how to make things right.

I know how to make things better.

This will all work out.

It has to.

It has to.

It has—

"Marco?"

It takes me a minute to realize the heap of blackness in the corner of the alley is Marco. I have that sinking feeling in my chest. Dread starts to fill me up like poison spreading through my body. And it only gets worse as I get closer. Soon there's no way my brain can create a plausible scenario to calm my heart.

My pulse races faster than should be humanly possible. I force myself to walk until the tips of my shoes bump up against his soles of his feet.

Leaning against the wall, his body is crumpled, his arms curled around himself, pulling his jacket closed. His clothes are ripped like he was attacked by a tiger, and I can see bruises on his face and arms. He looks worse than he did through the window, but I can tell all the wounds are survivable. They did that on purpose. They beat him to the brink of breaking, dangled him over the edge, and sneered, *You should be thanking us.*

I know, because in so many words, that's what they did to me.

"What happened to you?" I whisper, kneeling down to examine him. What a stupid question. I know what happened to him. I saw it.

And I did nothing to stop it.

No, that's not true—I did everything to stop it. I sacrificed other people's well-being to make sure this wouldn't happen to him. Which makes me wonder what would have happened if I hadn't paid the price I did. How badly would they have hurt him? What would they have done to me?

"Come on," I say gently, grabbing his body as softly as I can. He doesn't react except to mutter something under his breath—I think he's asking if I'm okay. Instead of worrying about himself, he's still worrying about me. I try to ignore the guilt that's welding itself to the bottom of my chest. Guilt for judging him before. Guilt for being so concerned with my own wounds on my wrists, which are nothing compared to his injuries. Guilt for what happened...and for what's about to happen.

I can worry about all that later. For now, I just need to get him somewhere safe.

"Solve the problem, Jamal. Solve the problem."

This is just like a math question. I can do this.

Spoiler: math is my worst subject.

Problem: Marco is hurt. Badly. He'll survive, sure. But being out here doesn't bode well for him.

Solution: get him somewhere safe.

Janna's home is too far. It took us about twenty minutes to walk from her place to the Nemesis meeting. That means it was at least a mile, maybe a mile and a half. But how far is the Red Lion from the police station? And if I go back there, what will I find? That place probably isn't safe anymore.

But then again, what place *is* safe right now?

"Shit," I curse, digging my heels into the ground and hoisting Marco up so I can grab him tighter. I have Mom's credit card, which is for emergencies only—but this probably qualifies as an emergency.

But will anyone take credit cards? I know technology is down inside the Dome. Does that mean we can't do anything that requires transactions? No, credit card machines probably connect to banks inside of Baltimore, which are inside the Dome. Especially if I can find some sort of off-brand motel or something. Yeah, that's where we need to go. A motel.

"I have an idea," I whisper. "I'm going to get us somewhere safe. I promise." That's the least I can do after what Marco did for me. He's right—I'd be dead without him. But now I'm alive, and I'm out here, not wherever they took all those other protesters. That's progress. That's something.

Once I have a strong grip on Marco, I steel my nerves and take one step after the next. There's no other way to do this. One step turns into two. Two turns into four. Eventually we'll get somewhere. Eventually we'll be safe.

But twenty steps in, I realize Marco's heavier than I thought, and I'm not nearly as strong as I'd hoped. Sweat is pooling on my brow, and my grip is slipping. He's going in and out of consciousness, so it's not easy to carry him. We're going nowhere.

It feels like someone is staring at me. I'm sure that's not true; the cops have more important things to do, and if they wanted to just stare at me, they wouldn't have let me go. But the heaviness of shame begins to weigh me down. I feel like I'm wearing lead shoes, and the way my heart is racing can't be healthy.

I rest against a wall, ignoring the sharpness of jagged bricks against my back. I focus on what I can control. We're farther along now than we were five minutes ago. That's something.

"Think," I hiss to myself, digging my heels into the concrete. "Fucking think, Jamal."

Finding somewhere safe for Marco can't be an impossible task. There has to be a solution. I just need to see it. I just need to think harder. I just—

Bright headlights blind me and make my eyes close. I hear the sound of large tires approaching me, closer and closer, no more than fifteen feet away. I hold Marco closer, maybe a bit too tight, but I can't worry about that right now. I'm more worried about who—or what—might be approaching us.

The truck comes to a slow stop just past us. The passenger door unlocks and opens, and a brown-skinned girl peers out at me.

"Look, you have no reason to trust me, but I think you should get in," she suggests. "I mean, what do you have to lose? Judging by your current…situation, not much."

I hold Marco's limp body close, staring at her. She's right. I don't have much of a choice. I don't know how long we can survive out here, and Marco is heavy and slipping. I can't get him across town on my own.

I bite my lip hard enough to taste blood and curse. I'll deal with the consequences later.

"Help me get him in the car?"

FIFTEEN

When I was little, my mother always told me to watch out for strangers.

I think every parent tells their children that, knowing that a stranger could try to lure them into a car and take them away from the safety and security of their home. I wonder if any parent guessed that in the new decade, people would have strangers pick them up in their cars to take them home, to work, or to friends' houses. Sometimes I wonder if the old adage even makes sense anymore, now that our world is so reliant on strangers and their cars.

But those things make sense to me. I understand why we meet people on dating apps. I understand why we get into strangers' cars to go from point A to point B. In some ways, this is just a new form of capitalism, a way to profit off people's loneliness.

However, getting into this girl's jeep is probably more dangerous than getting into an online stranger's car.

She helps me load Marco into the back seat, careful with his bruises and wounds. We lay him down, his lanky body sprawled over the seats. She folds them down quickly, as if it's second nature, tucking him into the makeshift bed with an old quilt—a little dingy, but who am I to judge. She studies him, just like I'm studying her.

I wonder what she's thinking. Two strange boys who most certainly don't look like they should be standing on the side of the road, beaten up and bruised. What assumptions has she made about me? About Marco? About what we're doing? About how we got here? Yet she was willing to pick up boys like us. Does that make her more or less trustworthy? Or is she just as lost as the rest of us?

The one thing I *can* make out about her is simple: she has more confidence than either of us. It's in the way she carries herself. She's wearing a plaid button-down shirt with the sleeves rolled up to her elbows, cuffed jeans, and Dr. Martens boots. Her brown hair is a shade or two darker than her brown skin and pulled into a ponytail. Also, she's wearing leather fingerless gloves. She's methodical in the way she moves; no movement goes to waste, and before long, she's back in the front seat, the jeep roaring to life.

"What happened?" she asks, but doesn't wait for an answer before she starts driving.

Can I trust her? She doesn't look like she's with the police, but then again, undercover cops can look like anyone—that's the freaking point. And after what happened to Marco and me, I don't think I can risk trusting somebody else. But she *did* pick us up—she didn't have to do that—and we *are* in her car, going god knows where.

Probably somewhere safe, if I'm to believe what she said. She didn't need to help us. She could have kept driving. That means something.

"You don't need to tell me," she says, taking a sharp right turn. "We all have our secrets. But answer one question. Can you do that for me?"

"Sure," I say, my voice scratchy.

"Are you part of Nemesis?"

"Are you?"

The response comes off as a snappy defensive quip, but she doesn't seem to care.

"I saw you at the meeting and saw the police take you away. I hung out by the station, hoping to get some info, and watched you both just...walk out."

Ice-cold water runs through my veins, threatening to short-circuit every vital organ I have. I'm gripping the plastic handhold on the side of the passenger door tightly when a piece of plastic splinters off and stabs my finger, coppery blood pooling around the pad. From the corner of my eye, I can see the woman looking at me, but she doesn't seem fazed.

Don't let panic take over, Jamal. Just think.

The next logical question is how she knew about the Nemesis meeting, and there are only two possible answers. One, she's actually a cop, or two, she's part of Nemesis and somehow got away. But I don't remember seeing her there, and I'm pretty good with faces—it's a skill many journalists have—which makes number one more likely. Which means I gambled on the wrong person.

I look behind me at Marco, checking his vitals as well as I can from a distance. He is still breathing, even shifting around to try and get comfortable. That's probably a good thing—if he's conscious enough to care about being comfortable, it means his wounds aren't getting the best of him.

"You didn't answer my question," the girl says.

"I'm thinking."

"Thinking about what? Either you were there, or you weren't. Seems like a pretty straightforward question. Unless you're going to lie to me, which would be a mistake."

"I'm thinking about whether I can trust you or not."

The girl lets out a hyenalike laugh that comes from the back of her throat and echoes through the car. She raises her right hand, waving it through the air like she's trying to push something out from under of her nose.

"I'm sorry," she wheezes. "That's funny. *You're* trying to decide if you can trust *me* when I'm the one risking it all by picking you up? When you don't even seem like the type of person who should be involved in protests and shit like this?"

I push my lips into a thin line, my hands squeezing each other tightly. She's not wrong—she's risking more than I am. But I know so little about her. I don't even know her name. Maybe that's a good place to start. But first...

"What does that mean?" I ask. "'Not the type of person to be involved in protests and shit like this?'"

She gestures wildly at me, not taking her eyes off the road. "You're too put together. Even with the scuffs and dirt and shit, you look too...stable. You were here for the protest, yeah?"

I nod. "For school."

"*Of course* you were here for school."

"I'm a journalist. I was taking photos."

"Sorry to hear that. It means you have a target on your back, like me."

I want to ask more about *that*, because something tells me there's information there that I could use—either to understand her or use to my advantage against her—but the girl doesn't give me an opening.

"Anyway, you're out of your depth. Yes, I was at the Nemesis meeting. No, I don't want to go into more detail. And also yes, I'm pretty sure you need me, especially with that friend of yours—"

"I'm Jamal," I say curtly. "That's Marco."

She doesn't say anything for two or three blocks. Then, "Catherine. My friends call me Cat."

"Are we friends?"

"Still trying to decide that. But like I was saying, you need me."

As I look around, I notice we are farther from the city center than before. I think we're on the north side of Baltimore. I haven't seen many police cars here, and I'm not sure if the silence and lack of streetlights makes me feel happy or scared.

"Most police officers aren't on this side of town," she says, answering my unspoken question. "We're in the 'rich' part of the city. The police don't feel like they need to worry about people here."

"You mean the *white* part of the city."

She shrugs. "Semantics."

Not only are we in the white part, we're also in the suburbs. There are no longer looming high-rises or boarded-up buildings, just rolling grass with picket fences and three-story houses. The sounds of the city are almost completely gone, and there's an idyllic quiet in the air. It's like we're in a world completely removed from what's happening in downtown Baltimore, and I'm not sure how I feel about it.

I glance over at Catherine again, looking her up and down.

"You never answered my question," she reminds me, turning down another road. "The Nemesis meeting?"

"I need to ask you one first." I don't give her a chance to argue with me. "How do I know I can trust you?"

Catherine's hands grip the steering wheel a little bit tighter than before. The jeep is moving slowly, like it's in neutral, gliding down the street, grumbling and rumbling like an old man. I can't help but wonder what goes through the mind of a person who just randomly picks up strangers. Is she a Good Samaritan, or is there something in it for her? Or both? It's probably both.

I remember hearing in class—I think it was AP Psychology—the debate around whether a good deed can also be selfish. Must a good deed *only* help others, with no selfish benefit? I like to think a good deed *can* still be good if you gain from it. I mean, how about something like giving money to a person in need? It helps with your taxes, so both of you benefit from it, but that doesn't make it any less good—it just makes it a good deed with personal gain attached to it.

I think you can determine a lot about a person based on their answer to that question.

But Catherine still shows no sign of speaking to me.

Finally, I cave.

"I was hoping I could get information about…I dunno—"

"Turning off the Dome?"

I don't answer her off the bat. The suggestion seems far-fetched. But the way our savior said that sounded almost like…

"Do you know something you're not telling me?"

Catherine doesn't say anything and turns toward a nondescript house. She presses a button on the dashboard, and the garage door slides open. The jeep slides smoothly into the slot, the door closing behind us.

"Help me with him, will you?" Catherine asks, already out of the car and opening the side door.

I jump out and open the other door. Catherine loops her arms around Marco, carrying him like a bride. I open my mouth to warn her he's too heavy, but she glares at me.

"I got him."

There's no reason for me not to trust her, so I do. She carries him effortlessly into the house, kicking the door open with her boot and walking down the hall.

"Fun fact: Did you know you're the only one I saw come out of that building?" she says, not even checking to see if I'm behind her. "The holding cell? I waited there for almost six hours. I was just hoping *someone* would come out. Just one person from that meeting. Which begs the question, what's going on in these holding cells, and where are all those people? What is being done to them?"

"If what happened to Marco and me is any reflection of what other people are going through, you don't want to know." I keep it at that and am happy she doesn't push.

Besides, there's something heavy in her voice…something familiar.

Pain. As if it hurts her to know Marco and I were the only ones who made it out.

I shake my head, knowing she can't see me, but I think my silence answers the question.

Catherine takes a right into a guest room. There's nothing fancy about it: plain grayish-blue decor with little personality. It looks like a three-star hotel—not good, not bad—but it has a bed, and it's safe, and that's more than we had before. She gently puts Marco down on the bed and sits on the edge, running her fingers over his arms, checking the bruises on his face and other worrisome spots.

"He'll be fine," Catherine confirms, shifting topics. "He just took one hell of a beating. I went to basic training, where they beat you up for fun. He'll need to rest, but he'll heal."

I flex my fingers, which ache more than I can stand. It feels like my body is rebelling against me, and I realize what I really need is sleep. The adrenaline of the past day is wearing off, and my body has been running on overdrive for the past twenty-six hours. Has it only been twenty-six hours? It feels longer.

"You need to sleep too." She's not asking if I'm tired. She walks past me into the hallway, and I hear a door slide open. A moment later, she returns with blankets. "You can sleep on the couch. Don't worry, you're safe here. Trust me."

Has Catherine given me reason to trust her? That's a question for tomorrow. Right now, I can feel the exhaustion weighing on me.

Catherine walks me down the hall and into the living room. It's spacious, with a nice-size fluffy couch, two chairs on each side, and an attached exposed kitchen. This is a family home. Someone was loved here and grew up here and made memories here. But I don't see any pictures of Catherine.

I sit on the edge of the couch, toeing off my shoes. A groan leaves my lips unexpectedly. I look at her, feeling a burn on my cheeks. I know, in the dark and with my dark skin, that she can't tell, but I'm still ashamed. Catherine makes no attempt to acknowledge it.

"We'll talk more after you get some rest. I'll check on him in the night."

"Catherine?"

"Hmm?" she asks, halfway out of the room.

"Thank you."

She doesn't say anything at first. Then, "You can thank me by answering some questions when you're feeling better. I might have a favor to ask of you."

"Anything."

"Don't say that until you hear it," she says, walking out.

I should probably be more concerned by how ominous that sounds, but the couch is just too damn comfortable for me to care.

SIXTEEN

I don't remember falling asleep. I remember closing my eyes, thinking about Catherine and Marco, and then a weightlessness. But when I wake up, even before opening my eyes, I can tell it's morning. I've always had a good sense of time—I usually wake up before my alarm goes off—so before sensation even returns to the rest of my body, my fingertips start to warm as my whole biological machine kicks into gear. I can tell it's probably six or seven a.m. Which means I got about three or four hours of sleep. Not as much as I wanted, but it will do.

It takes me a moment to realize I'm with Catherine.

It takes me a moment to realize what happened to Marco wasn't just a nightmare.

It takes me a moment to realize I'm still living in hell.

But once that moment passes, I notice something else, something that breaks through my haze of sleepiness. Someone is arguing. Loudly.

"Look, I don't know who you think you are, but that is an absolutely stupid idea."

That's Marco's voice. Deep, but still a little airy. Confident, with a live-wire crackle of mirth. "I'm not doing that. He's not doing that."

"And I don't know who *you* think you are, but just as a quick refresher, I saved your ass. You owe me. And not just you. He owes me. That was the deal."

Catherine's voice: sharp, but also solid, like a boulder blocking your way, immovable.

"Yeah, that's not going to fly."

"Excuse me?"

I'm not sure how long Marco's been awake, but a surge of cool water goes over my spine, forcing my whole frame to relax. He sounds just like he did before, which means he's doing better. Actually, he sounds like he's doing great. Sleep helps everything—helps your body heal, helps your mind heal, and helps you figure out solutions to problems you couldn't solve the night before. In hindsight, his wounds probably look worse than they actually are. Superficial cuts and bruises, like Catherine said. At least he seems well enough to be able to argue.

"You two can't leave."

"Says who?"

"Me."

"Listen, lady, you don't want to try me."

Catherine scoffs, "And what are you going to do? Look, I'm glad you're okay, but you can barely walk on your own, and even if you could, I'm pretty sure I could take you."

"You don't know anything about me," he spits back.

"And you don't know anything about *me*," she replies. "Care to find out?"

"Jesus," I mutter.

I force myself to stand, feeling the heaviness in my body. This is exhaustion—full-body, complete-and-total exhaustion.

I push through, walking down the hallway, one foot after the other. My mouth is dry, and my body aches like I overexerted myself on a six-mile run, followed by a rigorous workout. I take a deep breath and push that pain aside before entering the room. I don't want Marco to see me feeling weak, and I most definitely don't want Catherine to see.

"If we're talking about something I agreed to, I think I should have a say in it, don't you?" I ask.

Both Marco and Catherine look over at me, but Marco's the first to react. He stands up quickly, faster than he probably should, but I don't have time to comment on that before he bridges the space between us and hugs me.

My body tenses up as his whole form envelops me—which is an accomplishment, considering Marco's pretty lanky. He doesn't lean toward buff and strong; he leans toward thin and scrawny, if I had to put him on the spectrum of physicality. But he finds a way to wrap his whole body around me, his arms encompassing me like the protective wings of an angel. It's weird, considering that just twenty-four hours ago we were at each other's throats. But now I couldn't ask for anything better in the world, and I find myself wrapping my arms around him too, squeezing tighter than I should.

He pulls back and smiles. The wounds on his face are turning purple already. His bloody lip is caked in black. His black eye is more of a maroon eye, but overall, he looks okay.

"I'm glad you're all right," he says. "She said you were, but—"

"He didn't trust me."

"I can tell," I reply. "I wouldn't be safe—*we* wouldn't be safe without her."

Marco looks over his shoulder at Catherine and then back at me. "You can vouch for her?"

"I don't need anyone—"

"Yes," I say without hesitation. But can I?

I don't know much about Catherine, just that she was in the right place at the right time. I don't even know if she was being truthful about that. I don't know how she got this house. I don't know anything besides her name, if that even *is* her name, and that she went to boot camp. I'm sure there's more to that story than she's telling me.

Marco doesn't seem convinced. "I need to talk to him alone," he tells Catherine.

"Whatever," she says, throwing her hands up. "You two do what you need to do. I'll be in the kitchen. Making myself food. Which neither of you is welcome to anymore. Especially not you." She points to Marco.

"Sounds good," Marco says, watching her as she walks out. Once she's out of earshot, he turns to me. "I don't trust her. We should leave."

"You don't even know her. And we're not leaving."

"Do you? And why not?"

"No, I don't." A beat passes before I speak again. "But I'm not sure that matters right now."

Marco arches his brow in disapproval.

"I think everyone is just trying to survive," I explain. "In whatever manner they can. We're more likely to survive together. It's true that there's strength in numbers. And Catherine obviously knows how to handle herself. She was able to avoid the cops and get us across town without anyone noticing. We can handle the *why* part later. Right now, we need to try our best to get out of here and…"

"And what?"

I take a deep breath, wanting to fold in on myself and disappear into a black hole, never to be seen again. He needs to know. He deserves to know I sold out Nemesis and that the police know about Janna. I don't trust Chief Coles. I don't trust him to keep his end of the bargain, after all, if he's trying to take "us agitators" down.

"We have to go back to Janna's," I finally say.

Marco frowns, confused. "What do you mean? We're in North Baltimore, right? Nice place. A little too picket-fence-and-two-point-five children for me, but eh, to each their own. But anyway, it's on the opposite side of town, and I for one don't want—"

"We have to go back," I say, more firmly this time. "Now."

Marco frowns, studying me.

"You're leaving something out. What are you hiding from me? Less than three minutes ago, you were all 'we can't leave.'"

There's no easy way to say what I need to say, but I have to get it off my chest. Marco's like a pit bull; he won't stop until he's achieved his goal. And right now, his tunnel vision is focused on understanding what I'm hiding from him.

"I think Chief Coles is going to arrest her. If he hasn't already."

"What? Why would he do that?"

I nod slowly and take a shaky breath, grounding myself by sitting on the unmade bed. I rub my hands against my pants, feeling the sweat slide off.

"When we were arrested, Chief Coles wanted only one thing—information on Nemesis," I say quickly. Might as well get it out as soon as possible. "They told me to give them up, or you would…" I gesture to him, to his bruises, to everything on his skin. I don't need to say more.

"Okay," Marco says slowly. "But I don't know what Janna has to do with—"

"He knows what she's doing. He brought her up and knew all about her."

"And you think he's going to arrest her? She's a pillar of the community. People would fight back."

"I think people are more worried about other things right now. But I'm worried about what they'll do to her. To the kids."

Again, I can't help but look at Marco's bruises. They're starting to turn shades of purple and yellow. It's a sign of healing, but it looks like he was hit by a truck, twice.

Marco is smart enough to put two and two together. He nods slowly, leaning against the wall, crossing his arms over his chest.

"Then we need to go back," he says. "We have to help her. And them."

"Exactly what I was thinking."

"I—wait," Marco interjects. "Are we on the same page about this?"

I arch my brow. "Why wouldn't we be? It was my idea."

Marco shrugs. "I mean, just yesterday you were very 'ask three to five questions before actually acting,' so excuse me if I'm a bit surprised by this sudden shift."

I shrug. "People change." But Marco's right. I've always liked to think of myself as the type of person who would run into a fire head-first, but I remember how terrified I was a day and a half ago. How if it wasn't for Marco and Janna, I wouldn't have made it two hours. She helped all those kids, and she needs our help in return.

Pay it forward, and all that BS.

A knock on the door interrupts my train of thought; Catherine's standing there, looking at us.

"Sorry to interrupt," she says, "but, question. Did I hear you say last night that you're a journalist?"

"Aspiring, but yeah."

"And you take photos?"

"Yeah."

"Digital or film?"

"Film—better quality."

She nods. "Good, that's really good. Then I might have a way to help you, help your friend, whatever her name is—"

"Janna," Marco says.

"Yeah, that. I have an idea that can help her and help everyone else. Two birds, one stone."

"What's your idea?" Marco asks.

A sly smile, almost foxlike, spreads over Catherine's face, and I can tell I'm not going to like this.

SEVENTEEN

The plan is simple. Well, not *simple*, but it's straightforward.

We go back to Janna's house, where my camera is. We get the camera—since it's not digital, it's not affected by whatever the Dome and the cops' suits do that makes taking digital photos impossible—and get the photos I took of the Dome activating: the proof.

"What makes you think digital doesn't work?" Marco says, skeptical. "This seems like a lot of effort for something…"

Catherine pulls out her phone and shows us a flurry of photos, all of them filled with a bright white light in the center. Only the edges of the photos are remotely clear.

"I took these as soon as the Dome started."

I glance over at Marco. "You're the hacker, is this possible?"

"Possible, yeah," he mutters, taking the phone from her and examining it. "Celebrities have hoodies that can refract camera film, so you only see white. But to do it on a massive scale?"

"That would require money," I mutter.

"And connections. And power," Catherine adds.

"And intent," Marco finishes. "Intent to hide something you don't want the world to see."

"Which is why we need your camera," Catherine nods to me.

Then Marco uses his hacking skills to find a way to shut down a part of the Dome small enough for me to get through, and I take the photos to the police or a journalist or whoever will listen. And Catherine's in the role she says she has always wanted to play.

"The muscle," she smirks, cracking her knuckles for emphasis. The action is a little comical, I have to admit, but the chorus of cracks gets the point across. "I'll deal with any problems along the way."

It's a good plan. Not only will it give us leverage, but we can also check up on Janna, make sure everything is okay there. If she's not at her house, then we'll know Chief Coles lied. If she is, then we'll know he did something horrible to her. Either way, we'll have what we need: information.

"It's dangerous," Marco interjects.

"This whole town is filled with danger," Catherine says. "I don't see any difference, do you?"

"The place could be crawling with cops."

"And I'll deal with them if it is."

Marco scoffs. "Sorry, forgive me, but how are you going to deal with them?"

"How about you just focus on how you're going to get the Dome down? You're some great hacker, right? Do your part."

"I just want to make sure, if I'm trusting you with my life, that you're not going—"

"You're not trusting me with your life," Catherine says, cutting him off. "You're staying here."

"Excuse me?" Marco and I say together.

Catherine sighs, pinching her nose. She gestures for us to follow her down the hall, muttering, "I'm dealing with amateurs." Once we get to the living room, she pulls out a piece of paper and a pen, writing quickly.

"There are three of us," she says, drawing three stick figures: one with curly hair—me, one with an angry scowl—her, and one with a black eye—Marco.

"Rude," he mutters.

"Each of us has skills. I have military knowledge, Jamal is the journalist, and you, Marco, can hack. Each of us provides something: Jamal has the evidence, I provide safety while we're under the Dome, and you, Marco, are our best chance of getting out."

I nod. "I see where you're going with this."

"I don't, so…"

"We can't all be in one place," I say. "If all three of us are caught, then it's game over. If I go with Catherine, there's a chance—a high chance—at least one of us will make it back to you with the camera."

Catherine nods. "Exactly. We all have important roles to play, but it won't matter if we can't get the Dome down." She glances over at Marco. "You're part of Nemesis."

"An adjunct member."

"Whatever. Are you sure you can do it?"

For a moment, Marco falls silent. Catherine doesn't see it, but a shadow passes over his face, a shadow of doubt. I reach over, squeezing his hand for a moment.

"He can do it," I say. "I mean, what other redeeming qualities does he have?"

"Rude," Marco mutters.

"But true," she adds under her breath.

"There has to be another way," Marco interjects. "You could be going right into the lion's den. What if the area is cordoned off as a police investigation zone? What if you have to fight those cops?"

"There isn't another way," Catherine says curtly. "This is the best plan we have. And if we have to, then we have to. Simple as that. Right?" she asks, looking at me.

I didn't sign up to fight anyone, but I also didn't sign up to just let the police get away with anything they want. My pulse is racing, thinking of all the possible *what if*s, but I still nod.

"Right."

"Look, I understand you are all military or whatever, but I don't think you're actually thinking about the consequences of your actions here," Marco says. "If you go head-to-head with the police, even if you win, we're going to be labeled as terrorists without a doubt. There will be no place for us that's safe."

"We're standing up for what's right. Getting information to the people—that's not terrorism. And what's the difference between that and what you're doing already, Mr. Nemesis adjunct member?" she asks.

"It's not the same."

"And why not? You're hacking. That's illegal."

"We never actually put ourselves on the line; there are systems… protections…there…"

"Ah." She nods. "So you're only comfortable being a badass when there's no actual risk."

Marco balls his fists and opens his mouth, but he shut it quickly. A moment later, he opens his mouth again.

"We've already escaped the police once, and this happened." He gestures to the purple-and-black wounds on his body as a reminder. "They won't be so kind to us next time."

"We still have to try," I interject. Both of them look at me with the same puzzled expression. "Chief Coles isn't just going to stop. He's going to erase everything and everyone who stands against him. Janna, protesters, Nemesis..."

"Us," Catherine says.

I nod. "He might not be watching us right now, but eventually he'll find us. Or one of his underlings will, someone who's hungry for a promotion or something. He only let us go because he wanted to give us the appearance of freedom; we all know that, right?"

Marco nods.

"Then we've already lost. Might as well go down doing something worth the title we're being branded with anyway."

Accepting out loud that there's a chance we could be labeled as terrorists, locked up, or killed seems to strike a chord with Marco and Catherine. Marco's face twists with disgust, while Catherine lowers her eyes to the ground. It's as if she understands what being a terrorist means, as if she knows what the future holds for us and is sad that we're going to experience it because she's experienced it herself. I make a mental note to ask more about her, to find out what Catherine is really about—how she is so confident, and how she came to be in this situation. For now, I have to focus on what's ahead of us if we're going to actually make a dent in this Dome.

"I know my opinion doesn't mean much here," she says, "but I agree with Jamal. I don't believe in fate or anything, but we have a unique set of skills that gives us a chance to survive. We might as well use it. We have to try."

"And you?" Marco asks. "This whole G.I. Jane routine is cute, but what's your story? Care to share?"

Catherine's lips push into a thin line, and she clenches her fists tightly by her sides. I'm curious if she'll open up to us.

"We're both trusting you," I gently add. "You can trust us."

"Later," she promises. "If we survive this, then I'll tell you. Deal?"

Marco and I look at each other. The playfulness and softness in Marco's features is gone. He's sharper and more angular, like a piece obsidian has violently chiseled parts of him away. It hurts to look at him, but it hurts even more to know that I'm the reason why his edges, once round, are now rough. I give him a weak smile. He doesn't return it.

"Fine," he says. "You go to Janna's, and then, what, we regroup here?"

She nods. "I'll take Jamal to get the camera and check up on Janna—he's safer with me. Do you think you can get in touch with anyone from Nemesis? They must have some information about the Dome, something that can help you."

He nods. "I think so. I'll need a computer."

"An air gapped one?"

Marco pauses, obviously wanting to ask how she knows that, then nods. "Yeah."

Catherine points. "Down the hall, take the stairs, and go to the closet at the end. In the back there's a black box. One-nine-oh-four is the password—should be charged."

Marco pauses, shakes his head, and then stomps off quickly down the hallway. My eyes follow him until I can't see his form anymore.

"He'll come around," she promises and looks at me. "Boys are stubborn when their confidence is broken. We have more important things to worry about. Do you know how to change a tire?"

I spend the next twenty minutes with Catherine, checking methodically for anything that might hinder the truck on our journey. The last thing we want is a spark plug short-circuiting or a tire spinning out.

"This is like therapy for me," Catherine mutters, counting on her fingers the items she wants to check off her pre-drive list.

"Same." Not the same, but that felt like the right thing to say. My uncle tried to teach me how to change tire eighteen months ago with no success, and it was an embarrassing situation for us both. After that, my mother made sure our AAA membership was always updated. But learning the secrets from Catherine makes it so I'm able to do the last one by myself. I roll my eyes as she looks at me proudly.

"They grow up so quickly," she says, wiping her face with the back of her hand. I roll my eyes again, threatening to throw the wrench at her. She doesn't even flinch.

Instead she turns back and pulls out a rusty box, setting it on the floor beside her. Out of the corner of my eye, I see what she pulls out of it. My head twists around quickly, needing to look at it head-on to confirm what it is.

A gun.

Maryland isn't one of those states where you just…see guns lying around all the time. Sure, you can get a carry permit, and I know a friend or two whose parents have them, but they aren't common. Plus, as a Black man, I feel a sense of tightness whenever I see one—especially so close.

Catherine seems unbothered by it. She wields the revolver with ease, checking the magazine—I think that's the word—and then she straps the holster to her hip, slipping the gun inside. The whole time, she doesn't look at me. The expression on her face is calm, like this is normal for her. I can promise my face doesn't look the same, and she notices.

"It's for our protection," she says. "Those cops won't hesitate to use theirs."

"I know," I say. "It's just…"

"You don't know how to shoot one, do you?"

I shake my head. "And I don't want to know."

"Ever held one?"

I shake my head again. "I'm good."

"You sure? It might—"

"I'm good." I add emphasis in my voice so she knows I'm serious.

Catherine hesitates putting the toolbox back. She checks the tires one more time, kicking each one with her boot, and then checks her watch. "We should get going soon."

Almost as if on cue, Marco appears at the door.

Catherine nods at him. "We'll be back soon."

Marco lets out a sound of agreement before his eyes land on

mine. They don't have the same familiarity or warmth as they did before, and I don't like the feeling they give off, but I keep my gaze locked with his. I wish I could say something. I wish I could apologize. I know I should—even if I'm not sorry, it's the right thing to do. Because even if Catherine hasn't said it, there's a chance we won't see each other after this.

"Jamal and I should be back within three hours," she promises, walking around to the driver's side. "If we aren't back in five hours, though, you should change locations. That'll mean—"

"—you got caught by the cops again," Marco bluntly finishes for her. "I know."

There's bile in his voice, but that doesn't stop him from saying it. Marco looks away from us, down at the floor, scuffing his boot against the hard, cold concrete. I take a moment to look at him, to *really* look at him, knowing this might be the last time I see him. I have so much I want to say, so much I want to apologize for, so many mistakes I need to own up to. But before I can speak, before I can even take in a deep breath to start speaking, Catherine nudges me.

"Let's get going. We don't want to be out too long."

I jump into the passenger side of the car. The jeep rumbles to life as the garage opens slowly. Marco stands in the driveway, staring at us as we peel out and start our journey. And though I know he's staring at us collectively, deep down, I like to think he's looking at *me*. Only me. I nod at him before he disappears, hoping he knows what I mean: *I know, and I'm sorry too.*

EIGHTEEN

We drive in silence into the city we both want nothing to do with.

The light of day makes Baltimore look different—hell, it looks like a disaster zone, if I'm honest. There're people in the streets, still walking around doing their daily chores, because the city can't simply stop working just because it's under martial law.

But the air feels bitter; the people seem less lively, and there are more police than I've ever seen. In front of banks. On the corners. Aggressively invading people's space, rounding them up and throwing them into the backs of cars. It looks like something out of a really bad young adult novel that was adapted into a movie. But it's my reality right now. Every second we're driving feels like the second we're going to get caught. I feel like an officer is going to spot us, realize who we are, and stop the car—and then it's all going to be over.

But at no point does that happen. Even Catherine, who's driving, seems relaxed; two fingers on her right hand tap on the steering wheel in time to a song I don't recognize that's playing softly on the radio. Or maybe I do. I don't know, I can't think of anything besides the stunt we're about to pull.

"You have to act normal," Catherine says, glancing over at me. "You know the expression *Keep your friends close and your enemies closer?*"

I nod, unable to form words.

"That's exactly what we're doing. We're staying close to the belly of the beast because they won't expect us to be there." A crackle of a smile that's borderline manic appears on her face. "Isn't this fun?"

"I don't know if *fun* is the word I would use," I say honestly. *Exciting*, sure. *Panic-inducing?* Also yes. But *fun?* I don't know if I can agree with that.

I push the fear away and focus. There are two things at the forefront of my mind right now: the mission and Catherine.

Get in, get out, get the camera, get back to Marco. That's all we need to do. It's straightforward—we don't have to worry about anyone else, and I just have to remember why we're doing this. If I want to help the most people, we have to find a way to get me out of the Dome. Getting sidetracked will only put Catherine and me at risk of getting caught, and if Chief Coles finds me again, my punishment won't be as easy as it was last time…and it wasn't easy last time.

This is doable. Something inside of me makes me feel like we can do this. Maybe it's stubborn pride. Maybe it's stupidity. But with Catherine here with me, the fluttering of my heart doesn't feel as dizzying as before. If anything, it feels exactly like she said: excited.

I feel horrible saying that. Just looking out the window, I can see the way the police are treating people, images that will be branded on my brain no matter what happens. I know that, like so many other things in the news, even if we get information out there, the Baltimore Police Department's PR team will spin it in some way that will have America sympathizing with them. No one will care that a department with nearly a half a billion dollars in funding put its boot on the back of its citizens, especially its citizens of color, and did whatever it wanted to them.

The fact that Black and brown children are being eyed like criminals as they walk down the street, or that homeless African Americans' tents are being destroyed right in front of me, won't make the news. The footage will be cut, spliced, and crafted to win the police officers' favor. What's happening here might come up in the next presidential debate for three minutes. But at its core, the struggles of the people of Baltimore will be nothing more than a talking point.

And that makes me sick.

So instead I focus on something else. I focus on Catherine.

"If you want Marco and me to trust you, I think we've earned the right to know more about you," I blurt out, timing the words perfectly (unintentionally) to cut in the moment the song is done. "We're both risking our lives to help you, and sure, yes, you saved us, and we're grateful, but still. We deserve to know who you are."

"It's important for you to know that my parents are good people," she says. "But even good people can do bad things."

I steel myself for what she's about to say. Deep down, I agree. Of course I agree. But that doesn't mean it's something I want to hear. And usually when someone says something like that, what follows isn't great.

"My parents are—were—I don't know what tense to use—trained as engineers. They were assigned early on to a government-funded project that would change their lives. As you can see"—she holds up her hand and turns it left and right—"I'm Latina. My father's Mexican, and my mother is Guatemalan. It's not often that people like us get chances to work on government contracts; leading a multimillion-dollar project was an amazing opportunity my parents couldn't pass up. But halfway through, they realized what it was for."

Catherine pauses, as if she's unable to say it. But I'm already a step ahead, and I finish her thought. "Your parents helped make the Dome, didn't they?"

She nods curtly, and her hands tighten around the steering wheel to the point where her tan skin turns almost white. "You have to understand, they didn't know what they were doing," she says defensively. "And the moment they figured it out, they tried to stop it. They tried to talk to the governor, and they even threatened to go public. And that's when…" She takes a moment and swallows thickly. "That was a year and a half ago, and I haven't seen them or heard from them since.

"I was in basic training for the army the last time I heard from them. It was easy for me to brush it off as them just being wrapped up in a project or dealing with work stress, because I was so focused on being someone they could be proud of. Proving to them that this was my calling, even if it wasn't the same as theirs. But when I came back and I saw that the house was untouched, I knew something was wrong. None of my parents' coworkers would answer my questions.

When I confronted some of them, they pretended they didn't even know who I was and that my parents didn't exist.

"I was supposed to ship out a couple of weeks ago. The letter came in the mail, and a phone call followed, but none of it made sense. They wanted me to lead some peacekeeping mission in the Middle East. But I just graduated from basic training—there's no reason to give me that responsibility."

"Unless they wanted to shut you up," I suggest.

"Unless they wanted to shut me up," she agrees. "So I did what I could. I packed my bags, contacted a friend whose parents are off rekindling their relationship on a three-month cruise, convinced her I needed to use her home, and here I am," Catherine finishes. "I've made it my base of operations since then. That was a month and a half ago. I'm not going to stop until I get the Dome shut down and find the information I need to free my parents."

There's conviction in her voice, and I can tell that Catherine can't be stopped once she's put her mind to something.

I feel the jeep slow down and roll to a halt. I glance around, quickly noticing the area looks familiar. The broken streets, the empty alleyways, and the muted colors of the buildings look brighter and more spacious in the daytime. I haven't seen Janna's place in the sunlight; when we arrived and when we left, it was shrouded in darkness. But now I can see that this neighborhood looks like any other. It looks like home. And I wonder how many of her neighbors Janna knew personally. I wonder where they are now. I do my best to push that thought out of my head.

Catherine reaches over my lap, opening the glove compartment and pulling out her fingerless gloves. She slips them on, buckling the straps at her wrists, and clenches her fists. She takes a deep breath and closes her eyes, counting quietly under her breath. Each passing second feels like we're counting down to storming a castle, or like we're preparing for war. These are the last few moments I can still turn back.

"Let's go."

No turning back now. Once she's done, she turns to look at me with a smile that doesn't fully reach her eyes. I can tell she's nervous too.

"You know where the camera is?"

I nod. Assuming my bag hasn't been moved, I remember exactly where it is. I put that thought front and center in my head, forcing the images of Marco, the images of the streets, and everything else into the background.

Catherine nods. "Good. We get in, get it, get out. No distractions. This should be easy. Stay close to me, and if anything goes sideways…"

"I run."

She nods again, jumping out of the car. "Exactly. That camera has photos of the Dome going up. If Nemesis has been neutralized by the police, we could be the only ones with evidence. Getting those pictures is key."

"So are you," I point out, closing the door quietly behind me. "We wouldn't have gotten this far without you."

"That's absolutely true. But also—and don't tell Marco I said this—it doesn't matter how strong I am. If we can't find a way to shut down the Dome and get out of here, that won't matter."

"You don't think people will believe us without the photos?" I ask. "My mom called me before it happened. The Dome is huge. I'm sure people outside are already wondering and thinking—"

"I wouldn't underestimate our governor and the strength of her hunger for power or the governor's ability to spin a story."

She's right; our government has lied before. I can name a number of times the fourth estate and the government have changed the public's perception of crucial events.

"We need solid proof of the Dome going up, Jamal," she says. "You've documented it. You're the key here. Plus, your camera isn't digital. It's harder to fake film. The government can just say any digital photos were edited."

No plan is foolproof. I'm not some super soldier or special agent, but I know that to be true. Even the best-laid plans can easily turn upside down with a single mistake or missed detail. Our idea is pretty simple—to go in, get the camera, and get out—but there are so many things that could go wrong, so many things we can't plan for. I have to trust in myself, but more importantly, I have to trust Catherine. I have to trust that we will get through this, hope for the best, and keep my eyes on the prize, because it's not only my life on the line. It's Catherine's, and Marco's. If I want to make amends for what I've done to those kids in the house, I have to get this information out into the world. There is no other option.

"You ready?" Catherine asks as she stands next to me, Janna's house less than twenty feet in front of us.

"Yeah," I say. Because *fuck, no* doesn't seem like the right thing to say when you're about to jump into the belly of the beast.

NINETEEN

I don't know where Catherine learned all her life skills, but she seems to have a talent applicable to whatever problem we're facing.

We cross the street easily, keeping our bodies low to the ground as we head toward the house. I follow the same path Marco did yesterday, going through the back gate and across the lawn, keeping close to the wall as I head up the rickety stairs. I raise my hand to knock on the door, but Catherine stops me.

Silently, she pulls out a small kit from one of the lower pockets of her cargo pants and opens it. She extracts two thin metal rods and goes to work picking the lock. Thirty seconds later, the door quietly clicks open.

"Bingo," Catherine whispers.

I raise my eyebrows in surprise. Catherine seems to be the type of girl who fends for herself and knows how to survive.

She keeps low to the ground and raises one finger in the universal symbol for *quiet*. She doesn't need to tell me twice. As we walk into the house in a half-squatting position that makes my thighs burn, I notice something that makes my heart sink: the silence.

When I first arrived, there wasn't any silence in the house. There were kids running around, there was cooking, and the house was alive. Despite the upheaval going on outside, Janna did her best to keep her home warm. Now it's the opposite. There are no lights on, one of the windows is smashed, and clothes are strewn all over the place. The bookshelf in the living room is on its side, and the refrigerator door is open, letting a putrid scent fill the kitchen.

It takes all my energy to keep my heart from jumping out of my chest. I wish I wondered what happened here, but I don't need to wonder. Even if I don't know the details, the carnage is a perfect reminder of what the police in Baltimore can do when left to their own devices.

Catherine stays a few steps ahead of me as we wander through the house. I focus not only on her back but also on the image of where I left my camera. My mattress was in the corner of the living room with my bag against the wall. The camera should be in there.

I take a step forward and, before I can grab on to something, fall onto my back. A sharp pain shoots through my body, the heavy *thump* loud in the still-quiet air. Catherine whips her head around quickly, a look of panic, concern, and anger flashing over her face. I raise my left hand, waving to show I'm fine, and force myself up slowly. What made me slip? It takes me a moment to realize I stepped in something wet.

It takes me another moment to realize that wet something is blood.

I am standing in someone else's blood. A person I probably saw while I was here. A person I might have talked to, might have laughed with, maybe even one of the kids I helped tuck into bed. The blood is not fully dried, but it's not warm either, which means it's been here for a while…but not long enough to congeal.

I try to remember my forensics class from last year. Blood can dry out in thirty to forty minutes when exposed to air. A pool of blood, which will spread out and become a thin layer, will be tacky by afternoon and completely dry by the next day.

This blood is the definition of tacky.

My heart sinks when I put two and two together. Chief Coles didn't waste any time. After they let us go, he instantly came here and…and…

Catherine bridges the gap between us, and when she squeezes my shoulder, sending a jolt of pain through my body, it snaps me out of my downward spiral. I meet her gray eyes and see the seriousness in them. She whispers quietly, barely moving her lips, "Focus."

She's right. I can't let this derail us. This is just another reason to keep going. I have to use this as a catalyst, not a hindrance.

I stare at the blood one more time, letting the image seep into my mind like the liquid has seeped into the grooves of the floor-boards. This is why I'm here. This is what I'm here to stop.

Focus.

I drag my foot against the ground, pushing my shoe into the floor, doing my best to ignore it. Catherine and I continue forward, walking throughout the house and keeping as quiet as possible. When we reach the end of the hallway, Catherine glances over her shoulder and uses what I'm guessing is a military signal that means, *I'll go left, you go forward.*

Simple enough. I nod.

I'm not exactly sure what Catherine is looking for. Our goal is to get in and get out as quickly and as silently as possible. We're supposed to be focused on getting the camera, but she is almost halfway down the hallway. I open my mouth to hiss and grab her attention, but instead I swallow back my voice. I need to get the camera—that's all that matters. But she's doing her thing, I'm doing my thing.

The living room looks just like the kitchen. Mattresses are strewn all over the place along with blankets and books. The table where we had our buffet looks like somebody was slammed on top of it. There's broken glass, stacked clean plates, and cloth napkins in a pile to be washed. My mind wanders to the worst possible explanations for what happened here. It gives me a nauseated feeling, but I swallow it back.

I grit my teeth and walk toward where my mattress was. It only takes me a moment to find my bag, and a rush of relief flows over my body. At least something is going right.

I quickly unzip the worn metal zipper and scan the contents of the bag, feeling the familiar distressed leather. I bought this bag about two years ago with money I won from a photography competition freshman year. I'd always wanted one of those hipster bags all the photographers for *National Geographic* had, and this was the closest I could get with five hundred dollars. I'm not sure which I like more: the Pentax K1000 my mom got me for Christmas last year or the bag itself. Combined, they make me feel like an actual photographer.

Like there's space for a queer Black boy like me in the incredibly white-dominated field of photography.

I'm wearing the right clothes, I have the right tools, I have the right bag, and maybe, if I act like I belong, people won't look too closely at me. The bag and the camera make me feel like I'm somebody.

"Camera, lenses, notebook," I whisper to myself. Check, check, and check. Everything's where it's supposed to be. Good.

I zip up the bag as quickly as I opened it and slide it over my shoulder. I survey the room one more time, seeing if I've missed something. Part of me hopes that little girl I saved with Marco is here. She seemed like a survivor, so maybe she hid and they overlooked her. But I don't see her, which means one of three things:

One, she somehow escaped and is out there in the world, alone.

Two, she got taken with the rest of the kids and Janna.

And three, that blood is hers.

None of those are good options.

I swallow thickly and push the thought down. That little girl is important to me, but so are all the other kids whose names I don't remember. Each one of those children could have a parent looking for them who loves them, who needs them, who wants to know they are safe. We can give them that. Hopefully. Maybe. Possibly.

I walk quickly out of the room, afraid the ghosts of those who were taken might turn into shackles and keep me here permanently. I need to find Catherine. She's probably upstairs, rooting through Janna's things, wondering if there's anything of use. Normally, I wouldn't condone that, since it's technically—no, *literally*—stealing.

But desperate times call for desperate measures, and we need every tool we can get to survive.

I hear the sound of a car door shutting before I hear the voices. Two deep male voices, laughing and joking as they walk up the front steps.

Quickly, I press my back against the wall so hard I feel like I'm going to blend in with the wood. The voices sound too happy to be friends of Janna's who might be checking on her. And…I don't know how to say this…but the voices sound too *white* to be neighbors. The heaviness of the boots coming up the front porch stairs makes the whole house creak, and I know exactly who the men are without having to see their faces.

Cops.

"I'm telling you, Lewis," one of them says, "once this is all done, you have to let me hook you up with Cheryl. She's absolutely wild in bed; you'd love her."

"Come on, man, don't talk about her like that. She's a person," Lewis chides.

"Nah, she's a chick," the other man laughs.

Both men seem to find that joke hilarious, their bellowing laughter bouncing off the walls. There's no way Catherine can't hear them. She must know we're not alone anymore. Catherine seems like the type of girl who could jump from a second-story window, roll, and not make a single sound. I'm not saying she's the type who would run away from a fight, but she's smart enough to know when she can win and when to cut her losses.

I keep my body pressed as close to the wall as I can. Egress points: that's what I need.

Quickly, I survey the room. There's a window across the room, but it's closed, and I'm sure it will make a loud noise if I open it. There's the side door that Marco and I used, but I have to cross the hallway to get there, and that'll definitely put me in their line of sight. I can always hide; these cops are probably looking for things, not people. Looting like Catherine, or sent to retrieve something for Chief Coles. If I stay quiet…if I stay out of sight…they probably won't see me. I can wait this out.

At least, I hope I can.

"Ten-four, be advised there are protesters downtown, armed and dangerous. Requesting backup specifically from modified units," the crackling voice on their walkie-talkies says.

"Hey," the second man says, "you wanna go?"

Lewis grunts. "Nah, I'm good here. You go ahead."

"You sure?"

"Yeah, man," Lewis says. "No sweat. Just need to check upstairs for those papers. Circle back for me when you're done?"

"No promises."

The two men exchange a handshake, the sound of skin slapping skin loud. I hear the other man's footsteps disappear, the sound of the door opening and closing, the revving of the engine, and the car driving off into the distance. Less than thirty seconds later, it's just Officer Lewis and me on the first floor.

But that won't last long. He said he's looking for papers…papers on the second floor, where Catherine is. It doesn't matter what papers he's talking about. It doesn't matter if they give away information about protesters or something else Janna was doing, since Marco said she was an organizer in Baltimore. All that matters right now is that if Lewis goes upstairs, he's going to run into Catherine. And Catherine isn't going to go down without a fight.

And a fight with a cop means someone is going to die.

I weigh the pros and cons of my potential courses of action. Pro: if I stay hidden, I can probably sneak away when Officer Lewis goes upstairs. I may not be able to make it all the way back to Catherine's house, but I can make it pretty damn far. Con: What kind of person would I be if I did that? The police have already chipped away at my soul over the past couple of days, more than I would like to admit. I can't have Catherine's fate weighing on me too.

I bite my tongue until I taste copper. I squeeze my hands tightly until my body stops moving, as if my whole form is a live wire and I'm doing my best to ground myself. Officer Lewis is now across the entranceway from me. I can see the back of his crew-cut head less than five feet away. I have the advantage; I have element of surprise. I have to do something.

I can feel my heart pumping in my ears as I slowly release the energy from my fists. If I'm not going to do something, if I'm not going to stand up for what's right, then why am I even here? Why didn't I just let Chief Coles keep me in the barracks? If you want to be a hero—if you want to have a life worth living—you have to take risks. And risking my life for someone else is worth it.

I count to five in my head, using the seconds to steel my mind and focus my resolve. Once I reach five, I move quickly, plunging forward, intending to use the full force of my body to knock Lewis to the ground. After that, I'm not exactly sure what I have planned, but

I'll deal with that problem when I get there. Right now, I just need to alert Catherine to what's happening. If she's still in the house, she'll come down and help me—it will be two against one, with us having the element of surprise. It's a smart plan. It's a good plan. I think even Catherine and Marco would be proud of me.

But before I can reach Officer Lewis, his body whips around, and his hand darts out like a venomous snake. He grabs my throat, gloved hand wrapped tightly around my flesh, and slams me against the wall. Everything becomes dizzying, the world swirling like a watercolor. But I can make out the smirk on his face. And right then, I know what it's like to look into the eyes of pure, unadulterated evil.

"Found you," he sneers, squeezing tighter.

TWENTY

I can feel Officer Lewis's grip cutting into my skin. I know I'll probably have bruises in the shapes of his fingers. The skin will be purple and black and yellow, like a mixture of stamps rapidly pressed into a porous piece of paper. That should be what scares me the most—the way he grips my neck as if he's trying to break my spine but at the same time wants me to stay conscious enough to feel every second. The way I can feel his skin digging its way under my nails as I claw at his exposed arm. The way he ignores the red slash marks I leave on him. How his grip is too strong for me to fight, and no matter how much I punch and scratch and kick, he doesn't let go.

But what terrifies me most is the way his left hand, his free hand, moves casually down to something on his hip, flicking open a small pack. I see it happen, a wave of translucent light passing over the SWAT-like armor and then disappearing. The helmet's visor becomes darker, like those glasses that adjust to sunlight.

"You just had to stay away," he growls. "That's it. If you'd kept your head down and stayed out of the spotlight, you would have been fine."

His grip tightens more, and I let out a strangled scream that was caught in my throat. I feel my fingertips turn cold, the tingle in my feet from circulation being cut off.

I'm going to die like this, I realize.

"But no, you had to come back. Because *of course* you had to come back," he sneers, leaning forward and pressing his metal forehead against mine. "And I'm going to enjoy killing you."

"Fuck that."

Catherine's voice comes in loud and clear. Even with my blurry vision, I see her from the corner of my eye. She uses the steps to her advantage, practically jumping down them like a gazelle. When she's two or three steps away from us, a good three or four feet above Officer Lewis, she jumps off the step, flying at us with her knee out. I hear a sickening crack as her knee connects with his helmet. I'm not sure if she broke the helmet or her knee—I'm really hoping it's the former—but Officer Lewis lets me go. All three of us collapse at once, Officer Lewis growling in frustration, me gasping for air, and Catherine landing surprisingly lightly on her feet.

I take two quick breaths, enough to stop the blackening in the corner of my eyes. I rub my neck, feeling the sensitive, sore skin. Quickly, I look up at Catherine. "Are you—"

"Did you get the camera?" she barks out.

I nod, not sure if she saw me. She's totally focused on Lewis, her body slightly crouched in a predatory but protective manner.

"Get out of here," she says, simple and clear. "Keys."

She tosses them to me without looking, and I'm lucky I grab them.

"I'm not leaving—" I say hoarsely.

Slowly, Officer Lewis regains his bearings, the flying attack only enough to daze him for a moment.

"Get. Out. Of. Here," she says pointedly. "We're here for the camera, that's it."

I know she's right. But that doesn't mean I'm going to leave her. Catherine got the jump on Lewis—that's a fact. And the way his helmet is slightly cracked from the impact means she did a good amount of damage—also a fact. But the biggest fact of them all is that Catherine won't be able to hold her own against Lewis alone. Not because he's a better fighter than her, and not because I understand engineering, but because that suit he's wearing is going to give him advantages neither of us can comprehend. Catherine must be able to understand that—she *has* to know that.

Which can mean only one thing.

This is a suicide mission.

It's probably the soldier in her, I think—mission above all. Our goal was to get the camera, get out, and get the information on it to the public. Catherine's strengths are her strategy and physical combat skills. Her strategy got us this far, and her physical combat skills will ensure I make it out alive. Then Marco and I can use our skills to get out of the Dome and release the information. It's a completely solid plan. And I understand wholeheartedly why she's willing to sacrifice herself to give me an escape route.

But I'm not going to let another person sacrifice themselves for my well-being. Marco, Janna, Nemesis—all of them have in some way put my well-being above their own. I'm sick of being the person who has to be protected. I'm sick of being the person whose purpose is to be safeguarded.

I'm going to fight for my own destiny. Right here. Right now.

Catherine glances over at me, and her eyes lock with mine for a fraction of a second. I see frustration there, but I also see admiration shining through.

"You're not going to leave, are you?" she says. It's not really a question. Sighing, she stands up straighter, rolling her shoulders and taking a boxer's stance. "Stand behind me," she orders. "When you see an opening, you do whatever you can. I'll keep him busy enough. You just need to find the right opening."

"Got it."

She nods, moving fully in front of me. Officer Lewis also stands, refocused on his mission.

"Look at what we have here," he sneers. The cop opens his mouth, spewing out some of the most hateful, derogatory words toward Black and brown people as easily as someone asking for water.

I tense up, the words like hot knives stabbing into my most sensitive and exposed areas. But Catherine doesn't flinch or seem to care.

"Catherine and Jamal," she corrects him. "Remember those names when we beat your ass."

Without hesitation, she lunges forward. Catherine has the advantage. Not because she's stronger, but because she isn't weighed down by metal like Officer Lewis.

Her body moves with surprising flexibility and ease. Barely

avoiding Lewis's swipe, Catherine jumps up and kicks off the wall, striking him in the head again. When she lands, she's behind him, and she uses her advantage to swipe his legs out from under him. With a quick twist of his heavy body, Lewis falls faceup instead of facedown. Before he even hits the ground, Catherine grabs the end table next to her and slams it in his face. The helmet protects him, but he still lets out a frustrated growl. He punches upward, almost blindly, but she easily dodges the blow.

I stand and watch in awe as Catherine delivers blow after blow against Lewis. Anytime it looks like he might be able to get his footing, Catherine quickly takes it away from him and delivers more punches. It's not about delivering one giant hit to incapacitate him. It's about slowly chipping away at his armor—literally. About thirty seconds into the fight, Catherine has a few scratches and a bruise on her right leg, but Lewis's visor is completely ripped open, exposing his left eye. Each blow Catherine delivers causes the SWAT armor to ripple with the same translucent light as before. The color is different from the Dome, but it functions the same way, reducing the impact of her blows.

That just makes Catherine hit harder and harder.

She jumps back, taking a second to breathe. Lewis stands growling, panting, snarling like a wild animal.

"What's the matter?" Catherine asks. "Oh, I know, you thought that armor of yours would, what, give you an instant win? That's the problem with people like you. You think every advantage means you get to sit back and coast. I think we call that *privilege*. I'm here fighting for something—for someone—and I don't have the luxury of taking it easy. I'm going to fight to my death. Or yours. Whichever comes first."

Catherine's movements are more than just methodical; they're well practiced and precise. I wonder if this is what the army has taught her—how to not only exact revenge but engage in cold-blooded murder. Every single time Officer Lewis swings once, she delivers two blows. It doesn't matter that he has armor. Catherine has better training. And in many ways, I think its kind of like David and Goliath. Catherine is smart enough to know how to fight him, how to adapt. It becomes clear that the suit has similar properties to the Dome. Her punches and kicks make contact, but each time she strikes, a ripple of light comes from where she hit, and the officer stumbles back less than he should. Like he has a barrier around him.

But that doesn't stop her. Catherine tumbles out of the way, losing her footing. Lewis pays no attention to me, a lion with a single goal. Catherine scrambles to her feet just in time. Lewis uses his heel of his boot, which puts another hole in the weak wooden floor.

Like a gazelle, Catherine dances around the room, as if she's barely touching the ground. She moves around chairs and tables, sliding over the desk, using bookshelves as barriers. Officer Lewis is at a disadvantage. The suit weighs him down, and Catherine's spatial awareness is exceptional.

I could maybe help her fight. But I'm better off focusing on finding a way to give her more of an advantage.

"Think, think," I whisper, running to the kitchen. What can

I use to help? There are knives, ladles, plates, wooden spoons. All of those would be good against Lewis's flesh, but not against his exoskeleton.

And then I notice it. It's like everything comes together as pieces of the puzzle align and click into place.

The pool outside.

"Perfect."

It's risky—no, it's more than risky, it's *stupid*—but I have to do something.

Just in time, too. Catherine slips, losing her footing, but Officer Lewis doesn't let her hit the ground. He grabs her wrist and slams her into the table with his free hand raised. The gears sound heavy—some sort of mechanized punch charging, ready to punch Catherine through the table.

She's not strong enough to get out of his grip, no matter how much she struggles.

A wave of panic flows over me, but I know what I have to do. I have to be quick. I have to be relentless. I have to be filled with resolve. I can't hesitate. I can't chicken out. It's not only Catherine's life on the line, it's mine too.

"Hey, idiot!" I blurt out the most offensive thing I can think of. Grabbing a book from the bookshelf, I dig my heel into the ground like I was taught during baseball and hurl the book at Lewis. I'm not sure if it's luck or God or something in between, but the corner of the book strikes the exact point where his visor has been busted open, hitting the corner of his eye. He lets out a scream.

It's enough of an impact that Catherine is able to wiggle out of his grip and roll out of his line of sight. I hightail it out of there, running down the porch steps, knowing that in a few seconds, he'll follow me. But a few seconds are all I need. I jump the last few steps, almost stumbling, and quickly dart to the left, hiding under the steps. Officer Lewis is too blinded by the impact to see exactly where I've gone; he just knows I headed in this general direction, and his anger gives me the advantage I need.

"You little fucking…" he snarls out. I feel almost bad for him for a fraction of a second. He probably joined the police force thinking it would compensate for whatever he's lacking. Thinking he would become a man if he ascended through the ranks. But from what I'm guessing, he quickly learned that he's nothing more than a pawn. Some people aren't made for greatness; some people are just made to be followers, and Officer Lewis is the lowest of them all.

That moment of pity doesn't last long.

I hold as still as I possibly can, the throbbing in my head and chest making it hard to hold even the smallest of breaths. I just need to wait until Officer Lewis is past the steps. Just a little bit farther. A few feet. Three feet. Two feet. One foot. Six inches.

Now.

I use every ounce of strength I have, dig the balls of my feet into the dirt, and push off like a rocket. Letting out a guttural scream of anguish and frustration, I use my shoulder much like Catherine did and shove Officer Lewis and his armored body toward the pool. Since I have the element of surprise, it's enough of a force to make him stumble and fall the three steps. He trips over his clunky legs and falls into the pool headfirst, completely submerging.

177

I ignore the sharp pain in my shoulder. I don't think it's dislocated, but it hurts like hell.

But not as much as this is going to hurt Officer Lewis.

It's a gamble, sure, but whatever is giving Office Lewis's armor that veil of protection must use a lot of power. Electricity and water don't mix well. I just have to hope I paid attention enough in science class to put this concept to use. At the very least, it will give us a head start if we need to run.

I hold my breath as the officer disappears under the surface. The half a second before the blast of white light feels like an hour. It's almost as bright as the Dome when it first appeared, burning my eyes. Officer Lewis screams as electricity jumps across the surface of the water. His body flails quickly, then slowly, then not at all, and the light disappears as rapidly as it came.

I stand there in awe as I watch Officer Lewis's body float to the top. I should feel something, I think. I just electrocuted a man. There's a good chance he's dead. And not only is he dead, but he's a cop.

"What have I done?" I whisper, every ounce of feeling returning to me at once as the scene plays over and over again in my head. Panic begins to replace my adrenaline. The throbbing in my chest feels the same, but the sensations are fraternal twins, not identical twins.

I hear Catherine's footsteps behind me and glance over my shoulder. She's grabbing one arm with the other hand, and scuffs, bruises, and blood cover her, but she looks okay. She doesn't seem surprised to see Officer Lewis in the water, but maybe she doesn't know what just happened.

"I killed him," I say. The words come out more easily than I thought they would. "I—"

"No, you didn't," she says curtly, and walks—limps—forward.

Catherine looks around for a moment and finds whatever she's looking for about three feet from us. Walking over, she picks up what looks like a spoke for a volleyball net. She looks at me and juts her head in a silent gesture to stand back. I follow her orders, and she punctures the side of the pool.

All the water flows out, sparkling and crackling against the ground. It's less than an inch deep, and the light show only lasts a fraction of a moment. Stepping into the pool, Catherine uses her boot to roll Officer Lewis over. A fraction of a moment passes before she says, bluntly, words I never thought I'd be happy to hear: "He's still alive."

A wave of relief washes over me. It's good to know I'm not a murderer as well as a criminal, but still, I'm sure whoever saw that light or is in contact with Lewis is going to find us. I've seen many sci-fi TV shows; that suit probably sent some sort of message to his precinct the moment it went offline.

Shit.

"What do we do?" I ask.

Catherine taps his helmet with her knuckles. He lets out a wheezing, exhausted breath.

"Help me get him up," she says, using her good arm to hoist his heavy body over her shoulder. "Looks like we got ourselves a hostage."

TWENTY-ONE

Catherine and I load Officer Lewis's body into the back of her jeep and drive away as quickly as possible. We don't stop, doing our best to avoid traffic lights and trying not to be noticed, even as we speed through the streets. I don't even have to suggest that to Catherine— she just does it on her own. I think the incident at Janna's affected her as much as me.

"Your arm," I say, looking at it. It's limp, and she's hasn't touched it since we loaded up Office Lewis.

"Dislocated," she says. "I'll be fine." A moment passes. "You were good back there No. Great."

"Thanks."

"Seriously, you would make a badass solider."

Something about that makes my stomach turn. I've written anti-war articles. Gone to marches. Gotten into arguments in TikTok comment sections over war. I don't want to be this. But being Black in America means always being at war, in some way or another.

I look over my shoulder, checking on Officer Lewis in the back seat. His breathing is shallow and his mouth is slightly open. How long he'll stay out and what will happen when he wakes up are questions we will worry about when we get there.

"Are we taking him to your house?" I ask.

Catherine nods.

"Do you think that's wise? I mean, he'll know where we are when he wakes up. Don't you think he'll reach out for help or something?"

We have no idea what other tricks the suit has up its sleeve. But I don't think it's unreasonable to assume long-distance communication is one of its skills. I replay the fight in my head and gently touch at the skin around my neck. The wounds are still fresh, and the skin is still inflamed; it's at the point where the bruises are hypersensitive. I bite back a wince.

Lewis was a lot stronger than us, that's for sure. He was even faster. Had he not been in the close confines of the house, and had he been fighting someone less skilled than Catherine, he might have bested both of us. But I doubt the suit is just a combat suit; it has to have other capabilities too. And the idea of him waking up and sending out an SOS signal without us even knowing…that worries me.

"I've thought about that," she says, turning down her street.

"And?"

A moment of silence. "I'm still thinking."

I don't find it comforting that Catherine doesn't have a plan. Ever since this is all started, she's been one step ahead of Marco and me—hell, a step ahead of everyone else too. It's like she has planned everything out twenty-five steps ahead and we're just pawns in her game. But this situation seems to surprise her. She clearly didn't expect to have a hostage. She's smart enough to know that wounding a police officer, let alone holding him captive, is a crime that could send us to jail for many, many years. But I don't know if I care. I don't know if *she* cares. We're so far deep into this now, that's a problem we'll worry about later.

Right now, we're alive.

We arrive at the house and slide into the garage. I walk around and latch the car door quickly, opening the rear of the jeep and staring at Officer Lewis. My pulse races as I imagine him lunging forward, using surprise to get the advantage, and wrapping both of his hands around my neck. With one easy crack, he could break my spine in half, and I can practically hear the sickening *pop* echo through the garage. Everything would turn black.

Just like that, in a flash, our mission and my life would be over.

A warm hand on my shoulder snaps me out of my thoughts. I turn, expecting to see Catherine, but instead come face-to-face with Marco. He glances at my eyes, at my neck, and then looks down at Officer Lewis. He doesn't say anything at first, just slowly raises his right hand and traces the lines of fingerprints on my skin. I wince. He pulls back and frowns.

"I'm sorry," he whispers. "You okay?"

I don't know how to answer that, because I'm not. But in the literal sense of the word, I guess I am? So I settle on, "I'm fine." A beat passes. "Better off than him."

It's a weak joke, but Marco smiles faintly, which makes me feel lighter. He's not as mad at me anymore, I can tell. That's good.

"Hey," Catherine says. "Either of you know how to pop a shoulder back into place?"

"I got you."

Marco's hand leaves my neck, but it lingers and drags from my throat down to my shoulder, as if he's trying to maintain physical contact with me for as long as possible. But I'm probably just reading too much into it. Marco walks over to Catherine, gently sits her down on a pile of boxes, and stands behind her, one hand on her loose arm and the other right below her neck.

"You ready?"

Catherine grunts.

"One...two..."

A loud pop, a single cry of pain, and a grunt fill the air as Catherine's whole body shakes. She takes a shuddering breath, sighs, stands up, and rolls her shoulder. "I hated that."

"But you're alive, aren't you?" he cheekily replies, nodding to Officer Lewis. "Either of you want to tell me what happened?"

Catherine walks over to Lewis. "We fought, he almost killed us, and then your boy here almost killed him—"

"Wait, wait." Marco holds his hands up. "Rewind about ten seconds. You did what?"

"I didn't almost kill him," I clarify. I mean technically, I almost did, but I don't like the way that sounds—like I actually *tried* to kill him.

"Oh, you fully did," Catherine muses. "Went full G.I. Joe on his ass and everything. Our little journalist has turned into a warrior."

Marco's eyes go wide, but it's not in fear—he's surprised, in a good way. A slow grin spreads over his face as he crosses his arms. "Good on you."

"I wouldn't say that."

"I would," Catherine says. "Like I told you in the car, it was either him or us. You made the right choice. Don't dwell on it. You two, help me get him inside."

Marco and I follow Catherine's request and both help carry Officer Lewis. Marco grabs under his arms, I grab one of his legs, and Catherine grabs the other leg, not putting too much weight on her arm. We carry him inside and, at Catherine's command, take him down the hallway and into the large but mostly empty pantry.

"I'll be right back," she mutters, returning moments later with a chair from the kitchen and rope.

Lots and lots of rope.

"Do you think this'll hold him?" I ask as we set him down. "I mean, we saw what the suit can do."

"Absolutely not," Catherine says bluntly, wrapping him six times around at the waist, arms, and legs. "It'll stall him, maybe, but when he wakes up—and he will—we're going to have to deal with him."

"And what's your plan?"

Catherine stands, admiring her work, and says for the first time, "I don't know."

There's nothing good about Catherine saying, *I don't know*. It's the truth, and I appreciate that, but it feels like our leader is lost, and that means that we, her subordinates, are also lost. I flex my fingers once again, like pumping an engine, and let the blood run through my body. The adrenaline is starting to wear off, and a dizzy nip of exhaustion is taking over. I've used a lot of energy in the past few hours, and I haven't eaten a lot. The past few days have been hard, and it's catching up with me. I'm not thinking clearly.

But suddenly, Marco interjects. "I might have an idea."

Catherine and I give him space. Marco takes a step forward and squats in front of Officer Lewis, balancing on the balls of his feet, tilting his head to the side and examining him.

"This suit is sophisticated," he mutters, running his hands slowly over the metal. "Time and care went into making it. There are probably millions of dollars of technology in this. But it's not just armor; it's its own technological achievement. It has abilities like a computer does. That means it has to have a motherboard or something somewhere. That means it can be hacked."

"And you can do it?" I ask.

Marco chuckles, glancing over his shoulder at me. "I *think* I can do it. Give me a few hours, and we'll see."

"I don't think he'll be asleep for that long," Catherine notes.

"Then I'd better get started," Marco says.

Catherine nods. "I'm guessing you want privacy?"

"If you don't mind."

"Hey, plausible deniability. I'm into it."

"Considering all the crimes we've already committed," I mutter.

Marco and Catherine laugh—actually laugh. Catherine claps her hand on my back, using her injured arm and grimacing through the pain.

"That's the spirit!"

There's a moment of calm between us before anyone does anything. It's like no one knows how to move forward or what exactly to do next. We have an officer in our house, we're all fugitives, and the world is going to hell. I'm not sure making the right choice really matters anymore, because who knows what the right choice really is?

Marco cracks his knuckles and rolls his neck. "I'll let you know when I'm done."

"Wait." I quickly grab my camera and move past Marco, into the makeshift prison. The irony hasn't escaped me; Officer Lewis had Marco and me in a prison not that long ago, and now the tables have turned. I squat down to his eye level and snap a few pictures, making sure my flash is attached so the light bounces off his armor, illuminating everything in an eerie, almost holy glow.

"For evidence," I say, waving my camera. Marco and Catherine both nod in approval. Before I can turn to leave, Marco grabs my wrist and squeezes it gently.

"Thank you," he says. I don't have time to say anything else before he closes the door behind him.

Catherine and I spend the rest of the morning together. Neither of us really knows how to talk to the other when there isn't danger or some sort of mission guiding us. We hold light conversations, just enough to keep the air from going stale. Catherine takes a shower and spends a considerable amount of time in the bathroom tending to her wounds. It feels like everyone has their place.

But me? I'm fiddling with my camera, wondering how I'm going to get these photos developed.

A loud scream from the pantry snaps me out of my thoughts. I'm in the kitchen, but on the far side, closer to the garage, when I hear the noise.

Catherine pokes her head out of the bedroom. We look at each other, exchanging a *should we do anything?* look before she shakes her head.

"If he wants us, he'll ask," she says, slipping back into her room and closing the door.

I hear muffled screams coming from the pantry. Whatever Marco is doing seems to be working. I bite my lip, tasting blood, and do my best to forget about what's going on behind those closed doors. It doesn't concern me. It's not about me. And honestly…this is an eye for an eye.

It feels like days pass before Marco emerges from the room, but it's only been a few hours. I take a glimpse at the pantry-slash-prison before he closes the door. The officer is out of his suit, dressed in a black T-shirt and a pair of boxers. I want to know how Marco got him out of it, but he doesn't seem to be in the mood for questions. He looks exhausted, not physically but emotionally. Catherine comes out of her room at the same time, as if some light has gone off in her room telling her there's a team meeting about to happen.

Marco makes a beeline for the kitchen and pours himself a glass of water. One glass turns into two, and two turns into four, before he leans against the counter and finally starts speaking. "Do you want the good news or the bad news first?"

"Bad," we both say without hesitation.

"The bad news is that he didn't give me any information we can use. Whatever training they gave those guys is good."

"And the good news?"

He nods toward the room, arms crossed over his chest. "I got the suit off of him, and I think—I *think*—I know what makes it work. It's a pretty ingenious form of technology, actually. I didn't know the government had that level of tech. Using biometric rhythms and other technological code that allows the user to basically assimilate themselves—"

Catherine's holds up her hand. "English, please, and for the love of god, get to the point. I don't need to know all of this."

Marco narrows his eyes, but he clearly understands. "I think I can reprogram the suit to work for us."

The room falls silent for a moment. Catherine's face shows more emotion now than I thought it ever would, her eyes wide with shock.

"Are you serious?" she asks.

He nods. "I think. I mean, there's a chance it won't work. There's a chance it'll self-destruct or send out some distress signal or one of a dozen other things."

"But if you can," I say, "we'll have an advantage. Can you imagine what that would mean? A suit being under our control?"

"And they'd have no idea anything was happening. It could be the advantage we need," Catherine says.

"Exactly," Marco says. "The question is…"

"Does the risk outweigh the reward?" Catherine finishes.

"There's no real way to answer that question, though, is there?" I ask. "If we don't give it a shot, we're playing defense, like we have been. If we do…at least we're trying to go on the offensive. At least we're trying to, you know, even the playing field. We'll never gain ground any other way."

Marco nods in agreement. "We can't do this by majority rule.

This choice affects all of us. I have no idea what safeguard systems are in place with this suit. It could backfire horribly. So if we're going to do it, we decide together. All of us. I vote yes."

"Me too," I say, looking at Catherine. Her eyes are focused on the ground, slightly narrowed. I have no idea what's going on behind those gray orbs, but I know she's processing a lot of information.

"Do it," she finally says.

Marco nods. "Give me three hours."

TWENTY-TWO

More than three hours later—closer to six—Marco emerges from his spot in the back of the house. His shirt is off, tied around his wait, a layer of sweat and oil and a few new scrapes on his body, but he's grinning.

"I did it," he announces. "Was a bitch to get through the security, but I've hacked the suit. They're impressive. Not only have they found a way to take what makes the Dome, well, the Dome and use that technology in a the suit, but they've also created this visor that processes information, photos, and data faster than anything I've seen, and predicts patterns. The officers can also communicate with each other, see through each other's visors, and communicate with the technology. It's like a hive mind."

Catherine and I have been keeping ourselves busy in the living room. She showed me a few self-defense techniques, and in exchange, I made her some soup—from a can. Marco makes a beeline for his bowl, now lukewarm, practically slurping it up.

Catherine goes into the room first, and I follow close behind her. Officer Lewis is gagged with a rag and dressed only in his boxers and socks, zip ties around his wrists and ankles, a ripped shirt over his eyes and headphones covering his ears. Catherine's eyes dart from the suit to the officer.

"Good job. Do you know how to work it?"

"If you're asking me if it'll work on your body, I don't know. But I do know it's no longer active, which is good for us."

"We should test it," I suggest. "Make sure we know how to use it."

"Agreed," Catherine says. "But first…we need to get rid of him."

Being the strongest of the three of us, Catherine hoists Officer Lewis up with the help of Marco and loads him into the back of the truck. Once done, she walks over to the toolbox and pulls out a new license plate, which she swaps for the car's current plate. Now it looks like the jeep is from Kansas.

"I'm going to dump him somewhere. No, I'm not going to kill him, and no, don't ask any more questions. Don't make trouble, don't leave unless you have to, and for the love of god, please don't get into a fight, you two."

That last request is directed at Marco. When she glares at him, he gives a lopsided smirk and a shrug. I know it will be my responsibility to make sure he doesn't get us in trouble, a responsibility I'm uncertain I'll be able to handle, but I'll do my best. I'm not sure how Marco feels about me anymore.

Catherine nods. "I'll be back in a few. If I'm not back in two hours, you need to leave. Understand?"

"Understood," we both say.

"Come back safe," I add.

"I intend to." Catherine winks, getting in the truck. She gives a two-finger salute and then leaves Marco and me alone.

"I need a shower," Marco mutters, walking inside and letting out a loud sigh.

We spend most of the time doing nothing. I clean the house, because my mother taught me that cleaning is one of the best things to do when you're stressed out.

It isn't long, though, before Marco nudges me with his shoulder, rocketing me out of my mental dreamland with a suggestion.

"We should go out," he says casually.

I frown at him. *Going out* makes it sound like we are going to hit the town and go to a bar or something. Has he forgotten that we are under, for lack of a better term, martial law? Has he forgotten everything we just went through? His wounds are still pretty bad, the purple and yellow patches still slightly swollen. I wonder if they are still tender. I wonder if they still hurt. My right hand twitches for a moment as I think about reaching up and touching them, but I keep it by my side.

"I don't think that's a good idea," I settle on. "Catherine told—"

"Blah, blah, blah." Marco waves his hand. He reaches for one of the glasses on the drying rack, uses his shirt to quickly dry the inside, and gets himself a glass of water while leaning against the counter. His shirt rides up slightly, revealing his tight stomach and a few familiar bruises. Possibly from cops punching and kicking him while we were in custody.

"I'm not saying we should, like, go and party." He points to my camera on the counter. "Maybe we can even do something that's helpful to this 'mission.' Or just wander around. We don't need to wait for Catherine to give us instructions. We're our own people. And that way, if she barks at us for leaving, we can say we did it for a good reason."

I know what he's thinking: that we should go and take pictures downtown for evidence. It's part of the plan: to get as much photo evidence as possible so that when I leave the Dome—which Marco seems confident he'll be able to help me do—we'll have enough proof to take to the police. And let's hope they believe us and don't side with their brothers and sisters in blue.

Catherine was very clear—staying put was one of the three things she asked us to do. Following her directive isn't that hard. It's the least thing we can do. But still, I check my watch. It's going to be dark in six or seven hours. There's no reason why we can't go out; according to Chief Coles, we're just supposed to stay out of trouble. As long as we keep our heads down—as long as we don't cause a ruckus—we should be fine taking pictures discreetly.

"So…" Marco nudges me. "What do you say?"

At first, I don't have an answer. Well, I *do* have an answer, but it's not what he wants to hear. Because my instinct, every fiber in my flesh and bones and blood vessels and muscles, is telling me to push back against his brazen attitude.

But I would be lying if I said his smile and the way it spreads fully over his face, almost childlike, doesn't make me want to make Marco happy. I want to do everything in my power to keep that smile on his face, and a part of me feels like I owe him that. Like what I did to Janna means I'm indebted to him, and this is a small way to pay it back.

I mentally run through every possible iteration of what could happen as I chew gently on my nail. It isn't until my teeth brush the quick that I wince and speak.

"You have to promise me you're not going to cause any drama," I demand.

"I promise."

"And that we're only going to take photos."

"Yep." He nods.

"And if anything bad happens—"

"We'll steer clear of it," he says without me having to finish.

"Yes, but also, if Catherine yells at us, you'll take the blame."

He's already hopping around while slipping his worn sneakers onto his feet. Marco taps the heel of his right foot against the ground, getting his shoe situated. "Again, I promise. So, you ready?"

I'm fully dressed, feeling comfortable in my clothes and knowing that if we need to leave at a moment's notice, I will be able to do just that. I refuse to be deadweight; I think I've proven to myself and to Catherine that I'm a valuable member of this team, more than just a photographer.

I finish washing the last dish and put it away, writing a quick note for Catherine and putting it on the table before grabbing my camera, feeling the cool familiar metal against my fingers. The curves of the camera are well known to me, and just holding it with both hands, the worn strap against my neck, makes me feel safer and more like myself than I have in the past few days. More importantly, it makes me feel like I'm closer to my mom, which makes me feel like everything will be all right.

"Let's go."

We're in Hampton, too far from the Baltimore city center to head there by foot, but Marco suggests we head to Reservoir Hill or Remington, only about a mile and a half from where we are.

"Reservoir Hill," I suggest. "If we go to Remington, there's going to be more police, which could mean more violence." And that's the last thing I want right now.

"Sure," he says, nodding in agreement. "I'm sure we'll get some good action there too."

I grimace at the way he says *action*. He makes it sound like we're about to see two dogs fighting or a dance battle, when in fact we're going to see police officers brutally abusing people of color, poor people, and homeless people in the name of whatever civil protections they hide behind to make their actions feel noble. It makes my stomach sick to know this is happening, to know there's no one on the outside who has knowledge of what's going on. I look up at the sky, still seeing the faint white shimmer of the Dome. I want to grab a rock and use all my strength to hurl it against the barrier to see how strong it really is. I wonder if there's any chance, with any luck…I could just…break through it.

"It's like a rainbow," I mutter.

"Sorry?" Marco asks as we walk down the hill and cross 83 on the overpass, heading toward Reservoir Hill.

"The Dome," I clarify. "Where does it end? It's like a rainbow. Where's the pot of gold?"

"You never know, because you never see the starting point or end point of a rainbow." He nods. "I get you."

We walk in silence as we cross the overpass, and I notice there are very few cars on the road, far fewer than there should be on a busy highway in the middle of the week. Martial law is probably forcing people to keep off the roads. Catherine wouldn't let us listen to the radio or turn on the TV, saying there was nothing we could learn that would make us feel any better. She's probably right; it would likely just scare us and make us more worried about our future. For now, it's better to have tunnel vision focused on what we're trying to accomplish. Everything else is just a distraction.

"From what I know about the Dome," Marco says a moment later, "I think it's only surrounding Baltimore proper. Baltimore as a whole is what, one hundred square miles?"

"Ninety, I think."

He nods. "And some of that is water."

About 12 percent of it is water. Maryland history is something every Marylander is forced to take, and at my school, we had to write papers about Baltimore. I wrote about how land was taken from Black people years ago and never returned to them, with a focus on the role segregation played in weakening Black communities in Baltimore. Land area and distribution was part of that story, so these facts are burned into my brain.

"I don't think the Dome is that big. That's huge," he says. "I'm going to say it's probably closer to thirty square miles, maybe?"

"So you don't think it covers the whole city?"

He shakes his head. "Just the areas they need to contain. I don't think all of Baltimore's residents would be happy if they were unable to leave their city."

By *all of the residents*, he specifically means white people. Baltimore has a very big difference in the amount of money white people make compared to Black people. Most people know Baltimore from the TV show *The Wire* and because of the racial struggles it's had, the poverty, and the fact that there are more homes than there are people to fill them. They also know about the affluent white families who have been here for ages and about Hopkins and the Inner Harbor and the Ravens.

But they don't really know about the vibrant community here—or at least they refuse to talk about it. They refuse to mention the art scene, the local crab cake institutions, the dance troupes and musicians who have been born and cultivated in this city, or the intelligent Black community that has thrived since before the Harlem Renaissance. There are a lot of good things about Baltimore that don't make the news. There's a lot of rich history here that negates the bad things the news always wants to talk about. So often, cities like Baltimore and Detroit and Atlanta and Englewood and Chicago—predominantly Black communities—are regarded as places that can be forgotten and thrown away.

But when you inconvenience white people, all that goes out the window.

"We'll figure it out," Marco says, his hands behind his head as we walk. "How to shut the Dome down, I mean."

"You can't promise that."

I don't know if any of us has really thought about it, but there's a chance we could fail. The Dome could be too complicated, the code itself could be too complex, or we could all be captured, and this plan will go to hell. I think it's actually more likely that we'll fail than succeed. And there's no guarantee of when the Dome will come down. I'm sure it will someday—all human rights violations like this come to a head eventually—but how often have we seen our country let bad things slide just because they want to? Latinos in cages. Hate crimes across the United States. Black people lynched and killed in the streets.

These are all things that should be over and done with in America…but they just keep happening, and we just keep letting them. Who's to say the Dome will be any different?

Not to be a pessimist, because this makes me sound like I don't care about the work we're doing or like I think it's all in vain. It's actually the complete opposite. I look over at Marco and really study him, trying to pick up on his body language to see if he agrees with me. He's also a person of color, so he has to understand that the cards are stacked against us as Black and brown folks. It's more likely we'll be forgotten than receive justice. That's a shitty thing to come to realize. Even if I do like to think I have hope, that we will, as a society, grow and evolve, it's hard to keep that hope alive when you're living the bad years in real time.

Marco seems to pick up on what I'm feeling.

"I hope it'll get better too, even if I'm not that optimistic. There's a part of me that has to keep hoping, you know? Keep doing what I can, being part of the narrative that's making change," he says honestly as we cross the street. "Will anything good come from it? Who knows. Maybe I'll be a forgotten footnote in history, and things will actually get worse. But I can promise you I'm going to fight like hell.

I'm going to do everything I can to shut that thing down." He nods to the Dome.

There's conviction in his voice that feels like fire. I don't know if there's some specific reason why Marco is so focused on getting the Dome shut down. Maybe it's just cockiness or the need to prove himself to Nemesis, or maybe it's because of Janna and what happened to her, which is also my fault. But whatever it is, I know it's personal. I don't say anything as I keep walking, giving him the space to open up if he wants to—and sure enough, he does.

"I'm not actually part of Nemesis," he says quietly, like he's saying something forbidden. "I mean, I want to be, and I think I'm good enough, but I'm not an actual hacker for them. I've always wanted to work for them. I think they're making real change, you know?"

"Mm-hmm."

We reach one of the main streets and see the first people we've met since we started our walk. Sure enough, there's a police officer with the same activated armor as Officer Lewis, questioning a young woman with a kid. I think it's her younger brother, because the girl doesn't look old enough to have a child. The police officer is crowding her, definitely well into her personal space, close enough that it makes me tense up.

"What are you doing here?" he asks.

"Shopping," she says.

"Shopping? For what?"

"Food."

Good, I think. Keep answers short and sweet. That's how you stay alive.

"Isn't that kid—what is he, your brother—a little chunky?"

I watch her ball her fists by her sides. "He has a thyroid problem."

"Should get that checked out, then, huh?"

"Come on," Marco mutters.

"We should do something."

"Do what? How would interfering help her or us?"

"Because it's the right thing to do?"

Marco shakes his head. "Remember, long game. We can't help anyone if we're captured or dead. The right thing isn't always the *right* thing. We get involved and we get put in jail, or worse, and then this whole mission you, me, and Catherine are doing goes up in smoke. This is the long game, Jamal. You have to remember that."

I don't want to admit he's right. It makes me sick to think we're just going to go along with it and turn the other cheek. What makes us different than anyone else if we do that?

But, in this moment, what can the two of us really do? I've seen firsthand what the police can do with their new armor. And with the Dome, there's no one to hold them accountable. To stop them from living out whatever twisted fantasies of power and control they have.

I bite back my frustration and walk briskly with Marco to put some distance between us.

"So, Nemesis," I mutter, trying to right our conversation and forget about how I just left that girl to fend for herself. "You were saying?"

"Yeah, them. I just...have always looked up to them," Marco continues. "There aren't many places a brown hacker without an education can fit in. Nemesis seemed like the right group."

Once we're far enough away from the girl and the cop, I take a picture of them. It's a quick turn on my heel, a *snap*, and then I turn back before anyone can second-guess what I'm doing.

"And…"

"And?"

"I have a record," Marco says. "Which is kinda hilarious when you think about it, because Nemesis wants its people to either be perfect or only have a record for hacking. Protesting and being arrested doesn't fit their narrative. They can't have criminals like me in their ranks. It will undermine trust."

"Is that your assumption or what they said?"

"They said it to my face," he says without hesitation. "Or, well, as much to my face as they ever do. Nemesis is a fan of talking through objects. Very Big Brother."

I nod curtly. He seems like—no, he *is* the type of brash, headstrong person who would jump to someone's defense or into some social justice issue without thinking about its ramifications. It fits everything I know about him, and honestly, it makes me see him in a different light. Activism and standing up for the underdog defines who Marco is.

"You're smart."

He gives a fake bow. "Why, thank you."

"You must have known that going to a protest and getting arrested would close the book on you getting into Nemesis."

"Of course," he says without hesitation. "But that doesn't mean it wasn't the right thing to do. I don't regret it, Jamal, just so you know. People in North Carolina were terrorizing Asian business owners after—"

"Yeah, I remember." I saw it on the news. There was a lot happening then.

"And it wasn't being covered. No one cared, except for a small set of people."

"Sounds like if Nemesis doesn't see that as a strength of yours, then they don't deserve you," I say. "I get it. I'm not going to blame you for lying. We all have our secrets, and it's hard for people like us to get any sort of advantage. You did what you had to do. I think my only question is—"

"Why did I lie about it?" he finishes for me and shrugs. "Would you have helped me if I hadn't? Would you have followed me if I hadn't seemed like I had my shit together?"

I don't want to answer that, but I know what the truth is: no. I would have chalked him up as a wild guy who had no idea what he was doing. Maybe I have my own preconceptions about people that I need to work through. But he doesn't need to know that.

As we head toward the downtown area of Reservoir Hill, there are empty stands that, on a typical day, would be filled with farmers selling their fruits and vegetables. Most farmers markets in Maryland are open one day during the week and one day on the weekend. But the stalls are empty. Still. Quiet.

"I don't blame you for lying," I say after a moment. "I mean, we all have different reasons for keeping secrets."

"I know," he says. "But it still feels shitty."

"Probably not as shitty as I feel for giving up Nemesis. They were doing real good. I heard what Karma said. I mean, they'll probably figure out how to shut down the Dome, and I gave Chief Coles all the information he needs to take them down. I acted against my own interests to preserve myself."

Marco shakes his head. "Yeah, no, that's not it at all. I know why you did it. I mean, I understand what happened. You had an impossible choice. You were trying to protect Janna and me, trying to live to fight another day. You had your back against the wall. I'm not sure I would have done anything different. I'm not...I'm just not the best person to rely on when good people suffer bad things."

I smirk. "Sounds like you're not a fan of the way our world works."

He chuckles dryly and nods. "I'd agree."

"But more importantly, you consider me a good person. I'm flattered," I tease.

Marco doesn't miss a beat. I expect a snide comeback but get something far more real.

"You have no idea how good you truly are, Jamal."

Marco and I continue to walk through Reservoir Hill, snapping pictures and pointing out atrocities. We see a pair of police officers completely bash a person's car, another police officer destroying a homeless man's tent, and a third harassing kids. Each of the experiences leaves bile in my mouth that I have to swallow down, burning like fire as I snap my pictures and move along. There's nothing we can do about it right now. These photos are a protest. It will all be worth it in the long run. I hope.

I take a final photo, as discreetly as possible, of two cops in their gear forcing two teens into the back of their armored car before Marco gently taps my shoulder.

"We should get going," he mutters, inclining his head. Two people are staring at us. They aren't cops, but they have the look of people who want a quick buck and will do anything to get it—and what better way than to rat us out?

"Plus," Marco yawns, "I'm getting a little tired. Might need to lie down and take a nap."

I snap one more picture for good measure and nod. We don't double back the way we came; that would be too obvious. Instead, we take the long way home.

"I asked if you wanted to lie down with me," he says directly.

"Oh."

Oh.

We walk back mostly in silence, both of us filled with images of the things we just saw. I don't mind the silence, because even though Marco is fun to talk to, he's a *lot*, and all I want to do right now is absorb everything I saw and heard and try to fully understand this new world order that exists under the Dome. And if I'm being honest, just having Marco's body close to me is enough to make me feel warm and safe. I don't want to ruin that by talking. I want to stay in this moment as long as I can.

But the idea of lying in bed with him? The two of us, our bodies touching, vulnerable, but also protective of one another? Ready to spring into action if the world outside comes knocking, ready to be each other's saviors if ours dreams threaten to rip us apart?

Right now? There's little else in the world that I want more.

TWENTY-THREE

"If you want to join me for a nap, I'll be in the room."

Marco doesn't force an answer out of me, and he doesn't pull his hand back either. Instead he just gives me a soft squeeze, and I return the gesture.

Sleeping with someone—and I don't just mean having sex with them—is a pretty intimate affair.

There's a lot you learn about another person when sleeping in a bed with them. Do they spread out? Which side do they prefer? Do they instantly go to sleep, or do they like to linger and talk? Each of these things affects how you sleep with them, and finding somebody you work with in bed is hard. It's not like I've slept with anyone before besides a friend or two at a sleepover, but I'd like to think it's as important as understanding what position each person is in the bedroom.

Marco isn't shy about his desire to sleep in bed with me. Almost as soon as we get inside, he kicks his boots into the center of the room. His long body reaches for the skies, and his bones crack while he stretches. He walks up the steps, nodding for me to come along with him. I'm a little behind, and I take a few moments to steel myself. I don't know why my heart is racing so much. It's not like we're having sex. We're just two boys sharing a bed.

Two boys with obvious feelings with each other.

Two boys who have been to hell and back.

Oh god.

By the time I reach the top of the stairs and push open the door, bringing with me two glasses of water—Mom always taught me that if you're going to enter someone's space, you should always bring some sort of offering—Marco is already down to his black boxer briefs and jumping into the bed. This isn't the first time I've seen him shirtless, but it is the first time I've seen him with no pants on. There are scars on his lower body, just like on his upper body. Many of them I can chalk up to being a normal teenager, but I know some of them probably came from protests and the illegal activities he's committed. The bigger, thicker welts that look like skin grafts and the jagged ones that look like they came from cut glass stick out to me the most.

But more importantly, Marco just looks really, really good without any clothes on. He doesn't look like one of those jacked-up jocks who play teens on TV, but he definitely looks like he spends a little time working out, though it's not his focal point of his life. He runs his fingers through his shaggy black hair, shaking his head in frustration to get it out of his eyes, before looking at me with a dopey, boyish grin and patting the spot next to him.

"I don't bite," he whispers. I expect him to go with the usual joke that follows that statement—*unless you want me to*—but he doesn't. He just gives me space.

"Thanks for the water," he says as I lie down on the bed with him. I take off my pants, pause, and then follow up with my shirt, sliding under the covers. He takes a few sips before pulling the blanket up.

The blackout curtains make the room dark, even though it's just early afternoon. At first, neither Marco nor I knows what to do with our bodies, both stiff as wood. But slowly, Marco shifts and gingerly wraps one arm around my waist.

I tense up, but only for a second. I force my body to relax, remembering he's not a threat, and let him pull me closer.

Naturally, our bodies shift into position, with him taking the role of big spoon while I become the little spoon. I feel his face against the coils of my curls and hear him take what he probably thinks is a discreet deep breath. At first I'm self-conscious, worried I might stink from the day's activities, but Marco doesn't seem to care.

In fact, I'm pretty sure I hear him whisper, "You smell good."

One minute turns into two, which turns into five, which turns into ten. Slowly, I feel his body start to relax, and I can tell he's drifting off to sleep. My brain is still going a thousand miles an hour, bouncing between fear that we're in a war zone and guilt about how much I'm enjoying what I'm experiencing right now. There are just so many people dealing with so much horror, and I feel like I don't have the right to be happy, like I don't have the right to experience the joy that every teen wants to experience—the joy of being with someone you find attractive.

Twenty minutes of silence later, I feel my own body start to grow heavy, and the world begins to drift away. I wrap my arm around Marco's, which is across my chest like a safety harness. I'm not sure if it's a dream or not, but as I drift to sleep, I hear him whisper, "I'll protect you. Always."

I think I whisper back, "Same to you."

I'm not sure how long I'm asleep, but I when I wake up, everything feels quieter and stiller, like it is in the middle of the night.

Marco and I have separated; he has turned toward the wall, while I'm spread out on my back. I guess we each know how the other sleeps now. I stare at his back, noticing the way it expands and contracts He's still in a deep sleep, but with each passing moment, I'm becoming more and more awake. I've never been somebody who needs a lot of rest. It must be the journalist in me, or maybe it's the capitalist allure of working long hours on minimal amounts of sleep, but I'm more than ready to get up and go.

I reach over quietly and guzzle down the water that's still at the side of the bed, but it's not enough to quench my thirst. Sighing and slipping on my pants, I slowly tiptoe out of the room, careful not to wake Marco up. I close the door quietly behind me and carefully head down the hall into the living room. I let out a breath of relief when I see a scribbled note from Catherine on the table that wasn't there before.

> GOT HOME A FEW HOURS AGO. GOING
> TO SLEEP. THE COP IS TAKEN CARE
> OF. PIZZA ON THE COUNTER. —C

I'm not sure when *a few hours ago* was, but the pizza instantly makes my stomach grumble. I realize I haven't had a full meal since everything went to hell; I've been surviving on nuts and berries and scraps like some sort of forager. Just the idea of cold pizza makes me want to drool on the floor.

I quietly walk into the kitchen, not wanting to wake either of them up, and spot the pizza on the counter. There's also a six-pack of beer—Baltimore's quintessential brand of Natty Boh—with two cans missing. For a moment, I find myself thinking how Catherine is definitely not old enough to be drinking beer, but then I remember the world's going to hell, so why does it freaking matter?

I hesitate, staring at the beer. My mom would never let me have it, always reminding me that Black boys throw their whole lives away if they're caught with alcohol underage. But honestly, there's a chance I might not live till tomorrow. The thought flutters into my brain and out again as easily as if I just remembered what day of the week it is. Death shouldn't be that casual, and how relaxed I am thinking about it should give me pause.

That's a problem for tomorrow's Jamal.

"To hell with it," I mutter.

I grab one of the beers and quietly pop open the top. I keep it under the table, hoping that will block some of the noise. The can hisses, and some of the fizz bubbles over the side, dripping over my hand. The beer is lukewarm, which I know is not the way to drink it, but right now, I don't really think it matters.

On TV shows, everyone seems to think beer and pizza is a good combination, so I take a bite of the cold pepperoni pizza and chew it a few times before guzzling a slurp of the beer.

As a Maryland resident, you either like Natty Boh, or you hate beer. There's no middle ground. And I think I fall into the latter category.

I expected the tartness. I expected the bubbliness. But the…I guess you would say the *hoppiness* of it makes me want to vomit. I swallow it down, staring at the can, and try another sip, hoping maybe the second time will be better.

It isn't.

"Water it is."

I put the beer in the refrigerator, thinking Catherine or Marco will probably enjoy it. I finish two of the remaining five slices of pizza. I want more—I could probably eat a whole large pizza right now, if I'm being honest—but think about how Marco is going to be hungry when he gets up.

Just thinking about him makes the warmth in my stomach expand, the same warmth I assume people get from drinking too much. Part of me can't wait to go back upstairs and slide back into bed with him. A part of me—a *large* part of me—is missing the warmth he gives off that kept my body feeling safe and comfortable.

I smile to myself just thinking about it, idly chewing on the crust of the second piece of pizza.

Maybe there's a future for us after this. Part of me wants to scold myself for thinking that far ahead. Marco and I have a long way to go before we get out of this Dome, and even considering a relationship with him is probably premature. There is some psychological term for people bonding over a traumatic experience, and from what I remember reading, those relationships don't usually survive.

And there's little that's more traumatic than this real-life Hunger Games experiment we're a part of.

"That's a thought for next week's Jamal," I remind myself. Today's Jamal needs to think about surviving and getting out of the Dome. That needs to be my priority. Not some cute boy.

Some *very* cute boy.

I rub my eyes and slap both sides of my face to wake up. I can be productive, maybe clean the kitchen again. I don't want to sleep, even though the thought of being with Marco is beckoning me back to the bed. I need to stay busy. I feel guilty for sleeping and maybe even guiltier for finding any amount of joy right now.

I know that's not how it's supposed to be. I know that I've earned this little bit of joy. It is important to move forward, but that's not what my brain is telling me. Right now, the only emotion going through my body is...

A creak behind me alerts me that I'm not alone. I push off the counter quickly and narrow my eyes, looking into the darkness of the house. I don't see anybody, but it's probably Catherine. I'm sure I woke her up with my movements.

"Sorry," I say in a whisper, trying to make sure I don't wake Marco as well. "Was I too loud?"

And then I realize it's not Catherine.

It's a cop with his gun cocked and trained on me.

"Where is he?"

TWENTY-FOUR

It takes me a moment to figure out which *he* the cop is referring to, but then it clicks. I blame my slowness on panic and the overwhelming sense of dread that starts at the soles of my and works its way up my body. I'm breathing so heavily; I'm not breathing at all. My body is so tense that it feels cold.

Since we've been in Baltimore, this isn't the first time I've had a gun trained on me. In fact, I would argue that going head-to-head with Officer Lewis was more terrifying than the gun. But there's something so brutal about the cold metal. Its history, the way it's been used to kill people like me. I can't think of anything but the fear that's pulsing inside my chest. It's all-encompassing. It short-circuits every single circuit inside my body.

The cop takes a step forward, shaking his gun at me. "Where. Is. He?"

"Who?"

"You know who I'm taking about," he growls. My whole body tightens as he takes another step forward.

"I'm going to ask you one more time. Where. Is. Officer. Lewis?"

I glance at his name tag: OFFICER CONRAD.

The voice is familiar too, and it only takes me a moment to pinpoint. "You were at the house, weren't you?"

I didn't get a good look at the officer with Officer Lewis before we started fighting. He was long gone before Lewis discovered us. But I don't think I expected to see a Black officer. Being a police officer is a way out for a lot of people in bad situations. It allows them to provide for their families and gives them a sense of power and control over their lives that they didn't have before. I understand logically why people who are marginalized become the exact thing that threatens their communities. I can see how we get from point A to point B.

That doesn't mean I condone it.

This guy, Officer Conrad—he's like me. He looks almost exactly like I do when I have my hair cut short. His face is slightly round, and his hair is no more than half an inch long, making him almost bald. His form is stocky but not overweight, just middle-of-the-road average. He's only a couple of inches taller than me, maybe five foot ten with his boots on, but it's more the look in his eyes that resonates with me. He seems like he's actually concerned for his friend...for his partner.

To him, we're the antagonists of the story.

"I'm not going to ask again," he hisses, taking another step forward. "Where the hell is he?"

I hold my hands up defensively. "You don't have to do this, you know," I whisper. "What if I told you he's safe?"

"Then let me see him."

I bite my tongue and taste blood.

"That's what I thought," he growled. "You freakin' kids. You think you're actually doing something. That your actions mean something. What about the people who defend your asses? Where would you be without us?"

By *us*, he means the police. I've heard this argument before. We've all heard this argument before. How important the police officers are. How our system will collapse if we don't have people to enforce the law. It's based on the idea that humans are not naturally good, that they need someone good and strong and just to protect them. It has always felt very medieval to me. Like the excuse used during the Crusades when it came to slaughtering thousands of people.

But I guess you could argue that we haven't really evolved much since then. We're still killing people in the streets because of religion, or skin color, or other simple things we believe make us right and other people wrong.

"I'm going to ask you one more time, where the fuck is he?" Officer Conrad says. "And if you don't answer me…"

"Are you going to kill me?" I ask point-blank.

He doesn't answer that directly. I wonder, has he ever actually killed anyone? I remember hearing his words at the house, how he was excited to go downtown. It sounded like he got some sort of thrill out of this. But he hesitates. At least with Officer Lewis, I knew where his moral center was.

With Officer Conrad, I'm not sure.

And that scares me more. A scared, trapped animal is more dangerous than a confident one.

"I'm going to do what I need to do," Officer Conrad settles on. A diplomatic answer.

"Then I'm going to do the same," I whisper.

I count down in my head from five to zero. Each second feels like a pulse inside my chest, like atom bombs going off in rapid succession. With every second, I wish I'll wake up next to Marco in his bed and this will just be a bad dream. But I'm not given that luxury. And like before, just like before, I need to defend the people I care about.

Once I hit zero, I swipe my arm quickly and send the case of beer flying toward Officer Conrad. I dive to the ground behind the island, just in time to dodge the bullet that leaves his gun. It shoots through the window and shatters it—that and the crash of the beer falling to the floor will be enough to wake up Catherine and Marco.

I stay low, keeping my body flat against the floor, and crawl military-style toward the living room, keeping to the wall. Officer Conrad growls, and I hear his heavy metal footsteps thump against the wooden floor as he follows me.

"Where did you go?" he snarls.

My back is pressed against the couch, and I cover my mouth with my right hand in an attempt to keep my breathing as quiet as possible. I'm sure I can figure out what's happening upstairs. Marco will realize I'm not with him. He and Catherine will meet in the hallway and put two and two together. It won't be long now. I just need to wait. I just need to—

Click.

I feel the cool metal of the gun before I hear the sound. Officer Conrad presses it against my forehead with enough force to push my head backward until it rests against the side of the couch. He keeps pressing, as if he's trying to burrow a hole the size of the barrel into my forehead. There's anger—pure, unadulterated, white-hot anger—in his eyes, and his hand is shaking.

"You couldn't just leave well enough alone, could you?" he growls. "You couldn't just…"

One flick of his finger. That's all it'll take for the bullet to fire. That's all, and then my brains and blood and bone will be all over the couch. The last thing I see could be his pained, horrible, traitorous face.

Dying like this—so quickly and without putting up any sort of fight—is not how I thought this would end. But at the same time, when I think back to being in the holding cell, to the fight with Officer Lewis…I've been living on borrowed time since this Dome was erected.

Maybe, just maybe, it's time.

My desire to sit there and accept my fate lasts only a moment, though. A fire inside my belly awakens, and I can see everything more clearly. I'm not going down without a fight. That's not who I am. I've come too far for that.

Quickly, I roll to the side and stand up, shoving the cop out of the way. It's enough for him to lose his balance and stumble back, which allows me to put some space between us. I think it only works because he doesn't expect that of me. I think part of him has been hoping I'd sit there and take it, make his life easier.

I push away from him, putting more space between us, and move to the other side of the room. I hear thumps from upstairs; Catherine and Marco both hurry down the steps and stand next to me.

"Are you okay?" Marco asks.

"I'm fine," I lie. They don't need to know I literally almost died. That's not going to help anyone. "It's the cop from before. He's friends with Officer Lewis. I saw him when we were in the house. We need to get—"

"I'll handle this."

I didn't notice it at first, but Catherine isn't dressed normally. Maybe it's because it's so dark in the house, but the steel of the suit we took from Officer Lewis doesn't compute at first. It is not until her heavy footsteps fill the air when she moves in front of Marco and me that I see it. She flexes her arms and presses a button on the waistband. Metal panels fold out and layer on top of each other, the suit acting like an exoskeleton and encompassing her whole body.

Catherine rolls her shoulders, metal hydraulics hissing and contracting as she does so. She cracks her neck and grins, looking over her shoulder at us through black pane of the visor.

"Told you I got this." Her eyes are barely visible, but I see her wink.

The suit fits her well. It reinforces the confidence and strength Catherine drips. But we don't have time to marvel at her or at the fact that Marco's hacking skills were successful. The whine of metal fills the air as Officer Conrad's suit also comes to life.

"Shit," Marco hisses.

"Go," Catherine growls, not turning her back on him.

"I'm sorry, what? We're not going to leave you. I didn't leave you back at Janna's house, why would I leave you here?"

"We made a promise, Jamal," she says without looking at me. "The mission always comes first. Two and one. That's how we divide and how we survive. This is no different. Marco is key to shutting down this dome, and you"—her eyes flicker to me—"I underestimated you. You're braver and stronger than you look. He needs you."

"Two on one is better," I debate. "We can take him out. We did it before. We—"

"Marco," she says sternly, glancing over at him like I'm not there.

"I'm on it. You be safe, you hear?"

She doesn't say anything in return. It's like Marco and Catherine have some secret language, and I'm not privy to what's happening. Did they just suddenly decide they were going to start leaving me out of decisions? Before I can think it through, Marco grabs my arm and yanks me toward the door.

"Wait, hold up—"

But he doesn't stop; he doesn't listen. He just keeps tugging me, keeps pulling me out the door and toward the garage. The last thing I see before he shoves me is Officer Carter trying to get past Catherine as she blocks us. Just like with Officer Lewis.

Except this time, something deep inside my chest tells me she's not going to make it out.

"What are you doing?" I snarl. But Marco doesn't listen. He uses his newfound strength to force me into the passenger seat of the car and walks around to the other side.

"Listen to me," he says, slamming the door loudly behind him. "Jamal! Listen to me!"

I've never heard him yell that loudly before, like he's a lion trying to make a whole pride bend to his will.

Marco's hunches over the steering wheel, gripping it so tight his knuckles are white. His shaggy hair is in front of his eyes, so I can't see them clearly. "She's not going to make it, okay?" he whispers. "You have to… You're not stupid. You have to understand that. She has no idea how to use that suit. He does. She's buying us time, and Every second we spend discussing this is another second we're wasting. You understand that, right? She's doing this to keep us safe."

Marco takes a deep breath. The house shudders as Catherine and Officer Conrad fight. It won't be long before one of the neighbors figures out what's going on. I'm also sure Officer Conrad also has backup coming. Marco is right—Catherine won't win. Honestly, she'll be lucky if she makes it out alive. Which is why we need to get out of here as quickly as possible. It hurts to think that, but the mission, as she said, is most important. We have to shut down the Dome.

"Promise me one thing," I say quickly. "Promise me you can shut down the Dome. Because if you can't, then we might as well fight here with her. This one's on you. I'll get the photos out to the right people if you can keep your end of the bargain."

Hunched over, Marco turns his head slightly toward me, revealing one of his eyes. He's exhausted, and I know I look the same way. We've been running from the police for the past couple of days. And it's felt like Chief Coles has just been waiting in the wings to snatch us up. Like he released us from the holding cell just to prove that he could, so his officers had a little game to play.

"I promise," Marco finally says. "I can do it. You can count on me."

I take a half a second, 'cause that's all that we can afford, to look deep into his eyes. He seems to believe in himself more than he did before, and there's no reason for me to doubt him, either. I think he finally understands, just like me, how important what we're doing is. We don't have the luxury of waiting around. We don't have the luxury of making mistakes. We're going to have one shot, one chance at success. And Catherine is ensuring that we have the best chance possible.

"Let's go," I say.

TWENTY-FIVE

Marco and I drive in silence away from the house. We're lucky enough to get out of the neighborhood before anyone spots us.

Small miracles, I guess.

I'm tempted to turn on the radio, like a fish attracted to light at the bottom of the deep ocean, hoping I'll hear something about Catherine. My hand twitches toward the knob, but Marco shakes his head.

"I listened while you and Catherine were gone," he mutters. "Tried the TV too. None of the stations outside of Baltimore work, and those remaining are owned by the city. It's just propaganda. If they talk about Catherine at all, they'll probably say they killed her for good reason."

"You were hoping to hear something about Janna, weren't you?" I ask. Marco nods. "Did you? Hear anything?"

"That she's dead."

"And you don't believe them?"

"Not in the slightest. She's smarter than that, and too valuable."

We drive in silence for what feels like two hours, but I can tell from the clock that it's barely thirty minutes. We pass the same streets twice. I don't mind Marco's aimless driving. Sure, it puts us at risk of being stopped, but it's the complete opposite of Catherine's determined point-A-to-point-B driving. For a few brief moments, I don't think about her.

And where we left her.

"We'll get a hotel and regroup. We'll figure it out from there," Marco says.

"We can't seriously be thinking of just…leaving her there, can we? We have to go back for her."

"You heard what she said—two and one."

"I heard what she said, and I'm saying fuck that."

But I know we can't, deep down.

We keep driving, finally finding refuge at a motel with lights that are half flickering and half completely dead. It looks like a one-story house that was turned into a motel. I cringe at the idea of staying here. This is the type of place where *Law & Order* or *CSI* would set tons of episodes. But it's perfect for our needs; no one will find us here.

I try my best to stop thinking about Catherine. To ignore the pit in my stomach that feels like I let her down. Like we're abandoning her. I know we're doing this, trying to stop the Dome, for everyone in Baltimore, and that includes Catherine. But she saved us; shouldn't we try to save her?

Marco hands me some money: sixty bucks. "Get us a room?"

I don't ask him why he thinks I'll be better at it than him. I know: Marco's hotheaded. His anger switch can be turned on by the slightest of things. I'm useful for things like this. It's what I bring to the group.

I walk into the motel, smiling nervously at a woman with her hair in a messy bun, a cigarette hanging out of her mouth. There's a tabby cat sitting on the counter and a small TV playing in the corner that doesn't get great reception. The sound is down low, but I can make out multiple shots of cops rounding up Black and brown residents all across Baltimore. The chyron at the bottom reads: CLEANING UP BALTIMORE, ONE STREET AT A TIME.

"Hey," I say quietly. "I can get one room for the night?"

"Fifty bucks," she says without hesitation, without even looking up at me. "You got ID?"

I fish out my wallet, pull out my ID, and slide it across the table, but then I see a flash of something unfamiliar. I pull out a card. And there in my hand is Chief Cole's business card. It's bent in five different places, and some of the text is smudged, but I can still clearly make out his easily memorizable phone number.

I shove the business card into my pocket like it's a hot coal and focus on the one-page contract the woman gives me.

"Out by nine a.m. No smoking, but I won't tell if you don't. No loud parties. No drugs. Don't give me a reason to call the cops."

"Especially now, right?" I force out. Making a joke about the situation tastes like bile in my mouth, but I feel like it brings me closer to the woman. She looks like somebody who's pro-cop, pro what's going on in Baltimore, and it seems to work. Her leathery skin twitches into a smile.

I quickly sign my name and slide the paper back to her and receive a key in return.

"Up the stairs, turn right, third door on the left."

I give her a quick thanks before heading to the door, but I pause. A single word snaps my attention toward the TV: the word *Dome*, coming from Governor Ambrose.

"Do you mind turning that up?"

The woman arches a brow like the request annoys her.

"Please?"

She sighs and nods, grabbing the remote control and clicking it half a dozen times. Governor Ambrose's calm and steady voice, as she stands on the steps of the Baltimore courthouse, fills the air. Her brown hair is pulled back into a manicured bun; her skin is pale and flawless; her sharp, angular features are accented by the lights set up by her press team to make her look taller.

"I know a lot of you are scared, and you have a right to be," she says. "This is a scary time. Our city is under attack from all sides, and I, as Governor of Maryland, am doing what I can to help. To stop this. It's like when you have a bad habit and your parents need to break it. They will do anything to help you, because they know it's for your own good in the long run.

"I understand that many of you are upset about the Damon Kyles verdict. But Officer Kyles was judged by a jury of his peers. Even Chief Coles spoke against him. He was found guilty. The criminal justice system has done what it is supposed to do. And your solution is to riot?" She shakes her head. "I understand being in pain. I understand suffering and being upset. But this isn't how our country functions. This isn't how our city functions. The Dome will stay in place until I am sure our men in blue are safe, that each and every citizen is safe, and most importantly, that our city is safe. You are in control of when that happens. But until then, it will remain intact. I promise you that every citizen within the Dome is being treated with care. Chief Coles isn't your enemy. The police force isn't your enemy. I am not your enemy. We are here to serve and protect the people of this great city."

Journalists—the few that are still around—erupt in a flurry of questions that Governor Ambrose doesn't even attempt to answer. She calls on only one journalist from the *Blue City Star*, a well-known pro-cop paper. It's a softball question about who manufactured the suits. It completely ignores what's happening in the city and treats cops like they're interesting specimens, as if they're models wearing a new style of clothing everyone is going to want to get their hands on.

It's interesting to watch the governor try to spin what's happening in her favor. Yes, the Dome is up. She's not shying away from its purpose. But what's going on inside? That's the key. She's acting like everything in here is fine and peaceful, that the Dome is the cause of that peace, when in fact it's the complete opposite.

I know her game. When push comes to shove, she'll explain that she had to do this. That people were rallying against the cops. She'll cite a few incidents that no one will be able to confirm and spin that into a whole pro-Dome conspiracy. It's not about the Dome itself. It's what's going on inside of the Dome that's the problem. But by the time the governor is done playing the news like a fiddle, no one will question her motives.

That's why our mission matters. The photos of the Dome, the photos of the police brutality, the hacktivism—each is another layer of proof that might not be enough to take her down on its own, but together, it'll be impossible for the world to ignore.

"Thanks," I say quickly. I don't want to listen to this anymore. I've heard everything I need to hear. I quickly walk out and wave the key at Marco, who's leaning against the car. He has two bags in hand; one looks like a duffel bag full of clothes, and the other is a laptop bag.

"You brought it?" I ask, leading the way up the steps. I look through the grimy window to see if the woman at the front desk even notices I have another person with me, but she's too focused on the crossword puzzle on her desk.

"I thought I should. You know, we need to have something…"

"…to fight back with."

Marco nods. When we reach the door, I push the key into the lock. It takes two tries to open the door, and even then, the rusted metal fights against me. Finally, I get it open, revealing a nondescript room with two beds, a small TV about the size of the one in the office, and an ugly, green-painted bathroom. Marco's grimace matches my own.

"Home sweet home," he sighs, fiddling with the AC. It comes to life, but the whining sound of metal sliding against metal isn't worth the piss-poor excuse for cool air it gives. Quickly, he turns it off, sighs, and sits on the edge of one of the beds.

"Okay," he whispers, rubbing his fingers over his head. "We need a plan."

I sit opposite him, giving him space and quiet. He doesn't speak, so I decide to take the lead. "Have you found any new information about the Dome? You said you were going to talk to some contacts?"

He shrugs. "There are some Nemesis hackers who think they might know the base code they used, which means they should be able to rework it. But no one has tried it. It's too big to upload on Wi-Fi. We need some sort of direct access point, something that has a direct link to whatever is powering the Dome. And most of those points…"

"…are in places we don't want to be," I finish for him.

He nods. "I've narrowed it down based on probability and power surges." He opens the computer. A few clicks later, a map of Maryland appears with six dots appears. "We've got the state capitol and the governor's home. I'm sure she has one on her person. The police station in Baltimore, of course. The mayor's office…"

"And one in Fort Meade."

Judging by what Catherine told us, that's probably where they made the Dome. And then there's one that seems completely out of place in one of the ritzier neighborhoods of Baltimore.

"What's this one?" I ask, pointing to it.

Marco clicks on the dot, and the screen zooms in on it. An address appears that doesn't look familiar, along with the longitude and latitude.

"That's Chief Coles's home," he says. "It's a gamble, but I think he'd probably have one. He's so close to the governor, right?"

"He is the police chief of Baltimore," I reason. "It would make sense. If anyone would have direct access to being able to turn on and off the Dome or anything important related to it, it would be him. Two peas of the same pod who have the same goal in mind when it comes to the people of Maryland."

Marco scrunches his face. "You mean they're both racist." I nod, and he continues, "Also, no one uses that expression anymore. *Peas of the same pod.* That's not even the saying. *Two peas in a pod* is what you mean."

I shrug.

"Each one of these locations, I reckon, also has some sort of override code. If you trust a person with being able to access the Dome and control it, you trust them enough to turn it on and off."

"Another hunch?"

He nods. "Like backup codes when you have two-factor authentication turned on? I reckon the governor would be using these highly selected individuals as backup. If we can get to one of them…"

I stare at the little dot, as if looking at it long enough will teleport our bodies to the exact room where the code is. Marco's logic makes sense. If we can get that code, we can stop what's happening. We can take back control.

The business card in my pocket grows heavier and heavier the more I think about it. There's a plan forming deep in the crevices of my mind, somewhere between my subconscious and my consciousness. It's lingering there, just out of reach, because I know how completely far-fetched an idea it is.

A snap from Marco brings me back to reality.

"You tired?"

I'm not, but I nod anyway.

"Wanna lie down again?"

"Not yet," I say.

"I'm going to take a quick shower. I feel disgusting. Do you want to join me?" He waggles his brows playfully.

"Tempting." I grin. "But how about I go and get us food? I saw a vending machine in the office."

Marco walks toward the bathroom and turns on the hissing water. He pokes his head out, now shirtless. "Sure, that sounds great. Get me a Snickers if they have any."

"Will do," I promise.

Marco half closes the door, but I catch him with my voice before he can finish.

"Thanks for pulling me out of there," I say.

Marco's gaze lingers on my face softly. He doesn't say anything for a moment, and I enjoy us just looking at each other, drinking each other in.

"There's no one I'd rather be in this shithole with, Jamal," he says honestly, and closes the door.

I linger in the room for a moment, thinking things through. This is will be the second time I've betrayed Marco, and I'm not sure he'll forgive me, but like he and Catherine said, the mission has to come before everything else. And I can do this; I can help. If I tell Marco what I'm planning, he'll either immediately disagree or want to be involved, and this is something I have to do on my own. If I can get Chief Coles to give us information, maybe I can turn the tables in our favor and save Catherine. Chief Coles wants information—he always has—and I can give him that. Or I can pretend to. This won't be a repeat of Nemesis. I won't let it.

Trying not to overthink it, I quietly slip out of the hotel room and take the steps to the office again. The woman is still at the front desk, and in the ten minutes since we came upstairs, the tabby cat has fallen asleep.

"Do you have a phone I can borrow?" I ask.

TWENTY-SIX

It isn't Chief Coles who picks up when I call, but a woman with a high-pitched, incredibly happy voice. She sounds more like a kindergarten teacher than someone helping with the complete destruction of minority communities in Baltimore.

"Jamal, yes?" she chirps.

I'm thrown off but let out a grunt of assent.

"Ah, yes, Ian said you might be calling! I'll have the car pick you up. Do you mind giving me your address?"

I look around, seeing the street number of the motel written backward on the window. I read it off to her.

"Oh dear, that is a horrible part of town," she says. "That just won't do. Let's see. Can you head to one-fifty Broad Street?"

"I'm sure I can find my way there."

"Perfect!" she says happily. "I'll have food. Chicken pot pie?"

"Sure," I say hesitantly.

"Excellent. You'll be looking for a black Lexus. Should be there in about fifteen minutes. See you soon, Jamal. I'm so excited to meet you, and I'm so happy you called."

The line goes dead, and I'm left with my own aching, hollow thoughts. Who was that woman? She referred to Chief Coles with such familiarity. She sounded too nice to be married to a monster. But right now, that doesn't matter.

I say a quick thanks and leave the motel like a puff of air pushed out of a teakettle. I glance up at our room and see the light shining faintly through the curtains. Marco is probably still in the shower. He'll be out in a few minutes. After another five minutes or so, he'll start wondering what happened. He'll wonder why I left him alone.

A pain in my stomach ripples outward, almost making me vomit. We've already lost Catherine and have no idea what happened to her, and now I'm separating us again with no way to get back in contact with him.

That's a problem for future Jamal. If I need to get in touch with him, I'll find a way.

I turn away from the motel and walk at a brisk pace toward my destination. I wrap my arms around myself; it may be summertime, but there's a chill dripping down my spine that makes me shiver. I reach 150 Broad Street just in time to see the Lexus round the corner and flash its lights twice.

This must be what a hookup feels like, I think to myself, looking both ways and crossing the street. I slip into the right side of the car. The divider is up between the front and back seats, and the tinted windows keep me from seeing any features of my driver.

But the doors instantly lock when I get into the car.

"Buckle up," the driver curtly says. And that's the end of that conversation.

I obey his command. The leather of the Lexus is smooth and new with not a single sign of wear and tear on it. The windows are perfectly clean, no smudges, and there's a bottle of water in one of the compartments in the back seat. I don't usually take drinks inside of Ubers—my mom told me about some article she read about a woman who was drugged and kidnapped for three weeks by her driver—but my throat is parched, and it gives me something to do with my hands. I can't focus on anything outside because the windows are so dark there's nothing to see, like I'm in a cell all over again.

I'm not sure how long we drive. It could be five minutes, it could be fifteen minutes, but eventually the smooth drive turns rough and gravelly, and we climb a steady incline for at least a mile or two. Finally, the car comes to a stop. The driver gets out and opens the back door without a word.

I get out of the car and do a quick check of my surroundings. I don't know much about Baltimore, but the area doesn't look familiar at all, and the house...the house looks completely out of place. It's a three-story home made of painted gray brick with white and black accents. A three-car garage is on the right-hand side, and the land it's on looks like it's two or three acres.

A chief of police in the United States, I imagine, makes about a hundred thousand dollars a year. Unless Chief Coles has family money or a wife who is rolling in the deep, there's no way he can afford this house. The land itself is probably worth two or three million, and this house is massive. So how can he afford it?

And more importantly...

"Wait."

I look up at the sky and notice it's no longer bright. There's no eerie white glow that constantly illuminates the night. Well, no, that's not true. There is. It's just behind me.

Which means we're outside the fucking Dome.

How did we…*when* did we go through the Dome? I must look like some frantic animal that's finally seeing the outside for the first time, but I don't care. I know the air isn't actually cleaner or crisper outside of the shell, but it feels like it is. I take a deep breath and flex my fingers. It wasn't like I thought the Dome would never be shut down. One way or another, it would eventually disappear. But being outside it just feels so different. It feels like the world is literally my oyster.

"Come on," the driver mutters, his voice laced with annoyance. "We don't have all day. Ms. Coles is waiting for you."

Ms. Coles. I take one more moment to look at the city, to see how large the Dome actually is. It looks like half a sphere gently placed over Baltimore, perfectly measured so that none of the tallest skyscrapers in Baltimore break through its top. In a kind of twisted, sick way, it almost looks beautiful.

"Come on," the driver repeats.

This time, I follow him inside begrudgingly. The inside of the home is a stark contrast to the outside. There is a warmth here that's almost sugary sweet. The house is like a hug, thanks to the soft lights and the mahogany wood, and feels inviting and safe. The entryway looks like it belongs in the movie *Crazy Rich Asians*, with a staircase that peels off to the left and right. There's a large table in the three-roomed foyer, like three different paths to adventure, all open to me.

"Shoes and jacket off," the driver says. He points, like I don't know how to take my own shoes and jacket off, then demonstrates where to put the items in a corner. Before I can protest, or even decide if I'm going to follow through, Ms. Coles rounds the corner.

I take a second to look the woman in front of me, to see what type of person would marry a monster like Chief Coles. She is tall and slender, with a few flecks of gray in her mostly dark hair that's pulled into a neat braid. She has bright, vibrant eyes and a warm nature about her that pulses out like a beacon. She looks like a teacher, or maybe a nurse. Mentally, I kick myself for thinking those things. Just because she's a nice, kind-looking woman doesn't mean she has to have a job stereotypically assigned to nice, kind women.

And honestly, how kind can she be if she's married to Chief Coles?

She studies me up and down for a moment, scanning me like one of those machines in the airport the TSA uses.

"And a bath." The woman's voice I heard on the phone flits through the air as she wanders in. "I'm sorry to say this, but you stink, Jamal. Plus I think you'd appreciate a nice hot bath, yes?"

The idea of taking a bath in Chief Coles's house makes me tenser than I already am, but the softness of his wife's face isn't a gentle softness—it's the kind of softness that tells a person, *I'm being nice to you, but don't even think about betraying me.*

"Just down the hall, first room on your left. I left you towels. Feel free to use as much of the bubble bath as you want. Dinner will be ready in twenty minutes." She touches the driver's shoulder. "Meyers, do you mind helping me in the kitchen?"

"Of course not, ma'am," he says, following her.

I'm here for a specific reason, I remind myself. I'm not here to make friends or to win the Coleses' good favor. I'm here to get information. And the best way to do that is to make them think I'm cooperative. They won't think of me as a threat if they're not worried about me stabbing them in the back.

"Thank you," I say before wandering down the hall, following Ms. Coles's instructions.

It's not hard to find the bathroom; the door is partially open, and the aroma that comes from the room fills the whole hallway. It smells like a mixture of oranges, vanilla, and flowers. I push open the door and drink in the size of the bathroom, which is bigger than both of my bathrooms back home put together. The tub is one of those massive soaking tubs that you see in movies or in Instagram posts about Bali.

I quickly run a bath, getting the water as hot as possible and filling it to the brim with bubbles. It reminds me of one of those drinks at Starbucks that is more foam than coffee. I slip my body into the water, letting the hot liquid massage my sore muscles. I didn't know how exhausted I really was until I got into the water, and it feels like every part of my body breaks apart when it hits the heat. Like the water is separating the building blocks that make me who I am and putting me back together all at once. Like this bath is my safe space.

I could stay here forever, I think. Just in this bathtub. Nothing else in the world seems to matter besides the heat and the steam and the safety of this room. But I know what's outside that door, and outside this house—I know what's waiting for me back under the

Dome. Once the Coleses discover what I'm planning or guess that I'm going to turn against them, they'll send me back…and that's the nicest possible outcome. Besides, this is just a beautiful gilded cage made of expensive wood and porcelain. But it's nothing more than that. Nothing more than an imperfect illusion.

I wash up quickly, ending my moment of peace. I'm not here to relax. I dry off and slip my clothes back on. There's a pile of clothes on the toilet that Ms. Coles left me, and they look like they would fit, which makes me think Chief Coles must have a son around my age. But I'm not wearing some other man's clothing. I'm not letting my oppressors dress me up in whatever outfit is palatable for them. These clothes have seen me through war; they are my armor.

Once dressed, I take a deep breath. I just need to get through the next couple of minutes. Find an opening and do what I need to do. I look at myself in the mirror, noticing that my bones are sharper, if that's even possible. I know for a fact that my eyes look darker. There are healed cuts and bruises on my body that I didn't even realize I had and a few scars that will be permanent reminders of these nights.

Sighing and taking a deep breath, I force a smile three times on my face, trying to make the grin look natural. I need the smile to look authentic when I go downstairs. That's the only way I'm going to be able to convince them.

Once I'm done, I push open the door and walk quickly out and down the hall. The smell of starch in the air, maybe potatoes and bread, steers me into the living room and then into the dining room. I see the leather jacket of the driver hanging on the door as I walk past, and I hear Ms. Coles chatting with someone before I see them.

Half of me expects it to be the boy whose clothes I was offered, but when I see Chief Coles there in plain clothes, I tense up.

It's Ms. Coles who walks over quickly and pulls out a chair for me, gesturing for me to sit across from her husband, perpendicular to her. Chief Coles sips at his dark liquid, which I think is Coke, never breaking eye contact with me, like a lion looking at his prey, before gesturing at the seat.

"Sit, sit," he says. "I bet you're hungry, and the food is going to get cold."

Funny, I think as I take the seat. I've never been less hungry in my life.

TWENTY-SEVEN

My mother's cooking is the only cooking I actually love, but Ms. Coles's is probably a close second.

"It's the butter," she says, pointing her fork at me and then down at the mashed potatoes and gravy. "You have to go heavy with it. We only live once, am I right?"

It's such a common expression, but knowing her husband is responsible for killing people kind of makes me sick to my stomach. I give a small nod. I've managed to eat about half of my food: mashed potatoes, peas, and chicken with some sort of rosemary sauce.

Chief Coles has been pretty quiet throughout dinner, not looking at me or his wife but off into the distance. He has a completely different demeanor from the man I saw only a few days ago inside the jail cell. That man was cutting, in control, vengeful, and ruthless. This man kind of seems like a normal father and husband, home from work after a long day.

It reminds me of those stories I've heard about Hitler when he was visiting with family members. There's a video of him at some castle, playing with a girl whom I think was his niece, and people said how he looked like such a normal person and how you couldn't see the monster inside of him. But I think that's the point. Monsters don't have fangs, and they don't have masks, and they don't scream, *Look, I'm a monster!* Some of the most horrible people in the world are just normal-looking people. Darkness and pain and hate and anger come slowly, creeping like ivy, and they strangle you, and before long, you're a victim of it like everybody else.

So, no, I don't care that Chief Coles seems like a loving husband who is just distracted because he had a long day at work. This man is evil.

"Well, I'm full," Ms. Coles says, the only one of us who has cleaned her plate. "You boys, I believe, have a lot of catching up to do?"

Chief Coles flashes his wife a smile and squeezes her hand. His grip lingers for a moment longer than it would if it was forced, which just reinforces the idea that this man actually does love something. He's capable of love and kindness and still chooses to look at people like me with nothing more than anger.

I think that makes me hate him even more.

There's a palpable quietness in the air as Ms. Coles clears the table and wipes it down. She walks out of the room, closing the sliding oak doors behind her, leaving Chief Coles and me to have our conversation.

"So," I say after a moment's pause, "who starts?"

It feels like a do-over between Chief Coles and me. Before, he had the upper hand, and since we're on his turf, I suppose he still does. But this time, I know what I need out of the conversation. I know what cards I have and how to play them. What to say and what not to say. How to manipulate the flow of the narrative to get what I want. It's like being a lawyer in a criminal case; I don't need every juror to believe me, I just need one. I don't need to completely pull the wool over Chief Coles's eyes. I just need a few minutes of peace and quiet to find what I'm looking for.

"You reached out to me," he says, gesturing grandly with his hand. "I imagine you should start. What made you finally take me up on my offer? To be an informant?"

"I thought maybe you were right."

Chief Coles leans back in his chair and crosses his arms over his chest. The chair creaks as he puts his full weight on the rear two legs. "Oh?"

I take a shallow breath, steeling myself. I've never been a good liar, and stomaching this is going to take all the creativity I have. But if it gets me what I need—and Catherine and Marco—then it's worth it.

"You said something before that resonated with me. That eventually, I'll have to pick a side. That nothing ever happens if someone doesn't act. And the most important choices are the ones we make when our backs are against the wall. I think…" I pause and shake my head. "No, I *know* that what's happening out there, under the Dome, can be stopped. And maybe, just maybe, siding with you all is the right way to help that happen. I think I just didn't see that before. I think I was just too…"

"Driven and focused by madness?" he suggests. "Brainwashed

into hating the police because of the liberal media? Forgetting that the people who risk their lives every day to keep you and your family safe are doing their best and deserve your respect?"

I force words of anger down my throat by swallowing thickly.

"Yeah," I reply curtly. "Exactly that." Simple is best. It keeps me from lashing out and blowing my cover.

Officer Coles is quiet as he stares at me. Cops have to have a decent amount of intuition to survive, especially those who do interrogations, so I wonder if he can see through me and tell that I'm lying. I hear faint music from the kitchen and running water in the sink. I hear Ms. Coles singing a tune that's familiar, though I can't exactly place it. I focus on that instead of the way his eyes burn into me.

Finally he speaks. "I'm glad you came to your senses. It takes a big man to realize when he's wrong, and it takes a bigger man to turn against the people he believes are his friends in order to do the right thing. That's the type of person who makes changes, Jamal. Not those so-called revolutionaries that *he* runs with. People like cops? People like politicians? People like soldiers? Those are the ones who make a difference."

He leans forward in the chair, the front two legs clicking loudly as they hit the ground. He rest his large forearms on the table, making it wheeze with the weight as he leans forward. "I like you; you have a lot of promise. I see a lot of myself in you."

Nothing makes me so sick to my stomach as that.

"A rebel, someone who pushes boundaries, someone willing to stand up for the little guy. That's what a cop does. It's admirable. It'll help you go far, if you know how to cultivate it and if you have the right allies."

"And I'm guessing you're the right type of ally?"

He grins. "Exactly. See, I knew you were smart. You can't actually think you're going to do…whatever it is you and your little group of ruffians are trying to do, can you? Maybe that hacker group Nemesis could've, but—"

"You found them all."

He nods. "Thanks for that intel, by the way."

My stomach turns over, and I want to vomit. I saw how they beat up Marco; I can only imagine what they're doing to Karma and her crew. And Janna…is she really alive, like Marco hopes?

"So I'm glad you called. Means you're coming to your senses. You're a smart kid, so I'm sure you understand how the Dome can be good for everyone. You're on the wrong side of history here, son. I'm trying to help you find the light, so to speak. I promise you'll thank me when you're older.

"Now I'm going to really test you. Do you have any more information of value for me? Are we going to be friends, Jamal, or enemies?"

How long is too long before hesitation turns into an obviously brewing lie? I thought of this in the car, knowing Chief Coles would probably ask a question like this the test to me. There's no way he'll just trust my loyalty, considering I was willing to give up everything to protect Marco before. To have a complete change of heart and turn on him like this? It would be surprising if Chief Coles didn't question me.

But I'm always thinking. Mom has always said it's my greatest strength and will get me out of most dangerous situations if I trust myself.

"Marco knows how to turn off the Dome."

Surprise washes over Chief Coles's face, and I do my best to not smirk, knowing he didn't expect me to give Marco up that easily. He doesn't question me, though. Instead, he leans forward. "That's impossible."

I shake my head. "He's figured it out."

"How?"

I shrug. "I don't know. He didn't tell me. It's why I came to you. I don't trust him anymore."

I study Chief Coles's expression carefully. Worry, anger, fear, and confusion all wash over his face. It gives away more than he expects, even if those emotions are only visible for a second. It means the Dome *can* be shut down and that maybe, just maybe, this isn't all for naught.

Chief Coles stands up, pushing his chair back so hard it falls over. A string of curse words leaves his mouth as he pulls out his phone, dialing quickly.

"Find Marco Gonzales," he growls when the call connects. "I don't *care* if you don't know who he is! Do your damn job and find someone who does! Use every resource you have to find him, and that girl he was with too!"

A girl? Are they talking about Catherine? They have to be, right?

I do my best to not look like I'm eavesdropping, which I obviously am. Ms. Coles's singing is too loud and the phone is too quiet for me to make out any words from the other end, but the exasperated sigh that leaves Chief Coles's mouth releases a ball of tension I didn't know I was carrying.

Catherine got away. She won. Now I just need to hope Marco is able to do the same thing.

Chief Coles moves the phone away from his ear, looking at me. "Where did you last see him?"

Now comes the real challenge. How much information do I give away? If I don't say enough, Chief Coles won't believe me. If I give away too much, he might actually find Marco.

"Last time I saw him, when we went our separate ways, he was heading toward a hotel somewhere in the seventieth block."

Roughly ten blocks away from where we were—that'll buy him some time.

Chief Coles nods, relays that information curtly, and then hangs up his phone, shoving it into his pocket. "Come with me."

He doesn't hesitate, just opens the sliding doors and walks down a hall, different from the one I walked down earlier. I wipe my mouth quickly and follow him. This hallway is almost a mirror of the other one, where the bathroom is, except it has portraits of old white men lining the walls. Some, I can tell, are police officers. Judging by the age of the photos, they seem to go back all the way to when Baltimore was established. Some of them look like family members, and some of them, I'm guessing, are a combination of both—police officers and family.

At the end of the hall, Chief Coles pulls out a key and opens the door. Inside is a room lined with the one thing I never thought

I would associate with Chief Coles: books Books that surprise me to find Chief Coles owns. There are books in here in Latin, Greek, and even a few in Cantonese. There are more books than in my own home library, and my mother declares herself a lover of the written word.

Chief Coles walks over to the large mahogany desk and opens it, fishing out a phone and tossing it to me. I catch it and roll it around in my hands. It looks like a burner phone from a spy movie you might see on AMC.

"You helped me, and now I'm going to help you," he says. "You get one call. One less-than-five-minute call outside of the Dome. Use it wisely. I'll be back in five minutes to take you home."

Home. For a second, I think he means my home outside of Annapolis, but then I realize he means the Dome. He means the cage that he and his people have erected to trap me and all the others he's deemed a threat. And by calling it my home, he's saying that I am nothing more than an animal that needs to be caged.

That hits harder than anything the driver or Chief Coles or even Officer Lewis has said before. I'm not sure why, since the vitriol isn't as strong as those other words spat at Marco and Catherine and me with such poisonous bile. But the way he said it so casually, so calmly...it makes my stomach twist.

I barely notice I'm alone until the door clicks shut. I glance at it and see that it's one of those doors that locks from the outside. "So I'm stuck in here," I mutter.

Fine by me.

This is the only time I've had alone since I arrived in the Coleses' home, besides that weird bath situation. This room obviously means something to Chief Coles—putting me in here and offering me a phone call is his way of baring his neck in a show of truce. I gave him something, so he's giving me something in return.

Which makes me think there's something here I can use to figure out the code to take down the Dome. If there's a room where Chief Coles would put such precious information, it's this one.

I don't have time to sit with my feelings. This is a golden opportunity, and I can't waste it. Five minutes is all I have before Chief Coles comes back in, and I bet he's perceptive enough to notice if things in his sanctuary are out of place.

I move as quickly and quietly as possible around the room, searching for anything that could be of use. I open drawers and move picture frames. But I find nothing that can help me.

All the while, I try to keep track of how much time I have left. It's hard to multitask when your heart is racing so fast you feel dizzy. Between keeping my movements to a minimum, keeping an eye on the door in case Officer Coles decides to just barge in, and trying to keep track of time, I feel like I'm being split in three different directions. Not to mention the weight of the phone.

It's not physically heavier than any other phone, but it feels like a burning rock in my pocket. I could be using this time on something besides this fool's errand. Like calling my mother and telling her I love her, for example. Who knows if this might be the last time? But instead I'm trying to fight against the current. Trying to swim upstream against the riptide.

What makes me, a queer Black boy, think he can fight the

police force of Baltimore? Heroes like DeRay Mckesson, Janna, the members of Nemesis...they've all tried, and where are they now? Did I really think I was going to be able to waltz into this house, undetected behind enemy lines, and find the key to fixing everything? Instead I'm stuck in a room that looks almost sterile, like Chief Coles has an obsession with making sure everything is in its place. Every paper, every photo, every folder is perfectly aligned with one another. Even after my bath I feel like I'm too dirty to be here.

Except for one thing—one book slightly out of place on the bookshelf. One book that stands out.

"Wait."

Look for patterns, find what's missing or different, and pry it apart. That's what one of my journalism teachers told me. You follow those three steps, and you'll be able to uncover any story.

I look at the door and let my eyes trail down to the gap between the bottom and the floor. I don't see any movement. I walk to the opposite side of the room, pulling the book off the shelf. My breath hitches, half expecting some type of secret door to open up, but the book is lighter than I thought it would be.

Inside of pages upon pages of literature, there's a hole with something tucked snugly inside. A USB drive.

There's no guarantee that what I need is in here; this could just be an old everyday drive that everyone has dozens of. But it's the only chance I have.

I wish I had time to check it, to confirm this is what Marco would need, but I know my time is running out. I pocket the drive and make sure to put the book back exactly as I found it. I just hope I don't get searched on the way out of here.

With probably only a minute left, I open the phone and quickly dial the only number I have memorized. Only two rings pass before the familiar voice answers.

"Hello?"

It's been only three days since I last saw my mom, but it feels like it's been months, if not years. The simple two-syllable word says so much, and I can tell from the cracks in her voice that she hasn't slept. She's probably been up all night worrying about me, talking with the police, trying to find out where I am and if I'm even alive. We're not one of those rich families with lots of connections who can pull strings to get information. We're very middle-class, if not lower-middle-class, even if we don't live paycheck to paycheck. No one would listen to a forty-nine-year-old Black woman pleading for information about her Black son. We've talked about this, and we've always known that if something like this ever happened to me, I would be just another statistic.

And that's my mom's biggest fear.

I wish I could tell her everything is okay. I wish I could tell her that I'm doing all right and that I'll be home soon. But I don't have time for that, and all of those things are probably lies. I could die right here, right now. I could get back under the Dome and be arrested, tortured, and shot immediately. I've been living on borrowed time throughout my various encounters with the police, and that won't last. Math isn't on my side.

So I say the only thing I can. "I love you."

I hang up the phone just in time to hear the door open, and Chief Coles stick his head in. He surveys the room quickly before his eyes fall back on me.

"Time to go."

TWENTY-EIGHT

As if I was visiting her house to see her son, Ms. Coles gives me a Tupperware container of food.

"You need to eat more," she says, patting me on the head—actually *patting me* like I'm a freaking dog. "You're going to shrivel into nothing if you don't. Promise me you will?"

"I promise," I say hollowly. But she doesn't seem to care.

She kisses her husband on the lips. "Come home safely, okay?" she tells him. "Don't let those monsters take you from me."

"I promise," he says, kissing her back.

It's clear that the driver isn't taking me this time, which raises some alarms, but not enough for me to ask any questions. Chief Coles grabs his jacket, having changed into his uniform while I was in the office, and walks toward his cruiser, expecting me to follow. I say nothing and obey, opening the back door of the car, but he shakes his head.

"Front seat," he suggests. "You've earned it."

Oh, thank you, great one, I think, but I'm smart enough to keep it in my head. A few minutes later, we're zooming down the street, his siren blaring loudly, any cars still on the road moving obediently out of the way.

"I bet you're wondering why I'm taking you instead of having the driver drop you off," he says.

"I was just thinking that."

"There's a protest happening downtown, and I'm guessing some of your friends are part of it. They've got guns and everything."

I stare through the window to avoid looking directly at Chief Coles. I don't think the guns will do anything, considering I've seen those suits in action, but it's nice to know that people are still standing up, still fighting. It only took a few days, and already the citizens inside the Dome are willing to fight back. Imagine what it will be like in a week if the Dome is still up.

"They aren't my friends," I say, keeping the act going. "Like I said, I'm just trying to survive."

"I know." A beat passes. "I was just testing you again."

"Did I pass?"

"With flying colors."

We spend another five minutes driving with the road slowly growing brighter, like morning is approaching the horizon. The glow of the Dome is the only thing on the road, and it's getting closer and closer. It makes me think back to when Marco and I were talking about where the Dome ended. It seems to stop about five hundred feet past the WELCOME TO BALTIMORE sign on the south side. In another two minutes, we'll be within it, and I'll be back in my cage.

"How does the car get through the Dome?" I ask. It's a

gamble—he probably won't tell me—but it's also a test of how much trust I've gained with Chief Coles.

Another moment of silence passes, and I wonder if maybe I've poked the bear too much. Finally he answers by tapping the transponder on the roof.

"Essentially, to keep it simple for you, since it's pretty complicated and I wouldn't want to confuse you, I've got something here that tells the Dome we're good people. It'll let us through, no problem."

You have no idea how smart I am, I think.

But I keep my mouth shut. So the Dome has some way of recognizing who is and isn't allowed to exit. It's not just a catch-all net. Have the right fob and you're able to leave? That's good to know.

"I'm proud of you for making the right choice," Chief Coles says, turning down a dirt side road. There are police lining it, but aside from them, we're the only ones here. The car slows to a cruise, Chief Coles shows his ID, and the officer lets us pass, allowing us to approach the shimmering white wall. "That couldn't have been easy, but it was the right thing to do."

What does he know about doing the right thing? The right thing as a cop would be to actually protect everyone equally. The right thing would be to stand by the oath he took and use that gun and badge to do something good. But instead, Chief Coles and his subordinates are just puffing out their chests and holding on to their bruised egos, not willing to admit that maybe, just maybe, the system propping them up is the problem, not me and my community.

"We'll get through this," he promises. "The whole community."

But only if we do things your way, I think. There is no getting through this without Black and brown people suffering. The only way we're going to get through this in a way Chief Coles approves of is if his vision, his idea of Baltimore, is the sole guiding light.

I push that feeling down and focus on the glimmering wall ahead of us. Chief Coles doesn't slow down but continues to drive at a solid thirty miles an hour. Just as seamlessly as before, we pass through the barrier like its nothing. I remember the video of that Nemesis member, how he pressed his hand against it; this was like passing through light. Chief Coles doesn't even seem to care.

We turn onto another road that quickly becomes Martin Luther King Boulevard as we head into the city.

"I'm going to drop you off up there." He points to one of the light rail stops by the Ravens' M&T Bank Stadium. "And I expect you to stay out of the city, you understand? And call me if you hear anything else about Marco and Nemesis."

If he actually wanted me to stay out of the city, he would have left me at his house or kept me outside the Dome. I'm not sure what game he's playing, but I'm pretty sure he's expecting me to disobey him.

Well, he's right about one thing—I'm willing to kick and scream, to fight and bite and claw and rip to get what I want. Black people like me have to be twice as good, twice as passionate, twice as driven. That doesn't just extend to work ethic.

The blood of kings and queens runs through me. The souls of survivors and victors. Of lawyers. Of activists. Of politicians and revolutionaries. It fuels me.

Chief Coles may think we're all the same, that the protesters are nothing more than angry teens and pissed-off nobodies. But he's never met someone like me.

And he's going to live to regret it.

TWENTY-NINE

The first thing I do when I get out of the car is throw away the Tupperware.

The second thing I do is orient myself—that's easy. It isn't hard to figure out where the protests are that Chief Coles was talking about. The few people on the street, specifically the ones getting on the light rail, are all talking about it, even if they're not talking *directly* about it.

"Did you hear about the girl who defaced that statue?"

"Which one, the Columbus Monument or the Obelisk?"

"There was more than one?"

"Yeah, I heard it was a whole coordinated attack. Someone defaced the Confederate Soldiers and Sailors Monument too."

"Wasn't that taken down, like, three years ago?"

"Mayor had it put back up. Part of the mayor and governor's whole 'honoring Maryland's history, the good and the bad' act or some shit."

It isn't hard to figure out that the biggest protests are at the

Confederate Soldiers and Sailors Monument. It takes about forty minutes to get there, one mile by light rail and the last mile walking. Walking helps me control who sees me. I double back around blocks three times sometimes, make my way through alleys, and keep an eye on everyone I see. Anyone I see twice, or even three times, I keep a closer watch on.

But mostly, I just see people like me. People trying to survive. People trying to make their voices heard and people willing to risk it all to stand up against the police.

I walk with the flow of traffic toward the monument in the park about three blocks north. Cops—some in the reinforced armor I have become intimately acquainted with, some in plain clothes—line the streets. But there are more protesters than cops, about ten for every officer. It's a morbid thought, but I think that if we needed to, we could take them, even if we sustained pretty heavy casualties along the way.

I think the cops know this, because none of them is reacting to the protest. I've seen one of those suits in action, and they could easily take on a small crowd. Even if they might not win physically, the intimidation factor isn't something to overlook. But none of them move; they just stand awkwardly off to the side, watching us. Waiting for orders. Or maybe they're waiting for us to get into a confined space so they can take us out all at once.

As I enter the park, these thoughts fill my head to the brim and threaten to push my mind past capacity. I can feel the dull throb of a migraine at the back of my skull, beginning to spread. I do what I can to push it back, to remind myself that this isn't the time for blinding headaches, and do my best to stay focused on finding Marco.

I feel someone grab my shoulder and spin me around with such force that it would have knocked me off balance if I hadn't dug my shoe into the dirt. I'm ready to hit them in the neck with the side of my hand, hard enough to leave them dazed, but the face I see when I turn stops me.

"Where did you go?" Marco breathes out.

I can't hear any anger in his voice—no frustration, just fear. The same fear that's in his brown eyes and painted all over his face. He doesn't look like he's in bad health, doesn't look injured or beaten, doesn't look like he was captured by the police or had to sacrifice his own well-being to get out of the motel. He's changed his clothes and is now dressed in a hideous tie-dye T-shirt, a pair of pants that's a little bit too small, and ratty shoes.

A part of me knows I should answer. But first and foremost, all I want to do is pull him in close and hold him. I squeeze him so tightly, I'm afraid I might break his back or that his body might become one with mine, but at this point, I don't care..

"I'm sorry," I say in one breath. "I'm sorry for leaving you. I'm sorry for not telling you where I was going. I'm sorry for putting you in danger. I'm just…I'm really, really sorry." I murmur the words into his neck, not knowing if he can hear me at all but feeling like my voice vibrating against his skin must be sending signals to his brain.

Marco doesn't release his own hold on my waist, clutching me firmly—maybe not *as* firmly, but the sentiment is the same. "I know," he says quietly. He pulls back, holding me at arm's length, looking me up and down. "You good?"

I nod.

"They didn't hurt you or anything?"

I shake my head. "What about you?"

"Psh," he scoffs, rolling up the sleeve on his right arm and flexing his muscles. Marco isn't exceptionally fit, but there's some definition there. "When you didn't come back, I relocated. I saw the raid on the news."

"So you're not mad at me?"

"Oh, I'm furious," he says, cuffing my shoulder with his fist. "We're going to have to talk about this whole going-off-on-your-own bravado you've got. But no. I figured you had a plan." A beat passes. "You did have a plan, right? You didn't just leave me?"

I can hear the hurt in his voice. I reach forward, squeezing his shoulders. "I won't ever leave you again. I promise."

Marco studies my face, searching for a lie, but eventually he nods. "We're...we're stronger together. You know that, right? And I can't...I can't lose you."

"You won't, I promise," I say, and I know this time I can keep that promise to him. "But first we need to find Catherine. I—"

Marco's face screws into a puzzled expression. I open my mouth to let him know she's still alive, that I overheard it and that we can't—and won't—leave her again. But then Marco turns me around and points. About ten feet from us, standing against a large oak tree with a baseball cap on her head and her hair pulled into a tight bun, is Catherine, doing her best to look inconspicuous—which isn't easy when you're a tall Latinx girl who can punch your way through anything.

"She's alive," I breathe out. Without waiting for Marco, I quickly walk over to her.

Her eyes meet mine moments before I reach her. Catherine holds her hand out enough to stop me from hugging her, but her arm isn't rigid, and I get close enough to feel the warmth coming off her body.

"I'm not a hugger," she says without hesitation, "but I am happy to see you."

I grin. "I've never heard anything more Catherine." I didn't know how much I was going to miss these idiots until we separated. It felt like two-thirds of my body had been ripped off, each of third scattered to different sides of Baltimore. But now that we're together, I feel stronger, like when the sum of two parts is greater than the whole. That's what it's like to be with Catherine and Marco. If I thought before that I could accomplish something, that I could actually fight back against the police, now I feel like we can take on the world.

"What happened to you at the house?" I ask.

Catherine shrugs. "I survived. Barely. Took shoving him from a window on the third floor to escape. Some activists found me and sheltered me. They told me this was going on." She gestures to the protest.

I look around. There are so many people. More than I noticed before. Probably at least two hundred, all of them with signs, some with drums and trumpets and other musical instruments. It's a protest, sure, but one that perfectly and honestly describes our community—there's joy and camaraderie, support and brotherly love.

"I ran into Marco while I was here." She nods to him.

"After you left the motel, I knew something was up," Marco says.

"I was already packed before the cops came. I grabbed the laptop, and got out of there. I saw them break into the motel from across the street. Luckily, one of my Nemesis contacts sent me a message. Good news is, we have a place to stay, and it's not far." He points between two buildings to one of Baltimore's many abandoned complexes. The building, even from a distance, looks uninhabitable, but that's kind of the point, I'm guessing. "No one will look for us there."

"And all of these people are here for…what?" I ask.

"Janna," Marco says confidently.

A wave of panic surges through me. Sure, there are a lot of people here, and numbers are on our side, but I can't help but think about collateral damage and the bodies we saw in the street when this first began. "These people won't stand a chance against their suits. We should try and get as many of them, especially the women and children, somewhere safe."

"They don't care," Marco says. "I told you, Janna was a real pillar of this community. It wasn't long before people found out she'd been taken. Lawyers and other activists tried to get information. Nada. So the people are doing what they do best."

"They're standing up," Catherine finishes. "People protect their own. Janna is their own. She's worth risking it all for."

I curse myself for not asking Chief Coles about Janna. Would asking questions about her safety have given away my end goal? Maybe, or maybe not, but that's in the past now. I feel the USB drive in my pocket and reach out instinctively to grab it.

"About Janna," I say. "Well, about all of us. Is there somewhere we can talk? I have something I want to share with you both."

Catherine and Marco look at me, puzzled. I fish the drive out of my pocket and dangle it in front of them.

"I…" I swallow hard. Saying it makes it all real. It's not just a pipe dream in my head. I actually think this will work. "I think I might have a way to shut down the Dome. Seriously."

There it is. It's out there. There's no turning back now. We're really, actually doing this.

THIRTY

Marco leads us to a hideout a few streets over. "I knew I needed to find someplace to hole up. A Nemesis contact helped me, let me know this was one of their backup safe houses. Hadn't been set up yet, but they had done to work to scrub it from all the Baltimore County databases. It's essentially invisible if you aren't looking for it."

We've escaped just in time. As we cross an intersection, a silver van comes whizzing down one of the side streets. The van has the emblem of the Baltimore Police Department on it, and we all know what will follow.

My body barely tenses as the van zooms by, a stark difference from when this all began. Before, I would have felt immobilized with panic. Now I'm just focused on getting to our destination and counting all the points of egress in case things go south.

"We're here," Marco says. The building is one of those condemned places with caution tape, a lock, and a sign that says KEEP OUT in bright yellow letters. Marco walks around the side of the four-story building, pushing two wooden planks to the side. He holds them graciously so Catherine and I can walk through before pulling a tarp back and revealing an elevated window with a rusted metal frame. Catherine climbs into the room first, and then I follow with Marco helping me.

"You've been in contact with Nemesis?" Catherine asks. "You didn't tell me that."

Marco nods. "Again, when he"—he points to me—"left and I thought you'd been captured, I had to act. I found a website that was still being used for communications, and I was lucky enough that there were some members who avoided being arrested, so they saw the post and responded."

The ground floor is mostly empty. There are a few cots here and there, some bricks and cinder blocks stacked in the corner, and too many tarps to count. It looks like squatters were here at some point, but they probably abandoned it or got locked out. Marco's stuff is under one of the tarps, including his laptop. He grabs it and sits on the cot. I toss him the flash drive.

"What's that?" Catherine asks.

"I'm thinking it could be the code to the Dome. That's what you were thinking before, right? With those dots?"

Marco nods, quickly typing on his computer. "Hmm. It's encrypted. Give me a minute. And yeah, that's possible." His eyes flicker up to me over his laptop. "You went to his place, didn't you?"

I nod.

Marco stops typing. "That was dangerous."

"And it was stupid," Catherine chimes in from the other side of the room. She's casing the place, making sure it's safe. But how safe can it be? Either we'll get caught, or we'll die from whatever's generating that foul smell in the air—I'm pretty sure it's black mold.

"I did what had to be done," I say confidently. "If that's what we think it is, it was worth it, right?"

Catherine shrugs. "I guess."

Marco sighs and goes back to work, muttering, "You're going to be the death of me, aren't you?"

"Probably," I say.

I let Marco do his work in peace while walking around the edge of the room in the opposite direction from Catherine. Two of the windows are still intact, though they're covered with grime and a sickly yellow disgusting film that makes the world seem like I'm looking at it through a layer of water. A few people walk by the window, but no one pays any attention to the building. It's the perfect place to hide, if I'm being honest. For all intents and purposes, the building is on lockdown. No one is getting through those thick, multiple-pronged, government-issued locks.

"Hey, Jamal. Can you come here for a sec?"

I walk over to Marco, who pats the seat on the cot next to him.

"You need some help?" I ask, sitting down next to him. "Fair warning, I'm not good at—"

"You really scared me," he blurts out, never looking up. The screen shows me he's cracked three out of five passcodes. "When you left, you terrified me. I didn't know what had happened to you or where you'd gone. Yeah, I had an idea, but even that was terrifying."

I take a moment to think about how I want to respond to that. I knew he would feel betrayed, and I was pretty sure he'd feel angry—but scared? I guess it makes sense—we had gone from three to two, and then me leaving meant Marco was all alone. This isn't a place where anybody wants to be alone, especially after our run-ins with the police. We are stronger together.

I stand by what I did, especially considering it seems likely Marco will be able to crack the code. But that's not what Marco is saying. Him telling me he was scared is just like these codes. The five letters he's cracking might make a word, but they mean more than that. There's truth hidden behind his confession.

"I'm sorry," I say, reaching over, gripping his hand, and giving it a squeeze. "I didn't think that through."

"Do you ever think things through?" he asks, looking up with a smirk.

"There it is," I whisper out loud before I can stop myself. Marco arches his brow. "Your smile, that boyish charm of yours," I explain. "It's the first thing I noticed about you when you saved me."

The smirk on Marco's lips softens into a gentle smile. If his previous grin was like the sun, the softness of his face now is like a night-light. Comforting. Warm and trustworthy. He takes his right hand and brings it away from the computer, letting it rest against my cheek, his thumb stroking it, our eyes locked.

"Can I kiss you?" he whispers. "I know a run-down, probably hazardous building isn't the ideal place for a first kiss but…"

"We might die today, and it might be the last opportunity we have?"

"Morbid, but yes, basically."

"Well, since we're on the same page, I don't see why not," I say. "Gotta make the most of our last moments, right?"

"Exactly."

Marco leaned forward slowly. I turn my head slightly to the side, our lips connecting. It might sound foolish, but I remember listening to Taylor Swift's "Sparks Fly" a couple of months ago and thinking about how all I wanted to do was kiss Damian while the song played and literal fireworks exploded in the background. It was cliché, but our school always had fireworks for upperclassman prom. I was going to ask him to go with me at the protest. I had built a whole plan for us, culminating in that one kiss.

Marco may think that kissing in this derelict building ruins the moment, but there's no place else I'd rather be, and there's no one else I'd rather be kissing right now.

I don't know how long we kiss, but the computer chirps, and we break apart. Marco slowly pulls back, resting his forehead against my own. He doesn't instantly look at his computer; he doesn't open his eyes, either. He looks at peace just leaning against me. Just…being in the moment.

Slowly, we separate, turning our attention to the computer. There will be time for more kisses and romantic moments once we're done here.

"We're in," he says, loud enough for Catherine to hear.

"Finally." She walks over, standing behind us. Did she see? If she did, she's not commenting on it. Probably for the best.

Marco presses *access* on the screen now that all five passcode boxes are illuminated green. For a moment the computer goes dark, and then files upon files start to appear on his Mac. It's dozens of files—no, hundreds—that fill up the screen. Marco doesn't seem fazed, his fingers moving rapidly across the keyboard and the touch pad. Screen after screen is swiped to the right or the left like he's on Tinder, approving or disapproving information.

I glance up at Catherine, silently asking, *Do you understand what's happening?* She shrugs in reply.

A minute later, after the screen has gone still, Marco leans back, letting out an exhausted sigh. "Do you want the good news or the bad news?" he asks.

"Bad first," both Catherine and I say.

"These aren't plans for the Dome," Marco says.

"Then the good better be *really* good, or—"

Marco interrupts Catherine. "These are specs about their suits. How they were made, who made them, the first designs going all the way back to the eighties, even the first copy of a memo about starting the project…everything."

Marco types out a command. Three pages appear, all of them with one common piece of information: the name Maria Ortiz.

"That's my mom," Catherine gasps.

Marco nods. "Seems like your parents weren't involved only with the Dome but with the suits too. Your mom was an electrical engineer, yeah?"

She nods, leaning forward and resting her weight on both of our shoulders.

"According to this, your parents were against the direction the governor was going," he says. "Your mother was adamantly against the suits. See? This file is dated sixteen weeks ago, and it's a report she issued saying they should be dismantled immediately because of the threat to human lives they posed."

"That's two weeks before she went missing. My father went missing ten days after this."

"I'm guessing they both had issues with what they were working on and stood up to their superiors. Their complaints were deemed enough of a threat for them to be…" Marco pauses, hovering over the right word.

"Removed," I say. It's not the best word, but it doesn't speak into existence what we're all thinking. "Any information on where they are?"

"Give me a sec," Marco mutters.

Marco's fingers move deftly over the keyboard before the screen goes black again and then another file appears. Most of the documents are full of jargon I can't understand, but on every page, on every document, there's one signature that we all pick up on.

"Governor Lydia Ambrose," Marco says, his eyes flickering across the screen. "Her name is on every one of these documents."

"So she was in on this?" Catherine asked. "On all of this? She had to be, right?"

Marco nods. "We don't have proof of that. Correlation doesn't mean causation, but yes, I think it's safe to say that—Here it is." He taps the screen, finding the document about Catherine's parents that he was looking for. "Looks like they're in New York," he says. "The last document is from…six days ago. They're in a holding facility there. Camp Trevor?"

"It's a work camp," Catherine says, vitriol dripping from her voice. "I thought it was a rumor. One of my commanding officers joked about it. Like when a parent tells a kid, *If you misbehave, Santa is going to give you coal.* He was always dangling it over us. *Work hard, or I'll send you to Camp Trevor."*

"We'll get them back," I promise.

"How?!" Catherine booms, pushing back away from us. "We can't even get out of Baltimore, let alone get to New York. You think they're going to just, what, let us walk in and check my parents out like a library book? It's a government facility! It's not—"

"I have a plan," I interrupt.

That's only half true. The words leave my mouth before I've thought them through. I have an idea, or the beginnings of one. The pieces are floating around in my head like completely distinct thought bubbles that haven't yet come together to make one giant cohesive idea. But I can see it forming, and if I'm being honest, it's pretty out there. But considering everything I've seen, everything I've learned since being inside the Dome, and all of my history and psychology classes, this might actually work. Maybe. If we're lucky.

And we've been lucky so far.

Both Marco and Catherine look at me with surprise.

"Well," Marco says, "don't keep us waiting."

"It's insane."

"I don't care," Catherine promises. "If there's a chance it could help my parents, I'm down."

"It's one of those high-risk, high-reward things."

"Catherine seems like the type of person who thrives with those odds," Marco teases. "Besides, all your other plans have been successful. What's to say this one won't be? I, for one, trust you. Catherine?"

Catherine nods. "But look, don't let this go to your head. I was perfectly comfortable doing all this by myself. I just helped you and Marco because I could see you needed me. You were going to die out here."

"Real reassuring," I drone, and roll my eyes.

"But," she says, "you're smart. Both of you. You know how to react and when to act instinctively. That's not something you can teach. I wouldn't have gotten this far without you, and no matter what happens with your plan, if we succeed or if we fail, I'll know we tried, and there's no one else I'd rather fail or succeed with than you two. So whatever your plan is, I'm a hundred percent in. And I'm going to give it my all."

"Same." Marco smiles, standing up. "Lay it on us, babe."

"All right, all right." Catherine raises her hands. "I'm all for love, but can we keep that to a minimum until, you know, we actually succeed?"

Marco shrugs. "Seems fair to me."

"All right," I say, and take a deep breath. "Here's the plan."

THIRTY-ONE

Marco, Catherine, and I spend the next two hours going over the plan. Part of that time is me explaining it to them 234 times, while the other half is Catherine and Marco poking holes in it and patching them up with their own makeshift solutions. By the end of the discussion, we have a solid idea of what we're doing, and everybody has their roles.

"All right," Catherine says, checking the alleyway before jumping out of our hideout. "Coast is clear."

Marco and I follow. Marco, like before, helps me out the window even though I don't need it. I don't tell him that, though. I think helping me gives him a sense of purpose.

"Everyone know their jobs?" he asks. We both nod. "Repeat them back to me."

"I'm going to go and get the suit from where I hid it and meet you all in the park," Catherine says. "We're going to use it to draw the cops' attention away from any civilians protesting."

"I'm going to meet up with my Nemesis contact at the radio

station. That should give me the range I need to broadcast the override code I reverse engineered from tinkering with Catherine's suit we found and use it to shut down the barrier the suits produce." Marco explains. "I'm pretty confident I can make a feedback loop that'll incapacitate all of them."

"*Pretty* confident?" Catherine asks.

"I'm a hundred percent confident. The code is shoddy. That's what happens when you rush into building something. The suits have to be activated for me to make the loop. They're all connected; their visors allow them to share intel with one another. If there are enough active suits in one space, I'm confident I can hijack that signal—"

"And turn off all the suits." Catherine nods. "Genius."

"All of them except yours," he says. "You're off the network. You're on your own."

I nod to both of them. "And the other thing?" I ask Marco.

"The last-resort plan? Yeah, Nemesis can help with that, too. The code can be used for both plans." A beat passes, and Marco adds, "We're not going to have to use that, right? Right?"

Catherine and I glance at each other, a silent exchange. We both understand that there's a chance we won't make it out. Catherine's probably most at risk. But no one wants to say that out loud. No one wants to admit we could lose, or die. But if it comes to that—if we actually fail—we need to make sure our work doesn't die with us. That's what the last-resort program is for. To give other people the ammunition they need to continue this fight.

I hope.

"We should give it a name," Marco says. "All great programs that go down in history have a name."

"It doesn't need a name," Catherine rolls her eyes. "That's dumb."

"Oh, come on! That's what makes it cool." Marco looks to me for support.

I shrug. "If we make it out of here, we're going to want to have something the history books can use to describe what we did."

"Oh my god, you're actually entertaining this idea."

"How about Operation…" I pause. "Operation Zahn?"

Marco and Catherine look at me with a blank expression.

"Person to make the first camera?"

"No one is going to know who that is," Marco replies slowly.

"Do they need to know?"

"I mean, I imagine they should at least get the reference."

"I'm not sure that—"

"Operation Jamaica," Catherine interrupts. "*J* for Jamal, *M* for Marco, *C* for me. Jamaica."

Marco and I look at her, and then our eyes settle on each other. For a moment, I can't tell what he thinks about the name, but then he shrugs.

"It works," he says. "And it's clever."

"Works for me," I reply.

Silence falls between us. The debate on the title was a good distraction, for a moment, but soon we'll have to execute this risky plan. One wrong move, one thing that goes left instead of right, and it all goes to hell.

"Preparation is the key to success," I mutter under my breath.

"Sorry?" Catherine asks.

I shake my head, going back to the topic. "Marco you have your marching orders. You too, Catherine."

"And you?" Marco asks, gesturing to me.

"I'm going to National Harbor to be the bait."

That's not *exactly* what I'm going to do, but it's the easiest way to explain it. I have the closest connection with the police, and if I see Chief Coles, he's less likely to shoot and kill me then he is the other two. I understand Chief Coles. He is going to be where the action is, the biggest protest, the largest arrests. It's the narcissist in him.

And then, once we have them all incapacitated, we'll use *him* as bait for the governor. We're no longer on the defensive; we're not trying to get outside the Dome. We're going to bring her inside.

Catherine and Marco both have their own roles to play. The plan will fall apart if any one of us fails. We need to increase the likelihood of us all succeeding by separating and making our fates independent, not tied to one another.

Catherine nods. "We can do this," she says. "We've survived worse before, and we've made it out alive. We have the upper hand here."

"I'm not sure if that's your version of a pep talk, but it sucked," Marco scolds.

"Look, I'm trying."

He smiles and squeezes her shoulder. "I'm just playing with you."

Catherine smiles and squeezes back.

"All right," I choke out. "Let's go."

My feet feel like they're stuck to the pavement, as if my body doesn't want to move, but I forced myself to lift one foot at a time. Catherine nods and gives a two-finger salute before darting straight across the street, keeping her body low and leaving Marco and me alone.

"Hey," Marco says. "Be safe, all right?"

"I will."

"Promise me you'll come back," he says sternly.

"I could say the same to you. And Catherine."

"You could, but right now I'm concerned with you. Promise me."

"You've got me covered, right? You can—"

"I can do it," he promises. "I'm not going to abandon you."

"Then I'm not alone." I reach over and give his hand a squeeze. "Now, go. You have the longest distance to travel."

"Right." He pauses, then takes his watch off his right wrist and hands it to me. "You'll need this to keep track of time and for Catherine to find you. I put a tracking chip in it."

"Just in case?" I grin.

He quickly kisses my cheek. "Just in case."

My heart races, and my cheek burns. I want to kiss him back, to stay in this moment, but instead, I simply nod back.

"Go," I encourage. If he stays much longer, he won't leave at all—I know, because I'm thinking the same thing. Staying here with him is easier. Safer. Better.

But we have a job to do.

Marco stares at me before nodding and heading left. I watch his back until I can't see it anymore, then go right, back toward the city and one of the bigger protests—the one by National Harbor.

I don't take the light rail this time, instead relying on my own legs to get me there. There's something relaxing about the jog, about the burn in my legs and in my lungs. I was never a kid who really liked gym class, but I appreciated Coach Sawyer because of how much he instilled a concern for heart health in us. The mile-and-a-half jog barely winds me.

I'm hit with a wave of people the moment I get downtown. I've never estimated how many people are stuck under the Dome, but it seems like every brown and Black person inside is down here in National Harbor. It's reminiscent of before, when I first got to Baltimore. People have signs that say HANDS UP, DON'T SHOOT and LOWER THE WALLS AND LET US OUT and JUSTICE FOR JEROME.

A pang of panic pulses through my body, though not nearly as strong as before. I've come to accept that all these people know there will be consequences for their actions, and the consequences are going to come tenfold. Flashes of memories from history class flood my mind: pictures of people being sprayed with water cannons during civil rights protests or dogs biting people's legs on the streets of Alabama. But instead of generating a fear response, it generates something stronger. It grounds me like a live wire of electricity, once rogue, now under my control.

"Where are you, where are you…" I whisper, weaving through the crowd. I check my watch again. Marco and Catherine said they needed twenty minutes to get into place. It took about fourteen minutes for me to get downtown. Fourteen minutes for a mile and a half isn't horrible. But that only gives me six minutes to make this work. Six minutes to do what I need to do. Six…

A tug on my leg causes me to jump back. I turn quickly and notice a familiar face staring up at me.

"You," I breathe, grabbing the girl—the same girl from my first night under the Dome. I pick her up and rush into a side street. It's less crowded than the main street, which is flooded with people. Kneeling down at her level, I examine her. She looks fine—no bruises, no wounds, nothing. "You made it," I ask, not expecting a response. "You're not with the police?"

She shakes her head and wraps her arms around my neck.

"Oh, baby," I whisper, holding her close. "I got you, all right? I got you." I rub her back. How did she…but it doesn't matter. It means there might be others.

I pick her up and stand, not minding her weight as she clings to my body. For a moment, a brief moment, I think about abandoning this mission. I can't keep her safe and do what I promised Marco and Catherine. And taking her with me, putting her in harm's way, is wrong.

But what if this is our only chance?

"Hey," I whisper, nudging her. The girl turns her head toward me. "I need to do something. And it's going to be scary and danger-ous. Do you understand what I'm saying? It's going to be scarier and more dangerous than this." I gesture. "You don't need to come with me; I'll find you again. I won't leave you, I promise, but I have to—"

She clings to me, holding on to my body, tight enough that it makes my shoulder tingle from lack of blood flow.

"Okay, okay," I say, patting her side. "I guess that's not an option."

Either I don't do this, or I do it with her—there are no other choices. Neither option is good, and I don't have a way to communicate with Marco and Catherine to tell them we need to come up with a new plan. Sighing, I squeeze the girl tighter.

"I guess we're doing this," I whisper. "Into the beast we go."

I hike the girl up higher to lessen the weight on my arm and hip and get walking, one foot after the other. I go with the flow of traffic, heading toward the Hyatt downtown. From the top of a hill, I can see the wall of police officers, all in their mechanized suits, standing in a row. That's where I need to be. The watch on my wrist will act as a beacon. We're not going to get a second chance, so I need to get as close as possible.

"Okay," I whisper. "This is it." I smile at her nervously, hoping it reaches my eyes and she can't see my fear or feel my shaking. "We've got this."

I walk forward quickly, using my free arm like a battering ram to pierce through the sea of people. As I walk deeper and deeper into the protests, it gets denser and denser, harder to push through. But I don't stop. I just hold on to the girl tighter, making sure not to let go of her or hurt her, using my free hand to make a path for us.

Once we're at the front of the line, standing with other activists who are yelling and screaming at the cops, I survey the area. He has to be somewhere; Chief Coles wouldn't just leave. He was already downtown. It would be natural for—

"There you are."

He's standing with two other cops, dressed in their armored suits. Their helmets are down, except for Chief Coles's, and they're talking rapidly. It looks like Chief Coles is giving them orders, like a coach during a football game. I think that's a perfect analogy for how he views this. It's not a fight to the death or a discussion about who's right and who's wrong, who is viewed as more important. For him, this is just a game. It's just sport. He's the hunter, and we are the prey.

I hold on tighter to the girl and weave my way through the crowd until I'm standing relatively close to him. It only takes a few seconds for him to recognize me. There's surprise on his face, but there's also boiling anger. He claps the shoulder of one of the cops, gives it a squeeze, and I can see his mouth saying, *You have your orders* before he turns to me.

"I told you not to come here," he says loudly when he approaches, a barrier the only thing separating us.

"You knew I was going to come," I yell back.

"I was hoping I was wrong about you. That you weren't as stupid as everyone else."

"Funny," I retort. "I knew everything about you the first moment I met you, and you've yet to change my mind."

His jaw twitches in frustration, and he clenches both fists by his sides to still himself, like he's grounding himself during a thunderstorm. Chief Coles takes a deep breath before barking one of the officers' names. A short blond man appears almost instantly.

"Arrest him," Chief Coles says. "I'll deal with him later."

I take a step back. The blond officer pauses, looking at me and then at his superior. "And the girl?" he asks. "What should—"

"Take her too," Chief Coles says.

"Absolutely fucking not," I growl back. Bystanders nearby, who have mostly kept up their chanting until now, join the conversation.

"You're not taking this boy or this girl," a dark-skinned woman says.

"We are not letting you hurt our children anymore," an older man with stark white hair barks.

"You'll have to get through us," an Asian man about five years older than me says.

"I have absolutely no problem with that," Chief Coles says coolly. "Men!" he booms. "You heard them. If they aren't going to come quietly, then we'll treat them as hostile forces."

All at once, the officers smoothly stand at attention. There are only maybe twenty of them, all wearing the same SWAT-like uniforms with long pants and long-sleeve shirts that I've grown to fear. They each tap a button at their waist, and the same ripple of white light as when we fought Officer Lewis pools over their bodies, protecting them from damage.

Half the cops raise their guns. The other half raise their batons. But none of the protesters move. No one runs. Everyone stands together.

We win together, we lose together.

"Kneel," Chief Coles growls out, low enough for only me to hear. I take the girl and put her down. I slowly move in front of her, using my body as a shield. The dark-skinned Black woman on my left does the same, and the heavyset man on my right follows suit. Like centurions, we close our ranks.

"Fuck you," I spit out.

With a flick of Coles's right hand, the first wave of officers moves forward, the ones with the batons. In a flash, there are fists and kicks, screams and curses. It's like a giant pool of limbs and metal rods flailing together. But I'm focused on only one thing; keeping the girl safe.

Thwap!

The sound is hollow in my head, but the feeling of dizziness as I get hit by a cop floods my vision. I feel my body fall forward and hit the ground. I taste blood in my mouth. So much blood. I fold my body inward to protect both myself and the girl, curling around my vital organs. Each thump hurts, but it's not unbearable.

The question, of course, is for how long.

Eventually I won't be able to take it anymore. I'll be faced with two choices: beg for mercy, or watch my body be torn apart. Can I last until Catherine gets here? I keep telling myself, *Just five more seconds*, and then, when that passes, *Just five more seconds*. She'll be here. Our plan will succeed. I have to believe that. I have to trust them.

And then, just like that, everything stops. Not the pain—my whole body is throbbing. But the beating, the screams of agony, and the warlike cries from the cops. It's…silent. I loosen my grip on the girl, knowing I probably bruised her arms, but at least she's alive.

I open my eyes and look around. About three-quarters of the crowd is just like me: in defensive positions, bloody, beaten, bruised. But the cops? That's a different story. They're like statues, petrified, the glow around them much like the glow from the Dome, like an aura around their bodies.

And just like Marco promised, they can't move.

I slowly stand, still clutching the girl tightly in my arms. I pull her face away from my shoulder and examine her, noticing she doesn't have a single wound on her body. *Good*, I think. At least something positive came out of this.

"Hey," I hear a familiar voice say. Catherine weaves through the crowd, her visor activated so I can't see her eyes. Sure enough, there's no glow around her body. "You okay?"

I nod. "I'll be fine. You?"

She nods in return. "Sorry it took so long. I had to get the suit on, and then I ran into a cop, and it was a whole thing. Marco came through right on time."

"You got here; that's all that matters."

Catherine nods and gestures to me with a wide swipe of her hand. "Well, your move. This was your plan, after all. This all relies on you now."

I nod, looking to the girl in my arms again, smiling and pushing her baby hairs out of her face. I look around until I find someone who seems trustworthy. The woman with the dreadlocks who's standing about three feet from me seems perfect. I bridge the gap between us, gently handing the girl over.

"Take care of her for me, will you?" I ask.

The woman takes her cautiously and nods. "It would be my honor."

I walk back over to Catherine and step over the railing between the cops and us. Chief Coles did exactly what I expected him to do: he's ordered almost every cop here to suit up, which means almost every cop here is immobile. The few that aren't? They aren't going to be much of a match for Catherine or the hundreds of angry

Baltimore citizens they've been terrorizing. Their hesitation to do anything seems to mean they understand that.

"Go," I tell them. "You're not going to win this, and you know it. Chief Coles isn't worth this. Any of it. Just leave and go back to your families."

"Don't you even think about leaving," Chief Coles threatens.

Without hesitation, Catherine hits him on the side of the head. "You're not really in a place to make demands, are you? Just shut up for once in your life."

I watch the officers debate whether leaving is the right thing to do. They steal glances at one another as if silently communicating through some hive mind before coming to a decision. One steps back, then another, then another, until the whole group of them is fleeing.

"You COWARDS!" Officer Coles roars. "You can kiss your careers—"

"I. Said. Shut. Up. And. Listen," Catherine reminds him, hitting his head over and over. "Jesus, you white people can never learn to just sit and be quiet. Do you think there's a way for Marco to mute their mouths?"

"Sorry, I can't do that," Marco chimes in.

I turn to see him jogging down the street about five feet behind us. He waves, weaving through the crowd to join us at the front, smiling proudly.

"Wow," he says, surveying his work. "I really did that, didn't I?"

"Don't let it go to your head," Catherine warns. "We aren't out of the woods yet. Jamal?"

I nod. "Right." I move over to stand in front of Chief Coles.

"What in the hell do you want?" he growls.

"Simple," I say, making sure my voice doesn't vibrate with nervousness. "I want you to get the governor down here right now."

THIRTY-TWO

Marco uses his skills to allow Chief Coles's suit to perform one outgoing call to a specific number after vetting that the number is the governor's. The call lasts barely a minute before Chief Coles tells us the good news.

"She'll be here in an hour."

Everyone, and I mean everyone, does their part, even the people I haven't assigned roles. Catherine gets to work hauling Chief Coles's immobile body into the nearest building. Even without instructions, the rest of the protesters, the Black and brown community of Baltimore, does what it does best when empowered: It takes care of its own. People who aren't wounded help people who are get to the side of the street and patch up their injuries with the few medical supplies we find in abandoned stores.

The woman holding the little girl finds me and taps me on my shoulder. "I'm going to take her to my home," she says. "Are you okay with that?"

"Is it out of the danger zone?" I ask.

"As much as any of us can be." There's a sardonic smile playing on her lips, and I can't help but smile back. She's right—especially now, everywhere is dangerous. "But yes, it's far from here. Twelve-forty Rockwood Ave. She'll be safe there. It's far away from the protests."

My eyes grow wide. "There are more?"

"Hell yeah, there are more!" cheers a random guy with tattoos all over his arms from about ten feet away. "All over the city, especially now that everyone knows what you all just did."

It takes me a moment to understand what he means. What he's referring to is how Marco and Catherine and I shut down the cops' suits. I guess it didn't really hit me what an accomplishment that is until now. These cops have been terrorizing Baltimore, and their suits have given them a stranglehold on the city with no repercussions. And here we are—three teens with a little bit of luck, intelligence, and perseverance, who found a way to cripple their system. Will it last? Probably not. But that doesn't matter. It's a victory for now.

And a victory is what we needed.

"Sure," I say to the woman. "I'll find her when I can."

She nods and smiles, reaching over and cupping my cheek. I don't mind the softness of her hand, and her golden-brown eyes calm me in a way I didn't even know I needed. It's refreshing to be still, just for a moment.

"Your mother would be proud of you," she says softly.

A pang of emotion almost makes me double over, but I force myself to stand tall. I smile at her, and then at the girl, then lean over and kiss her cheek. "I'll be back, and once this is all over, we'll find your mom and dad. Promise."

I hope I can keep that promise.

"Jamal!" I hear Marco call from the building across the street. He points in the opposite direction, and I see what he's referring to.

A fleet of black cars coming this way.

"You need to get out of here," I say to the woman. "All of you."

Do I think the governor of Maryland will drop a metaphorical atom bomb on this street? No, but I know she's connected to the Dome somehow, and the suits. Her name was on every document we read. And if this is her creation, that means this monstrous reality is something she's comfortable with. And a person who thinks like that, who's willing to sacrifice people's lives like that, is someone we have to be wary of.

The woman nods, and the man with the tattoos joins her. "I can help. I have a motorcycle up ahead."

"I'm hoping you have some helmets too?" she asks.

"Yeah, I do."

The woman arches her brows. The man sighs. "Yes, ma'am, I do."

"Better." Turning back to me for the last time, the woman whispers, "Be safe."

"I promise I will," I tell her. That's not just a hope anymore, or wishful thinking. I'm not going down without a fight. We've come so far, and I can practically taste and smell the fresh air, like I did when I was at Chief Coles's house. There's an end in sight, an end where this Dome gets shut down, allowing everyone here to get out safely.

I can do it.

We can do it.

We got this.

"Wait!" I yell, turning to the man I jog over, take a deep breath, and say words I never thought I'd say. "Weird question, but...you don't happen to have a gun, by any chance?"

———

"I hate department stores."

It feels a little weird that our last stand is, yes, inside an abandoned department store. And it's not just abandoned because of looting or the chaos of the Dome; this department store probably hasn't been occupied for at least a year. There are mannequins all over the place, warped floorboards and walls, and old sale signs promising 20 percent off if we open a store card. The building has an open floor plan. There are only two exits: one behind us, and one in front of us, allowing us to control the flow of this conversation. There's enough space, and there are places to hide if we need to. This is the best place we could find.

"Where do you shop for your clothes, then?" Marco mutters.

"Amazon," Catherine replies, shifting her weight from right to left. "They have great deals."

"Oh, that's...tragic. Once this is all over, we're going shopping. For real."

"That's what you want to do with your newfound life? Shop for clothes?"

Marco shrugs. "I miss looking good. And how am I going to stomach taking this hunk"—he juts his thumb toward me—"on a date if I don't look spicy?"

"Is that a joke because you're Latino?" I ask.

"Shut up," Catherine and Marco say together, smirking at me.

While waiting and trying our best to ignore the grumbles and curse words Chief Coles is lobbing into the air, we're all thinking the same thing, even if we don't talk about it. Everything we've worked for has come down to this one moment. Despite how hard we've tried to take it back, the power lies with the governor. And if she's the person who came up with the Dome and the suits, how generous and kind can she be?

"Whatever happens," Catherine mutters, "we've got each other's backs, right?"

"Of course," I say without hesitation.

"You know it," Marco adds. "I wouldn't want to be with any other losers besides you two."

I open my mouth to reply with what I think is a pretty stellar comeback, but before I can, the far doors burst open. Two men enter in boxy black suits, obviously hiding some sort of body armor and gun holsters, and there she is: Governor Ambrose.

Governor Ambrose is a good-looking woman in her midforties, flawless skin, a small nose, and sharp, alert eyes. She's tall, five foot eleven or so, but she stands even taller in her cigarette pants and black stiletto heels. She's fashionable, which is one of the main things people noted on the campaign trail, wearing a jacket, a purple ascot, and a dark shirt with white trim. Considering everything that's happening, considering Baltimore is practically in flames, I'm surprised she looks so poised and relaxed.

Her heels click as she walks toward us, stopping about five feet away. Her guards stand six feet behind her.

"Showtime," Marco mutters, nodding at me. "You're up. You got this."

I swallow thickly and nod. It feels like the start of a sports game, how the two captains meet in the middle of the room. Except this is a game of life and death.

I don't have a speech planned, though I wish I did, so going with my gut is probably best. I open my mouth to speak, but she holds her hand up.

"I have one question," she says. "You got me here. You've got my attention. What next? Have you thought this through?"

Elegantly, she gestures to Chief Coles. "You've bested the chief of police—bravo. He's an idiot, so that's not that hard. But what's next? You're smart enough to know that when you have your opponent against the ropes, that's the time to ask for what you want. An internship, perhaps? We can make that happen."

Does she think I just did this to get her *attention*? I stare at her, trying to see if there's any remorse or shame on her face. But all I see is a woman who's annoyed to be here. Like the only thing that matters here is her and her time.

And then it clicks.

"You don't care, do you?" I finally say. "About what you did here? About what your Dome—"

"Let me stop you there...Jamal, that's your name, right?" I don't nod, but she continues, "What I've created, this Dome, is the future of dealing with insurgents and violent areas. Do you know how many soldiers we lose per year because we force them to go into harm's way? Too many. Do you know how many cops we lose because of violence? Those are men and women willing to risk their lives to help keep our cities safe. This Dome will allow...how do I put it...it will allow violent areas to fight among themselves, to keep our people, our citizens, from dying."

"Citizens you deem are worth living," I add. "The Dome doesn't stop people from fighting, it just stops people from seeing it. You're just isolating those you don't want the rest of the world to see."

"If people cannot act properly, they deserve to be isolated," she replies without missing a beat. "Think of it as creating a sort of *time-out* so the violent offenders can calm down. I'm doing a service not only to our country, but to the whole world."

"And let me guess—you needed to advertise your service to the world, and Baltimore was your test subject?"

She grins. "See? You're as smart as I thought you were."

"But it's not only that, is it?" I ask. "The press conferences, how cavalierly you talk about everything in public...you know how to play the game. You picked Baltimore on purpose. Because you know, or at least you assume, that the United States will move on and forget the atrocities you've done to Black people the moment you 'prove' that the Dome makes their lives better, even in the smallest way. No one will say it out loud, of course. But if you can market it as a tool that keeps families together, that prevents people from going to war, then people will side with you. They'll think this is all worth it. That you did the right thing."

"My, my, you *are* smart."

My blood begins to boil, like it's trying to erode my veins and flood out of every orifice. The screams and panicked sounds from when we first arrived here fill my brain, but that's not what I'm thinking about the most. It's not the beatings Marco and I received, not the multiple run-ins with the police that almost cost me my life. It's that little girl. We have no idea if her parents are alive, or where they are, and it's reasonable to assume she might never see them again.

That's all I can picture when I see Governor Ambrose's face.

"Then I know what I want," I say quietly. I walk over to Chief Coles, who's tied up, arms behind his back around one of the columns. Standing at his side, I pull out the gun I got from the protester and hold it to his head. "You either shut down the Dome, or I'm going to blow a hole in his head. Your choice."

THIRTY-THREE

A heavy silence takes over the room as I point the gun at Chief Coles's head. My arm is shaking, but I can't feel it. In fact, I can't feel anything. My whole body is numb. The blood pumping in my head is so loud, so overwhelming, that it takes all of my energy to focus on Governor Ambrose. Two of her security details raise their guns and point them at me. Catherine, in the corner of my eye, activates her suit, pointing the AK-47 on the right arm at them. Marco has found shelter behind one of the pillars, because right now, hacking isn't really a useful skill.

But Governor Ambrose hasn't moved. She doesn't seem flustered or angry. She's just studying me, trying to understand me, without saying a single word.

Finally she speaks, but due to the blood in my head, all I can do is read her lips.

"You think I care?"

I take a moment to let my body recalibrate, for the sounds and feelings to return, before I speak. The gun is heavier than I thought it would be, and the metal is warm from my hand. It fits snugly, more snugly than I'd like to admit, and I can feel the power it has. I can understand why people have guns, how they make them feel like… *more* than others.

"The reason I ask that, Jamal, is because I fail to see the point of this whole charade. You have a suit—bravo—but I have more men than you, at least in this room. Two here, three outside, and two more cars. We have the numbers and the training. You won't make it out of here if you shoot him."

"Getting out was never my goal."

The words surprise even me when they come out of my mouth, but they fit into a slot I've been trying to fill since we arrived here. Everything has felt off since we've been in the Dome, and I've just chalked it up to the fact that we were like caged animals. But I think the truth of the matter is that I never really thought we would make it out alive. Not really, not deep down. Marco, Catherine, and I have been playing at being heroes this whole time. But when would our luck run out? Logically speaking, it would be before we achieved our goal of exposing Governor Ambrose.

But in the long run, survival isn't what's important; proving those in power can be thwarted is. Because ideas never die—that's one thing I've learned from my mom when she talks about our history as Black people. People may not live on, but the impressions they leave last forever.

"Do you hear that sound? Outside?" I ask her.

"I don't hear—"

"Listen," I seethe. "Really listen."

Governor Ambrose sighs in frustration, crossing her arms over her chest, but she does as I ask. She closes her eyes, showing an amount of trust that I think is unwise in this situation. Her breath stills, and her brows furrow slightly, like she's picking up on what I'm referring to.

"That's the sound of people all over the city fighting back. You may have the numbers here in this room, but there are thousands, if not tens of thousands, of angry people of color willing to lay down their lives for what they believe in. For their freedom.

"You're a smart woman, Governor Ambrose. You're one of the youngest governors in history, and you're definitely the youngest governor of Maryland, in addition to being the first female governor. I'm a journalist, and I like to think I'm a pretty good student. I did a report on you last year for class. This Dome is a horrible idea, but it personifies something you've always been: bold. You have something that few politicians have—forethought and foresight. I imagine you think that will take you far, maybe all the way to the White House. I'm sure you can see when I'm trying to tell you. I have a feeling you're a type of person who can see three to five moves ahead during a chess game.

"In the long run, even if you take my friends and me down, even if you leave the Dome up, and even if you find comfort in the fact that no information can leave Baltimore right now, eventually everyone will know what happened here. The news will get out, and you'll lose any hope you have of seeing your dreams become a reality."

"And you'll have to deal with jail time," Marco chimes in.

"Something tells me you're not the type of person who would do well in prison."

In AP Psychology, we learned that if you want to get someone to do something, you have to present it in a way that's related to their interests. Very few people do things because they're the right things to do; they do them because their actions, or lack thereof, affect their own well-being. Governor Ambrose is the perfect example of that. She doesn't care that the Dome is unethical or that people are dying; all she cares about is how it affects her trajectory to success. So I'm hoping that if I show her she's putting her own well-being in danger by keeping it up and ignoring our demands, she'll be more susceptible to doing what we want.

But it could completely backfire. She could see the threat as a challenge and feel the need to assert her authority. She's a woman in the very male-dominated field of politics, and showing any weakness isn't beneficial for a president-to-be.

What's that saying? *The United States of America does not negotiate with terrorists?*

Something tells me that when the history books are written about this situation, we'll be viewed as the terrorists. Not much different from how history usually views Black and brown people.

Finally, the governor's porcelain right cheek twitches once. I hold my breath and tighten my sweaty grip on the gun, waiting for her to give her verdict. Even now, when I have a weapon pointed at the chief of police, she still has all the power.

"What's to stop me from just killing you all right here, including Chief Coles?" she says.

"The fail-safe," Marco, Catherine, and I say together.

"If I don't enter a certain code on a certain computer in the next two hours, it'll trigger a chain reaction code that'll send a file filled with videos of all the atrocities done to the people of Baltimore to every major news network on the East Coast. You won't be able to escape that."

"And people say hacking isn't a valuable skill," Marco grins.

"See, now I know you're lying," Governor Ambrose says. "The Dome keeps everything inside; you should know that by now. Surely you've tried to get a message out. And besides, the suits keep you from recording them with any digital device."

"And you don't know technology," Marco snaps, "or understand its power. Nemesis says hi, by the way. All we need is one computer constantly trying to upload a file, and eventually it'll get through; the moment you lower the Dome, that video is going online."

"And you underestimate the power of people," I add. "We're not uploading videos of your cops. We're uploading firsthand accounts: videos of bruised, beaten people, blood in the streets, destroyed homes. We're going to make people see. We're going to make people *feel* what you did."

"Where did you even get—"

"The suits," Catherine chimes in. "Those body cameras you had installed? I'm not a super tech nerd like my friend here, but hacking them wasn't hard."

"Every video any of your cops took from their suits has been compiled into a video to be uploaded. That's all the proof we need, a first-person perspective," Marco adds.

"Kinda poetic, isn't it?" I ask. "The thing you thought, I'm guessing, you could use as a last resort, the photos and videos you could manipulate to tell the narrative you want, will be the nail in your coffin?"

For a moment—just a moment—I see Governor Ambrose's face break. Anger explodes across her features for a fraction of a second. But they return to smooth, calm perfection a moment later.

"And if I were to do what you want—and I'm not saying I will—what are your demands?"

My eyes flicker to Catherine and Marco, who both nod.

"We have some ideas," I say. "Six of them, actually. One, which I think is pretty obvious, is that you shut down the Dome immediately. Give us the code, and you forget about this little project of yours. That is nonnegotiable."

Governor Ambrose pushes her lips into a thin line, her eyes narrowing. Her chest expands, and a slow sigh leaves her lips. "And the others?"

"Two," Catherine says, "you let Maria and Hernando Ortiz go. They are—"

"I know exactly who they are," Governor Ambrose interrupts. "You're their daughter, aren't you? You have your mother's eyes and your father's spunk."

"Cute. Three: you resign. And before you say that's too much, you've served as governor of Maryland once already. You have a good record. Not a great one, but a good one. Say that you think someone else could lead Maryland better after what happened here in Baltimore."

"Four," I chime in, "and this helps cover your ass, actually—you pin everything that happened on Chief Coles."

"You don't seriously think—"

"I don't care what lie you tell to make it happen," I bark. "You're going to do it. Not only does it help you, but Chief Coles here needs to answer for what happened to Jerome Thomas. The law has let him off. This is his punishment. I'm sure you have the resources to make the story stick."

"People won't believe he's responsible for the Dome. I held a press conference praising it as my invention."

"You're smart, I'm sure you can spin some story about how a man drunk on power and vision seduced you with his hope for the future. Say you finally came to your senses or something. I don't care. One thing you are, Governor Ambrose, is a good manipulator. You won't come out unscathed, but the other option is far worse."

The room falls silent. I should be shaking, I should be terrified, but the adrenaline pumping through me keeps me going. Governor Ambrose could say no; she could turn around and spit in my face. This could turn into a bloodbath if we aren't careful, and then what?

All of this basically hinges on how strong Governor Ambrose's sense of self-preservation is.

Finally, she speaks. "I suppose I can make that work."

"Are you fucking serious?!" Chief Coles roars, yanking at his restraints like a wild animal. "I did *everything* for you! This was your idea! And you're just going to—"

"Quiet. The adults are talking," Governor Ambrose scolds, never breaking eye contact with me. "You have two more requests?"

"Five," Marco says, stepping forward, "you let Janna Williams go with no charges—I know you have her—along with any other protesters you're keeping locked up. And six, you give me every single fragment of code you have on the Dome and let me watch you and your people turn it off."

"None of these things, I remind you, are negotiable," I say. "All six of them need—"

"I agree," she interrupts. "I agree to your terms. And in return, you'll not only give me that suit you have and that video you claim exists, but you'll also sign an affidavit swearing you to secrecy."

I look over at Catherine and Marco, who nod without hesitation.

"Once we're out of the Dome and safe, Marco will send you the location of the laptop," I say, lowering the gun slowly from Chief Coles's head and pocketing it. I rub my palms together to get rid of any evidence, like that will actually do anything. It's not like the gun is loaded. I don't even know how to shoot a gun.

I turn to Governor Ambrose and nod as well.

"Now, shall we get to work?"

THIRTY-FOUR

As I imagine everything in Governor Ambrose's life is, following the six rules we set forth is a very methodical process.

First, her men untie Chief Coles and escort him outside with handcuffs around his wrists. The whole time, he spits and snarls and curses and throws a creative volley of derogatory slang I have never heard before at the three of us—and Governor Ambrose. She seems unfazed. She doesn't even look his way when he screams her name and promises she'll regret this.

"If I were a dollar richer every single time a man said I would regret something…" she muses.

Next, after we all walk outside, one of the men in her security detail pulls Marco aside and makes several phone calls with him standing next to her. I see his face light up when she confirms that Janna has been let go. The man pulls a laptop out of the car, enters a string of code—which Marco watches diligently. He then turns the laptop to Governor Ambrose, who presses her finger against a scanner on the computer, and then hands it to Marco.

"Access to the Dome's code is through this terminal here," she says. "You'll want to…"

"I know how a shut-down works," Marco says, rolling his eyes and snatching the laptop from the man. "Do I trust you to actually say the code does what it says it does, though? Absolutely not."

Marco steps off to the side, leaning against a wall, scanning the screen. He stands by himself for at least fifteen minutes, eyes darting back and forth. Leaning against Catherine and feeling exhaustion take over me, I let my eyes settle on Marco and how diligently he works.

He's attractive when he's focused.

A moment later, Marco walks back over to us, patting the laptop. "It's all here."

"Everything you need?" I ask.

He nods. "Direct access to the Dome's mainframe." He turns his gaze to Governor Ambrose. "I'm keeping this. I'm sure you guessed that, though."

"I'd expect nothing less."

"Now your parents," Governor Ambrose says to Catherine, typing on her iPhone. She shows us both the screen, a conversation with some man named Scofield, who confirms that they are going to be released.

"I want photos," Catherine says with more urgency and desperation than I've ever seen her show. "And I want to call them."

"Of course you do." A beat passes, and then Governor Ambrose's phone vibrates again, and there we see it—a man and a woman who look exactly like two halves of Catherine, smiling weakly at the camera.

Catherine covers her mouth, tears rolling down her face. I don't think I've ever seen her facade break. Ever when she was afraid. Even when death threatened to claim us, she was never emotional like this. It's refreshing to see.

"You can meet them at Andrews Air Force Base in one hour," the governor says, pulling her phone back. A few rapid-fire clicks later, she glances up at Marco. "And Ms. Williams? She's free too. Twenty-fifth precinct."

"I know where that is," Marco chimes in, walking over. "I can take us there."

"Nonsense," she muses. "Consider this…an extra bonus. I'll take you three there. Personally."

We glance at one another, exchanging silent concern.

Governor Ambrose sighs in frustration. "If I wanted to arrest you or kill you, I would have done it already," she says, opening the side of her car. "Come on, now. Are you going to stand there and waste more of my time, or can we get going?"

"She's not wrong," I mutter to Catherine and Marco.

"Yeah, no, I agree," Catherine adds. "I have the suit…"

"And I have the code." Marco shows the computer.

"And you have…" Catherine looks me over. "Charisma, uniqueness, nerve, and talent."

"Did you just make—"

"A RuPaul reference? Yes, I did." She grins cheekily, opening the door to the black SUV that's closest to us. "Come on, we're almost home."

Home. That sounds so foreign to me, so weird, but she's right.

We did it. We actually did it. Despite everything, all the odds against us, this is almost—almost—over.

"Jamal?"

I turn to look at Governor Ambrose as she buckles her seat belt in the back of her car. "I understand most of your plan, and it was... flawless."

"I'm not going to thank you for complimenting me."

"I don't expect you to," she says. "I'm just telling you I recognize your...prowess, if you will. If I could jail you and your friends right now and throw away the key, I would do it without hesitation."

"Naturally."

"But I have to ask, what was the point of bringing Chief Coles here? You could have mentioned him in your ultimatum without going through the struggle of placing him on the chessboard. That was risky."

I don't hesitate to answer her question. "I wanted to show that you people aren't immune, and your Achilles' heel isn't as hidden as you think."

She arches her brows. "And by *you people*, you mean..."

"Take that as you will."

We ride across town in silence for the next twenty minutes. I think everyone is just exhausted, not sure what to say or do. We've been running at a hundred miles per hour for so long that we need a break, and this is it.

Catherine sits in the front seat, her suit folded in on itself. She's fidgeting, unable to keep still, bouncing her right leg, tugging at her seat belt. Marco's drifting in and out of consciousness, his head lolling heavily against my shoulder. I don't mind. I love it, actually. It's nice to be needed by someone, and not out of some life-changing, live-or-die necessity. Maybe it's possible for us, when this is all over, to be normal.

And that's when it hits me: I haven't thought about what happens next. After the Dome, after we survive, what then? What are our lives going to be like?

We get out of the car when it cruises to a stop. Governor Ambrose is already there. But no one cares about her and her slender, fashionable form. The only thing any of us cares about as we get out of the car is Janna.

"Oh my god, it's you," Marco says in a rush. "Mom…you're all right."

Janna holds Marco close, calming him as he mutters, "I'm sorry," over and over again.

"I know," she whispers, combing her fingers through his dark curly hair. "I know."

My eyes lock with hers. Janna smiles and beckons Catherine and me over.

"I was wrong," she says softly. "You three did it."

"We're not done yet." Marco says, pulling back, wiping his nose unceremoniously. He pulls the laptop out of his bag, balancing it on one hand.

"Just need to adjust a bit of code here…change a line of code there…modify this and…" he grins, hovering his finger over the enter key. "It's done. Once we press this, the code will cannibalize itself like a virus. No one is going to activate this tower again. You ready?"

He looks over at Catherine and me. "Together? We started this together, we end this together."

"Oh my god, you're such a dork," Catherine groans, rolling her eyes, but there's a twinkle of a smile in her eyes.

"Shush, you love me," he says. "Now, come on, before I hog the moment for myself."

We both flank him, putting our hands over his, hovering over the enter key. Janna takes the laptop, letting it rest on her forearms.

"One…" Marco says.

"Two…" Catherine continues.

"Three," I add.

With that, we press the enter button together. At first, nothing happens. Time continues to move forward, and the crowd of people at the precinct continues to reconnect with anyone who's there to celebrate their freedom.

And then, all at once, everything happens.

The Dome flickers half a dozen times. At the apex, a pinpoint appears, slowly growing. A moment later, it's a few feet in diameter. Then ten, twenty, fifty. The hole expands downward, the sides of the Dome cracking and disappearing, fragments of hard light dissolving into the air.

Two minutes later, the phone in my pocket chirps once. Twice. Three times. Ten times. Twenty times. Texts from Mom. News alerts. Emails. All of them coming in like a deluge.

I'm not the only one. Everyone's phones begin singing, a chorus of digital notifications filling the crowd.

Oh, and cheers too. So many cheers.

"*Now* it's done," Janna says with a proud smile. "All because of you three."

I look up at Marco and Catherine, seeing exhaustion washing over their faces. I know mine looks the same. Everywhere people are cheering, the streets shaking with excitement and jubilation.

"Now it's done," I repeat.

I take a deep breath, a really deep one, for what feels like the first time since this all began. I hold the air in my lungs and breathe it out. Is this air any different than the air inside the Dome? Probably not, but does it feel different? Absolutely.

"What happens now?" Marco asks, looking between the three of us. "Do we stay? Do we help? Do we just go home?"

"You don't stay." Janna shakes her head. "You leave this to us."

"But—" Marco begins.

"No," Janna says firmly. "You've done enough. It's time the rest of us join in the fight to make this city what we know it can become."

"Not to be rude, but how are you going to do that?" Catherine asks as respectfully as Catherine can. "I mean, if the last few days taught us anything…"

"It's that when people stand up, amazing things can happen?" Janna asks, grinning.

Catherine opens her mouth, but then closes it. "Fair."

"I imagine," I interject, "that Janna is going to do what she does best, right? Organize."

She nods, a twinkle in her eyes. "The governorship of Maryland is up for grabs next year."

"And Ambrose is going to resign," Marco reminds us. "It was part of our deal."

"I think I have a pretty good chance of winning, don't you?" Janna asks.

"I'd vote for you," Catherine says.

"Me too," Marco adds.

"I'll be able to vote this year, so…yes."

"I would hope so." Janna grins brightly. "But that's an issue for later. For now…"

She looks around and points to a boy about our age across the street. She beckons him over with a single curl of her finger. "What's your name?"

"Taylor, ma'am."

"Taylor, can you do me a favor and take these three kids somewhere? They might not look like much, but they're the reason why that"—she points up—"is gone. It's the least we can do, don't you think?"

Taylor nods, gesturing to his truck. "Yeah, sure, where do you want to go?"

"Andrews Air Force Base?" I ask Catherine. "To see your parents?"

Catherine lowers her eyes and stares at the ground for a minute before she finally answers, "No, not yet." She doesn't offer any explanation. But I can see the gears turning in her head.

"Then my place?" I suggest. "My mom would be happy to make us a meal and give us a place to sleep."

"Yes, please," Marco groans. "I'm starving. Let's go—pronto." He turns to Janna and smiles. "I'll be back, I promise."

"I know you will, baby, I know," she says.

Catherine shakes Janna's hand, and then she and Marco head to Taylor's oversize truck. I take two steps forward, pause, and turn back.

"Janna," I say, "can I ask a favor?"

"You can ask me anything, baby," she promises. "And I'm sure everyone here feels the same."

"There's a girl. The one from before, at your house. With the pink ties in her hair?"

Janna nods. "I know her."

"She's at twelve-forty Rockwood Ave. Can you find her parents for me? I promised her."

Janna smiles softly, cupping my cheek and giving it a squeeze. "You have my word. Now, go. There's nothing for you here—not now, anyway."

She's right, I think, as I get into the car with the rest of them. I fought so hard to get back to my life, to have a chance at living it. It's about time I do that.

THIRTY-FIVE

Taylor drives us to the parking lot where I left my car. I'm surprised I remember the location.

"Stay safe out there." Taylor waves when we're finally situated in the car. Marco's in the front with me, while Catherine is sprawled out in the back.

While I drive, Marco reaches over and threads his fingers with mine. The three of us drive in silence—a comfortable, well-earned silence—all the way to Annapolis. I think it's probably thirty or forty minutes before any of us speaks, and if I had to guess why, it's because silence previously meant that one of our minds was racing to the worst possible scenario. Talking not only helped us work through our issues but also kept us from overthinking. Now we have the luxury to do just that.

"So after we rest up, we should go to find your parents, yeah?" I ask, looking at Catherine in the rearview mirror. "Do you want to call the base? I mean, Andrews Air Force Base isn't that far from here. We can drive there tomorrow?"

"I'm down for a road trip," Marco chimes in. "But I'm picking the music. I can just tell neither of you has good taste."

Catherine doesn't instantly retort with some sharp, quick-witted reply, and the quiet is a little bit concerning. I glance over at Marco, who shrugs and looks over his shoulder at her. She's no longer lying on her back; instead she's sitting up, forearms on her knees, her right leg bouncing incessantly.

"I've been thinking…maybe we shouldn't go get my parents."

"That…isn't at all what I was expecting you to say."

"Think about it," she explains. "Governor Ambrose let us off too easy. I don't know how to explain it, but I've been thinking about that since she agreed to our terms. She didn't fight, she didn't argue—she just made some witty quip, then agreed to everything."

"It's because she knew she was boxed into a corner," Marco replies. "She's not stupid. She knew she couldn't win."

"She didn't have to agree so easily," Catherine counters. "I mean, face it—we were in a good position, but did any of us really think we would get *everything* we asked for? Did we really think she was going to resign that easily?"

Catherine just said the quiet part loud. She's right. Everything fell perfectly into place with little to no resistance. As I rethink the last few hours, I can't help but see, with the gift of hindsight, how right Catherine is.

Marco turns around in his seat, unbuckling his seat belt to look back at Catherine. "What are you saying?"

"She's saying that this isn't done," I say. "You think she's setting us up, don't you?"

Catherine curtly nods. "It's the only thing that makes sense, right? This was just too easy. She has to be planning something, some way to make us take the fall. Even if it's for something small, she can pile charges on, using each charge to justify the next one."

"And before we know it, somehow the narrative has turned into us being responsible for the Dome," Marco mutters under his breath. He turns around and hits the dashboard. "SHIT, SHIT, SHIT!"

I don't immediately react to Catherine's declaration. I turn into my subdivision. My house at the bottom of the hill is a good minute-long drive away. That gives me a minute to decide what to say, to come up with a solution. Marco's listing off ideas, but neither Catherine nor I says anything to validate or invalidate his suggestions. I look at her with a flick of my eyes and notice she's doing the same thing as me: thinking, processing, trying to come up with a solution.

Our eyes lock for one brief moment, both knowing what we have to suggest.

"We need to go on the run," Catherine says. I don't know if she wants to spare me from saying it or if she just spoke first, but I'm grateful. "It's the only solution, at least for now. We have to get far from Baltimore."

"Far enough away that no one we care about is in danger. And to give them plausible deniability."

I pull to a stop in front of my house. The lights are on in the living room, and the curtains are drawn. I bet my mom is glued to the TV, trying to get any scrap of information she can. I hope she's finding solace in the fact that the news is reporting the Dome's disappearance.

I could just text her, let her know I'm okay. But if I'm going to do this, join Marco and Catherine and cut all ties with our past lives—at least for now—I need to go all in. Even being here, outside her house, feels like too much of a risk. We've seen how technology can be used against people. Who's to say a text I send or a phone call I make won't be warped into a confession or something more nefarious? I can't risk it. I can't put *her* at risk like that. I won't.

"So, wait," Marco says. "We have to run, after we just did all that? Correct me if I'm wrong, but we got through that hell by fighting back."

"This time it's different," I say. "We're running to protect the people we care about."

"It's not permanent," Catherine reminds Marco. "It's just...until we can figure out what to do."

Marco falls silent, his brows knitting together. His lips push into a thin line, the angular shape of his jaw more pronounced. Catherine and I sit quietly, giving him time to process what he needs to.

"We do this together, or we don't do it at all," I say at last, squeezing his hand. "We got through this, like you said, by doing it together. That still stands."

"A hundred percent," Catherine promises. "Either we run together, or we stand and fight together. There's no middle ground."

"No, no," Marco says. "I agree. You're right. This is something we need to do. It's the right thing to do. Live to fight another day and keep the casualties to a minimum. And like you said, it's not for forever, right?"

"Right," Catherine and I say together. She reaches forward and squeezes his shoulder.

It doesn't escape me what we're all giving up by making this choice. Not only are we becoming fugitives and choosing to do whatever we can to avoid the law, we're all sacrificing something. Catherine is sacrificing being reunited with her family. Marco is sacrificing any chance at having a normal life by once again becoming a criminal. And I'm sacrificing a future I have worked so hard for. None of us can know what will happen in the next day, hour, or even minute, but we're okay with that. At least, *I'm* okay with that. Because as long as we are half a step ahead, we can survive.

"We should get going then, yeah?" Marco asks. "Not to be a shitty boy—friend?"

"Are you saying you're my boyfriend or my friend?" I ask.

He shrugs. "I think that's up to you, isn't it?"

"For what it's worth," Catherine interrupts, "I think you two look pretty cute together. I mean, I've never had much interest in the whole romance and sex thing, but it suits you two."

I smile softly at her and squeeze Marco's hand again. "I guess it's boyfriend, then."

A wave of relaxation washes over Marco's face as he squeezes back. "Well, as your boyfriend...not to put a damper on things, but we should probably go, shouldn't we? Not go into your place? I mean..."

"No," I interrupt, no hesitation. No time to overthink. "You're right." If our goal is to put fewer people at risk, then we can't stay here. I could go inside for a minute and say goodbye. But I know myself. I know a minute will turn to five, and then ten, and it'll be harder and harder to leave. Plus, this is only temporary. A momentary setback to protect the woman who has given so much for me.

I stare at the window and imagine what Mom might be doing. What she might be wearing. When my mom is stressed, she goes for comfort clothes, and her comfiest outfit is a pink-and-silver jumpsuit I had a custom made on Etsy with the Howard logo on the back, her class year on her right leg, and her major on her left leg. It was a random gift, but she has always said she loves it. She insists it brings together her two favorite things—her past, when she met my father, and her future, because I bought it for her.

She says it keeps us close.

A lump in my throat threatens to block my airway. I swallow hard and let out a short sigh. Gripping the steering wheel tightly, I take five slow breaths. When I reach five, we'll go.

One. For the hell we just went through.

Two. For the friends I made along the way.

Three. For the choices I had to make.

Four. For the lessons I learned.

And *five*. For—

"Jamal," Marco whispers, nudging me.

I open my eyes and turn to see him pointing. Standing at the door is my mom, in the jumpsuit I imagined her in. Elation, joy, and sadness fill her face. It's the perfect combination to express what she's feeling: relief that I'm alive, and all of the panic and fear she has probably been holding on to, suddenly released by seeing me.

I feel hot tears roll down my face as I stare back at her. I want nothing more than to jump out of the car and run into her arms, to introduce her to my boyfriend and Catherine, a sister and a friend I never thought I would have. I'd give anything to have her homemade nachos, her meatloaf, or her soup—just to talk with her and tell her everything I've been through. Every fiber of my being is telling me to forget what we just agreed to do. Who would it hurt?

But I can't. No matter how much I want to, my body won't move, because it knows it's not the right thing to do. If I've learned one thing since this Dome shit began, it's the difference between right and wrong, good and evil, and what you *want* to do and what you *need* to. And going is something I need to do.

I swallow any fear and pain I'm feeling and mouth to her through the window, *I'm sorry*.

Confusion pulses across Mom's face, but only for a moment. She's a smart woman—she graduated at the top of her class at Howard's nursing school. Relaxation settles onto her smooth brown skin but the tears, soft and few, stay.

I know she wants to cry more. I know she wants to say and do more. But she's doing what a mother is supposed to do: being strong for me.

Putting her right hand over her chest, she holds it there. Her left hand moves to her mouth, and she blows a kiss to me. And then she mouths back something that almost makes me break apart right there.

I'm proud of you, and I love you.

I love you too, I reply silently. I reach behind me and grab my backpack, pulling out the piece of shawl and showing it to her. I don't know if it's solace or happiness that passes over my mom's face, but I can tell she's glad to see that a piece of her—and of our family—is still with me. And always will be.

We stay like that for a minute, in this little world of ours where nothing else, not even time, exists. Mom is the first to pull away, slip inside, and close the door behind her.

Neither Marco nor Catherine touches me. I don't know how long I sit there, but I know that when I'm ready, when I return to my body, the lap of my pants is covered with tears.

"You okay?" Marco whispers.

I nod; the words are too hard to say. Wiping my face with my right sleeve, I swallow shakily. "Where to?"

"The South?" Catherine asks. "We're three people of color—I doubt they'll think we're going there."

"I have a friend who owns a beach house in Florida. We can use that," Marco offers.

"He won't mind?" I ask.

He shrugs. "He owes me for…long story. Here." He brings up the GPS system on the console and types in the address.

"Calculating route," the British voice says. "Estimated time… sixteen…sixteen…six…six…s-s-s-s-s-…"

The screen flickers and becomes pixelated, covered in thousands of small squares, like someone hit it with a hammer. It whines loudly from deep inside.

"What the hell did you do?" Catherine groans.

"I didn't do anything!" Marco yells, tapping hard at the screen. "It just…did…*that*!"

The pixels continue to flicker, almost as if the screen is fighting against something. And then it happens. The screen turns black, and a white symbol begins to appear, faint at first, then brighter and brighter, until it illuminates almost the whole small screen.

A symbol I've seen before.

Three rings—one thin, one thick, one thin—with dots along different parts of the rings like planets. In the center there is a triskelion.

The symbol of Nemesis.

"Hello, Jamal, Marco, and Catherine," the clear and crisp British voice of the GPS says. "It's nice to finally meet you three. Do you have a moment to talk about an opportunity?"

THIRTY-SIX

The three of us sit in silence, just watching the Nemesis symbol flash on the GPS screen. My heart plummets to my feet. I've seen enough movies to know that nothing good comes of a hacking group contacting you by hijacking your GPS.

"How do we know it's you?" Catherine speaks up, no longer sitting fully in her seat.

"Who else do you think could hack a car's navigation system?"

"Any decent hacker," Marco chimes in. "It's not that hard nowadays."

The voice goes silent for a moment.

"You, Catherine Ortiz, graduated at the top of your class with specialties in sniping and hand-to-hand combat. You used those hand-to-hand skills to take down Officer Lewis, with the help of Jamal here, and Officer Conrad. Nice use of that jujitsu throw, by the way.

"You, Marco Gonzales, are a well-known hacker, known mostly for local jobs. You helped get undocumented citizens' overdraft fees in Florida erased. That's what put you on our radar. Apologies for not getting back to you about your application; we hope this conversation will make up for that.

"And you, Jamal Lawson. A budding journalist. Top of your class at an elite private school. Your whole life is in front of you, and you decided to help others, to bring the truth to light. That's admirable."

"Yeah, that's cute and all," I interject, "but if you know all this, especially about Catherine's fighting, that means you were there, waiting in the wings like some creeper. And you chose not the help."

The voice falls silent, as if I've caught him in some type of trap. Frustration builds inside me. I don't have the time or patience for this.

"Look," I say, "if you know so much, then you know we've been through a lot—a fucking lot—and I'm pretty sure I can speak for the group when I say that I'm not here to be yanked around or to become a pawn in some bigger scheme. We literally just got out of that, and we saw what happens when people on high seem to think they know what's best for other people. I'm tired of it. So if this is all you came here to say…"

"On the contrary. I'm actually offering you a job."

"Well, that isn't what I expected," Marco mutters.

"A job? Doing what?" Catherine questions.

"You three were able to accomplish what months of research and hacking were unable to do. There is something to be said for the power of on-the-ground activism, for people working in the trenches. Nemesis is an excellent shadow group, but we are not an in-person operation. We were never meant to be. But we think you three may be able to change that. So we're offering you exactly what I said—a job working for us, being our eyes and ears on the ground and helping us address issues we can't fix with technology alone."

"You want us to be your muscle," I correct. "That's what you really mean."

"What do you have to lose?" the voice asks. "You don't have anywhere to go. How long do you think you can stay ahead of the police before they find you? And once they do, do you really think they're going to give you a fair trial? You're people of color, you're teens, and you're terrorists in the eyes of the law. No lawyer is going to be able to help you. The board has unanimously decided to offer you the money to do any operation you want. With our digital prowess, you'll never leave a trace. Anything you want or need can and will be yours. You'll have full control over how you accomplish these missions and the life you live. Your life will be your own, to change and shape how you see fit. You'll be agents of change, you three, not just agents of reaction. Few people can say that."

"So why us, then?" Catherine asks.

"Simple. You have something few people have."

"And what's that?" Marco asks. "Our dashing good looks?"

"Your desire to make the world a better place for those who have been forgotten and thrown to the side."

"What do we have to lose?" Catherine asks.

"Our *lives*?" Marco replies.

"I imagine we might lose those sooner or later anyway, given the direction we're going."

"Morbid?"

"But true."

They're right. There's no other way to say it. It's a pipe dream to think we'll be able to stay ahead of the police for as long as we need to after what just happened in Baltimore. If we really want to do good work, if we really want to change the world, we're going to need help. And why not have the help of one of the most powerful shadow organizations the world has ever seen?

"We have three demands," I say.

"Anything," the voice replies.

"One, you keep our parents safe. *All* of our parents. I don't want anyone to ever hurt them. I want people constantly checking on them. Scrubbing the internet, private networks, anything. I want their presence off the internet so no one can find them, and I want them relocated somewhere safe. Protecting them needs to be your top priority for as long as we work for you."

"Agreed."

"Two, we work independently. Whatever mission we agree upon, we need to have authority to do it as we see fit. We know how to get results, and we don't need you all telling us what to do while we risk our lives. This isn't the military." I glance at Catherine. "Sorry."

"No, you're right," she says.

"Also agreed. Anything else?"

"Three, Marco joins your board."

"Wait, what?" Marco snaps his head toward me. I reach over, putting my finger against his lips.

"I see no problem with that. So do we have an agreement?"

"Do we?" I ask Catherine and Marco.

Catherine reaches forward, grabbing Marco's left shoulder with her right hand and my right one with her left. I grab Marco's left hand with my right, making a circle. We squeeze each other, a silent pact made.

"Agreed," we all say together.

"Excellent," the digital voice says with its first flicker of joy. "Please head to the location in your GPS. You'll receive new clothes, identities, money, and tools for your missions, along with instructions on how to contact us, the locations of safe houses around the world, and contacts you may find useful. You deserve a break."

"And when we're ready?" I ask, tapping the screen as the directions appear. Looks like we're heading to Philadelphia. "What's next for us?"

"We have some options for you, but I'm curious…how do you feel about New York City? And what do you know about Governor Angelo?"

"I know he's a shit human being who cares more about getting in with Silicon Valley than he cares about New York City," I say. "Does that answer your question?"

The voice on the other end chuckles, then distorts as the screen begins to become pixelated again. "Oh, we will get along very, very well. Until next time, you three. And welcome to Nemesis."

ACKNOWLEDGMENTS

Survive the Dome is a book of resistance.

I created the idea three days after George Floyd was killed, in the midst of the pandemic, when I was stuck in an eight-by-ten-foot room in a city that had dealt with an apocalyptic first wave of COVID-19. This book helped give me something to focus on in a time when being me—a Black male New York resident—all felt like a death sentence. It was my therapy.

A lot of people helped make this book a reality. More than I can count and list here, if I'm being honest. To my book world community—my support system—and network: thank you. To my agent, Jim McCarthy, who believed in the idea the moment I pitched it to him. This book wouldn't be what it is with you. Now check your email; I sent you five more ideas. To my editor, Annie Berger, who let me shift from another book idea we had been working on to write this: thank you for being flexible and seeing how important this book was to me. To friends in the Please Scream Inside Your Heart group chat, who helped keep me sane for the past year and a half—somehow, we haven't murdered one another, and that's a blessing. Thank you to Makeda Braithwaite, who helped with this book's dedication, and to my Sourcebooks team, who always comes through with exceptional support. And, of course, my trusty friend Mary Averling, who helped make this book a polished draft before Annie saw it. You're the real star.

To my personal network, who helped keep me, a Black man in America, living in a time when the world said they love Black people but didn't truly stand behind Black people, sane. I adore you. My boyfriend, Jordan, who gave me the time, the space, and the support to write. My coworker (at the time of this book's inception) and Aquarius sister, Talya, who never stopped believing in me (and was a bad boba influence!). My friend, Leah Johnson, who is always just an audio message away. Cam Montgomery, my West Coast sister. As we get older, many of us find discovering friendships harder and harder. You all prove it's not the number of friends that matter, but the quality of them. And, of course, I wouldn't be here without my parents' undying and unconditional support. Thank you.

And then there's the network of activists: Alicia Garza, Patrisse Cullors, Opal Tometi, Stacey Abrams, just to name a few. Movements are made on the backs of women, usually Black women, and there are so many, known and unknown, who have made our world a better place. I won't forget you. Every person who has stood up against racial injustice, donated, canvassed, voted—every single one of you, big and small, brought us here.

Survive the Dome is a fiction book, but the reality in America isn't far off. If you learn one thing from this book, it's that one person—or three persons—can change the world. Never forget that.

ABOUT THE AUTHOR

Born and raised in the DC Metro Area, Kosoko Jackson has worked in digital communications for the past five years. He has an MFA in fiction from Southern New Hampshire University, is currently receiving his master's of public health from the University of South Florida. He has a strange love for indie folk, disaster movies, and odd tea flavors. He is also the author of *Yesterday Is History*. Visit him at kosokojackson.com.

FIREreads

 #getbooklit

Your hub for the hottest in young adult books!

Visit us online and sign up for our
newsletter at FIREreads.com

@sourcebooksfire

sourcebooksfire

firereads.tumblr.com